"You look…glowing," Tyler said, realising he sucked at compliments.

"Thank you. I guess." Her smile made her aura illuminate even brighter, making a glowing halo around her head.

For whatever reason, he felt the need to elaborate. "I don't just mean your aura, though yours is spectacular. But your human form is beautiful."

Anabel's smile widened, making her whiskey eyes sparkle. "Wow. Thanks. You kind of made my day."

He found himself smiling back. Maybe he wasn't so bad at this complimenting thing after all.

He let his gaze drink her up, his entire body burning. Funny how he still felt as if he had a body, even though he didn't. Even when she turned away, completely unaware of his desire, he tracked her with his gaze.

Focus, he reminded himself. He'd come back for a reason, to save Dena, not ache for a woman he could never have.

D0522779

SHADES OF THE WOLF

KAREN WHIDDON

MILLS
BOON

Published in Great Britain 2015
by Mills & Boon, an imprint of Harlequin (UK) Limited,
Eton House, 18-24 Paradise Road, Richmond, Surrey, TW9 1SR

© 2015 Karen Whiddon

ISBN: 978-0-263-25349-8

89-0115

Harlequin (UK) Limited's policy is to use papers that are natural, renewable and recyclable products and made from wood grown in sustainable forests. The logging and manufacturing processes conform to the legal environmental regulations of the country of origin.

Printed and bound in Spain
by CPI, Barcelona

Karen Whiddon started weaving fanciful tales for her younger brothers at eleven. Amid the Catskill Mountains, then the Rocky Mountains, she fueled her imagination with the natural beauty surrounding her. Karen lives in north Texas and shares her life with her hero of a husband and three doting dogs. You can e-mail Karen at KWhiddon1@aol.com or write to her at PO Box 820807, Fort Worth, TX 76182, USA. Fans can also check out her website, karenwhiddon.com.

Once again, to my husband. I can never thank him
enough for loving me and supporting me.
He is a special man and I love him very much.

Chapter 1

The man appeared in her peripheral vision, just like all the others who had come before. A hazy shape, flickering into mist before solidifying somewhat. Her black cat, Leroy, hissed his usual back-arched warning. Anabel Lee clenched her teeth and ignored the apparition, willing the ghost's ethereal form to dissipate so she wouldn't have to look at him.

Or worse, hear him try to speak to her. Mentally, she cringed. The voices were what bothered her the most. Whispers and muffled laughter. Wisps of conversation drifting on the breeze.

And pleas for help. Almost always cries for help. She had come to realize ghosts never appeared unless they wanted something. For whatever reason, they all seemed to think she could give it to them. Instead she steeled herself and sent them away.

This wasn't the first time one had appeared inside her

home either. They were prone to popping up in all kinds of places, everywhere. Some wailed; some screamed. Others simply glared at her with burning eyes, as if she could read whatever was left of their mind. And most asked—begged, actually. Until she ordered them gone. Doing so cut off the voices.

Since there seemed to be a method to her madness, she simply closed her eyes. "Go away," she ordered, speaking slowly and loud. "I don't want you here."

Having spoken, she counted silently to ten, quite confident that when she opened her eyes again the apparition would be gone. They always went, once she ordered them gone.

Only he wasn't. Instead it seemed he'd moved closer. Her eyes widened. Dimly, she registered he was—or had been—a beautiful man. Tall and broad-shouldered, with a narrow waist and capable, long-fingered hands. He wore his dark hair unfashionably long, which she also appreciated, since she too made a practice of skirting the edge of current style. This hair did not go with his camouflaged military fatigues and combat boots.

Leroy hissed again, then gave an indignant yowl and stalked away, his yellow cat's eyes flashing.

"What do you want?" she asked rudely, pretty sure she already knew the answer. And she got ready to strain to hear the whisper or brace herself for the shriek, since ghosts apparently couldn't speak in a normal tone.

"I need your help," he said, his deep voice strong and edged with velvet. Such a sexy voice, she felt the impact all the way to her toes.

Stunned, she stared at him. "I didn't expect that."

One corner of his well-shaped mouth quirked. Damned if she didn't feel a little electric tingle deep inside.

"What, that I'd need your assistance?"

"No, not that." She waved him away. "All the ghosts want some kind of help. But you're different. You can talk. Not whisper, but speak. That's unusual."

"Is it?" Appearing unconcerned, he shrugged. To her consternation, he appeared to be solidifying the longer she looked at him. Handsome, sexy and getting more real by the second. Maybe she finally *had* lost her mind.

"I've been sent back here for a reason," he continued. "And your energy is strong. It directed me to you."

This was new. Of course, she'd never gotten this far with a specter before. This ghost was different. For one thing, he was massive. And ruggedly handsome. His self-confidence was even sexy, making her feel something she hadn't since David's death. Things she definitely shouldn't be feeling.

Resolutely, Anabel ignored him. Eventually, he'd disappear. He had to. He had no reason to hang around haunting her. She'd brought her vegetables in from her garden for dinner. She planned to roast summer squash, zucchini, tomatoes and onions. Not only did she love the fresh taste, but the bright colors made eating feel like artwork. This, along with some quinoa, had become one of her favorite meals ever since she'd decided to give vegetarianism a try.

Which had given the townspeople of Leaning Tree even more to talk about. After all, who'd ever heard of a shape-shifter who didn't eat meat?

Anabel didn't care. At least that was what she told herself—ever since David had been killed and she'd lost her mind, she'd long ago stopped caring about what other people thought of her.

"Earth to Anabel." The ghost snapped his fingers. At her. And she could actually hear them. "Shutting me out won't make me go away."

Ignoring him should have worked. Sometimes she'd

found she could actually *will* them away, as if she had magical power over ghosts or something. Closing her eyes, she wished him gone.

"Hello? I know you can hear me. This is really important. Otherwise I wouldn't have come."

Him again. Still here. Worse, he actually knew her name. None of the other ghosts had called her anything but *lady*, or *ma'am*, or even *Ms*.

"Fine." Sighing, she crossed her arms and faced him. "I'm listening. Go ahead and tell me what you want."

She expected him to immediately start listing his demands. If they followed along with the other spirits who'd visited her, they'd be along the lines of *find so-and-so, my wife, my mother, my father, and tell them I love them and that I'm at peace.* Which she absolutely refused to do. Mostly since she knew no one would believe her. She already had a reputation as a nut job anyway.

So she waited for him to begin his laundry list of demands before she could shoot him down.

Instead he cocked his head and studied her. Anabel realized she'd never seen eyes that hazel, in either a live man or a ghost. Especially a ghost.

"You miss him, don't you?" he asked, his deep voice kind. "Your husband, that is."

She started, only the slightest twitch, but she thought he noticed it anyway. "If you're here to tell me he's all right, that he's not in pain and that he's happy, don't."

Even though she tried to keep the misery out of her tone, she knew she'd failed. "After all," she continued, "if he really wanted me to know, he'd have told me himself."

"I'm sure he couldn't." Again the flash of a smile, far too radiant for an apparition. "It seems to be some kind of rule or something, prohibiting us from appearing to those who loved us the most."

Which made sense. Though it didn't lessen the hurt. "I see ghosts. Not everyone can do that. I would appreciate just a short visit, or even a message…" She broke off, squinting at him and not bothering to hide her suspicion. "And don't take that as a good excuse to hand me some syrupy fake message. I'll see right through you. David and I had our own form of code. He'd definitely use it to prove to me that any communication actually was from him."

As she wound down, she noticed how his mouth quirked upward in amusement. He had a ruggedness and vital power she found very attractive. Which felt not only weird—he was a ghost, after all—but entirely unwelcome.

"I don't have a message from anyone," he said, not sounding the slightest bit regretful. "I'm sorry."

"Don't be." Irritated, embarrassed and more than a little bit flustered, she waved his words away. "Just tell me what you want so I can get on with the rest of my day."

"What I want…" His expression stilled and grew serious. "I need you to help find my sister. Somehow she managed to reach out to me. She's in danger."

This was a new one. "But you're a…ghost. You should be able to find her yourself."

"I have tried." He sounded frustrated. "And all I can tell is she's in some dark, windowless place. Underground, maybe. No matter how long I search, her exact location is blocked. She's still alive, though her light is beginning to fade. She is running out of time. The man who has her will kill her soon."

Her heart skipped a beat. "The man who has her? Are you talking about a serial killer? Or just some sort of psycho?"

"I don't know." His lips thinned as his expression turned inward. "He's probably killed more than once, because when I'm around my sister, I can also feel the whispers of other lost souls."

A shiver snaked up her spine. This just kept getting stranger. Not only did a ghost too good-looking to be real show up, but now he was spouting stuff about serial killers? She really, really needed him to go away.

Crossing her arms, she studied him. His massive shoulders filled out army camouflage. Her stomach swooped. The combat uniform had been exactly what David was wearing when he was killed. Coincidence? She thought not.

Steeling herself, she took a deep breath. "I have to ask. Why me? I don't even know you. Did someone else, some other *ghost*, send you to me?"

"No." His quick answer crushed all her hopes. "Your energy drew me to you. I need someone with your power. Not only that, but you live in the same town as I used to. My sister still lives here." He frowned. "Don't you ever wonder why you can hear the voices of the dead?"

"Not really. Mostly I only hear whispers."

"You can hear me. And the energy you send out directs the spirits to you."

Pain stabbed her. "Funny thing, that. You're right. I do attract a lot of departed spirits. All of them want something from me. But the one voice I most want to hear has never come to me."

"Your husband, of course…" Gaze intense, he frowned. "Maybe I can help with that."

"I received word David was killed in Afghanistan eighteen months ago. I just knew he'd come to me, at least to say goodbye. But he never did."

His frown deepened. "I cannot appear physically to my sister, even though she's in danger."

"That's nonsense." The words burst from her, practically vibrating with hurt. "I hear all the time of people seeing the shade of someone close to them. I don't understand why…" Tears pricking at the backs of her eyes, she couldn't finish the sentence.

He dipped his chin, as if he understood. "All I can say is I'm sorry."

"So am I." Though for once, she'd been able to say David's name without her voice cracking. "It's been really tough. David and I were mates. That's why I just don't understand."

"Mates. Interesting. During my time on earth, I never had the privilege of meeting my mate."

"Not everyone does. I got lucky. And I don't think it's too much to ask that he contact me. Or, if there's a rule to prevent that, he could reach out to someone else and send a message to me." It dawned on her that was what all the other spirits she'd sent away had been trying to do and for all she knew, David might have had the same luck if he'd made the attempt.

"Sometimes, when a soul has suffered a traumatic injury, he is taken away and given positive, healing energy," the handsome ghost continued. "Time passes differently there. Your David may not even be aware eighteen months has passed since his death. For him, it may feel merely like minutes."

His words felt like a soothing salve poured on a festering wound. They helped, even if she didn't really understand the logic behind what he'd said. The connection between mates should have transcended both space and time.

This ghost simply didn't understand. She felt bad for him; she really did. And she felt worse for his poor sister. Being held prisoner in a dark place sounded like her worst nightmare come to life. Add in serial killer, and it went way beyond the realm of terrifying. So much so that she knew she didn't want to have anything to do with it.

Now to convince him of that. She swallowed hard, lifted her chin and boldly met his gaze.

"Your eyes are the color of burnished copper," he said.

Nonplussed, she completely lost her train of thought. "Uh. Thanks. I guess."

The quick flash of a devastating smile further derailed her. "You're welcome. And I should thank you, for agreeing to help."

That snapped her out of whatever twilight land she'd gone to. "That's just it. I haven't agreed to anything. Look, I understand that I can hear you. But I'm just one person, a widow who, quite frankly, isn't well regarded in this town. Serial killers scare the heck out of me too. So what do you think I can do to find your sister?"

"More than I can," he shot back, his smile vanishing. "You have a physical presence. You can talk to people and be heard. You can ignite a fire under law enforcement. And you are able to research and hunt down the clues that occasionally flash into my consciousness. Once you and I figure out who this man is, we can have him arrested."

Still, she considered. Lately, she'd made a career out of avoiding just about everyone in town. For all she knew, they'd laugh at her if she started asking questions about a missing girl.

"How did you die?" she asked, feeling as if she needed to know.

"In Afghanistan," he said, his voice curt. Clearly, he didn't like discussing his death. "Like your husband and a lot of others. For me, it was a suicide bomber at a roadside checkpoint."

A chill snaked over her. This ghost and David had both

lost their lives in a similar fashion. It couldn't be a coincidence, even if she wasn't sure how she felt about that.

"I'll find your husband," he offered. "And try to bring him to you. If I can't, I'll bring back to you exactly what he'd like you to know. But time is of the essence. The longer Dena—my sister—is in that place, the weaker she becomes."

Again the image. A poor woman, curled up on the cold concrete floor, hoping to ward off blows—or worse. That could be any woman, even Anabel. She had to try to save her. Just like that, she decided.

"If I help you find your sister," she said, pretending she still didn't know, "you say you'll make sure David comes to me."

"Yes." A muscle worked in his jaw. "But not just find. *Save* my sister. And not *if*, but *when*."

"Fine." She cleared her throat. "I promise you, when I commit to something, I go all out. I will devote every spare second I have—when I'm not working, that is." These days, unlike the job she'd had as an executive secretary when she was married to David, she worked as a cook in the back of the diner, which suited her perfectly. It was easier spending her time interacting with food rather than people.

He continued watching her, his hazel eyes both intelligent and insolent. "I'll need your word."

Of course he did. She decided not to tell him that her word wasn't worth anything around this town. "Then I give you my word. I will do whatever I'm permitted to do."

Gliding closer, in that disconcerting way of all ghosts, he held out his hand. It looked remarkably solid. Even though she knew it wasn't. For a second, she pictured how such sensual fingers would feel on her skin.

Seriously. She gave herself a mental shake. What on earth had gotten into her?

"Tyler Rogers," he said, the velvet murmur of his voice filling her with longing.

Damn.

"You do know I won't be able to shake that," she said, hoping he didn't notice how breathless she sounded.

For half a second, he appeared abashed. And then he grinned, an irresistible, devastating grin that made her knees go weak and her entire body tingle. "You're right," he said, lowering his hand.

"I'll do some checking," they both said at the same time. Anabel found herself smiling, something she didn't do very often. It felt good. And wrong. Again she wondered if she'd finally lost what was left of her mind.

"I'll make sure no other ghosts bother you," he told her, apparently not noticing her inner struggle.

As distractions went, his statement was pretty good. Intrigued, she tilted her head. "How will you do that?"

"Simple. I'll ask my spirit guide to put a circle of protection around you."

"What?" she started to ask. But he was gone. Just like a candle flame snuffed out by a gust of wind.

Alone again, she sighed. Maybe she'd dreamed all this up. It was entirely possible the eighteen months of celibacy since David's death had made her come completely unhinged.

Except for one thing. Why would she even think about serial killers and sisters in need of rescue?

Whichever Tyler Rogers turned out to be, a genuine ghost or a figment of her lonely imagination, she'd do what she could to find out information on his sister. Dena, he'd said. Surely it wouldn't be too difficult to find someone named Dena Rogers in a town the size of Leaning Tree.

That night, when she turned out the light, she went to sleep in blissful silence. No ghostly specters haunted her, not in her house or in her dreams.

The next morning, she opened her eyes and sat up in bed, feeling completely rested and refreshed. Outside, bright sunshine hinted at the heat to come, but since it was only seven in the morning, she knew it would still be comfortable outside.

In the time since David had died, she'd gradually changed her bedroom, adding little feminine touches here and there. David had hated flowers, though Anabel loved them. A new comforter—floral—and some artwork that she loved had made the room totally hers. She'd told herself she might as well like it, since she'd be spending the rest of her life alone.

Stretching, she thought of her ghostly visitor. Today was her day off. Originally she'd planned to spend it puttering in her garden and hanging out with her cat, Leroy. He was big and fluffy and black and the laziest cat she'd ever known. She loved him so much it hurt.

Instead she guessed she'd better get busy seeing what she could find out about missing girls from Leaning Tree and the surrounding area.

"Good morning," a sexy male voice said behind her, making her jump. "I trust you slept well."

Gasping, she spun around so fast she nearly fell. "Rule number one. You can't just pop in and out of here whenever you feel like it."

Boldly handsome, he stood between her bed and her window. The sunlight made copper highlights in his brown hair.

"Why not?" He sounded genuinely puzzled. "It's what I do."

"Well, stop it. And rule number two, no reading my

mind." She stomped off toward her bathroom, shooting him a warning look. "And stay out here until after I've showered and dressed."

Once she'd closed the door, she looked at herself in the mirror and grimaced. She'd braided her long hair before bed, to keep it from tangling. That, combined with the oversize (and to be honest, ratty) T-shirt she slept in, made her look a little witchy. Since half the people in Leaning Tree thought she was a witch, she guessed it didn't matter.

Shaking her head at her weird and out-of-place vanity, she turned the shower on hot, pulled off her T-shirt and jumped in.

Though she normally rushed through her morning preparations, since she usually had to be at the diner to cook for the breakfast crowd, this morning she took her time and enjoyed the peace and quiet. No ghostly images swirled in the steamy mirror as she blow-dried her hair. No voices cried out their muted torment while she dressed. She hadn't realized how much she appreciated the silence until now. Maybe she wasn't going crazy after all.

Finally, she emerged to find Tyler reclining on her sofa, long, muscular legs spread out in front of him. Today she saw he again wore a soldier's combat uniform, camouflaged desert colors, and boots. She froze, flashing back to the last time she'd seen David, wearing the exact same thing as she'd taken him to the airport to make the long flight back to Afghanistan.

"Are you okay?" Peering closely at her, her ghostly visitor seemed a bit more solid than he had the day before.

"Don't you know?" she asked crossly, turning away so she wouldn't have to look at him.

"You asked me not to read your mind."

"Oh. Right." Crossing into the kitchen, she made herself a cup of coffee. "Thank you. And also thanks for the protection-circle thing or whatever you said. It worked. I didn't have a single ghost last night."

The fragrant smell of coffee made her mouth water. She poured herself a cup, adding a spoonful of powdered creamer and a packet of sweetener.

When she turned, she caught him eyeing her mug with a wistful expression.

"I miss that," he rumbled. "Among other things."

Heat flashed through her, so intense she nearly staggered. Not good, especially if Tyler could intuitively guess how she felt.

Deciding to let that comment go, she scowled at him. "Why are you here?"

One dark eyebrow arched. Sexy, again. "You didn't really think I'd retreat into the ether and wait for you to summon me, did you? We're working together on this."

She shrugged, pretending not to care. "Fine. I'm going to do some research on the internet first. I need to find any news stories about missing girls. I also want to do a search for Dena Rogers."

"Plus, I can tell you where she works and lives," he offered. "We might even go there."

"Of course." Rummaging in the refrigerator, she grabbed the roll of bagels, sprayed each side with vegetable oil, popped them in the toaster and, when they were done, spread a generous dollop of peanut butter on each one.

Tyler watched, his hazel eyes glittering, as she retrieved her breakfast and sat down to eat it.

"What?" she finally asked. "Have you never seen anyone cook breakfast before?"

"Cook?" he snorted. "I don't call that cooking."

She rolled her eyes in response. Since her mouth was full, she didn't deign to reply. Protein and carbs, and tasty too. When she'd finished, she got up, rinsed the plate off and placed it in the dishwasher. Taking a deep sip of her coffee, she padded to the room she used as an office and booted up her ancient desktop. She sensed Tyler right behind her, her awareness of him a prickling along her spine.

"You don't have a laptop?" Tyler asked, the astonished tone in his voice making it clear he thought she lived in the Dark Ages. The mischievous look in his eyes filled her with unwanted longing. To cover, she shook her head.

"Ghosts don't get to be picky," she pointed out, sitting back in her chair while she waited for the computer to finish booting up. If she didn't look at him, maybe she could manage to avoid all these unwanted feelings. "And yes, I had a laptop. David took it with him to Afghanistan. It never made it back, so I'm guessing someone from his unit kept it."

Finishing her coffee, she got up to make another cup, walking right past his still surprisingly solid form, her heart pounding, without him commenting.

When she returned, she checked on her computer, which appeared to be ready, and clicked on the icon for Google Chrome.

"Doesn't that drive you crazy?" he asked. "Computers aren't that expensive anymore. I'd think it'd be worth it to spring for a new one."

"Maybe." Concentrating on the screen, she searched for the local newspaper. "But not today." Once she had the paper up, she searched the archives, using keywords *missing* and *lost* and even *runaway*.

"I'll be—"

Suddenly, he materialized right next to her, practically on top of her, making her jump and bump her knee on the bottom of her desk. "What?" he asked. "Let me see."

"Don't. Do. That." Rubbing at her knee, she glared at

him, though he didn't even notice as he was busy reading the on-screen text.

"There *are* more missing women," he breathed. "Four, including Dena. And they're all from different towns in Ulster County."

Immediately, she began reading too. "Your sister's the only one from Leaning Tree." Hitting the print icon, she eyed him. "But it doesn't appear the police are even considering them to be linked in any way."

"That's where you come in." He stretched, causing the material of his shirt to expand over his muscular arms. Suddenly, she realized he'd changed and no longer wore the camo. Instead he had on civilian clothes, a tight black T-shirt and faded, well-worn jeans, though he still wore his combat boots.

For a ghost, he looked virile as hell. Tantalizing. Captivating.

No. This had to stop. Time to shut this ridiculous and unwanted attraction down. She no longer thought about sex, or at least she tried not to. Her mate was gone and she didn't want anyone else. Ever.

Chapter 2

Now that Anabel had settled the matter, she felt better. Straightening her shoulders, she knew she was strong enough to resist Tyler Rogers's ghostly allure.

"Let's go talk to the police," he said, flickering in and out, his form alternating between solid and ethereal. She figured this was probably due to the enthusiasm vibrating in his husky voice.

Maybe she'd do better if she treated him like a brother. At least that way, his nearness would no longer be so overwhelming.

"You know, for a ghost, you sure look concrete sometimes," she commented, clicking her computer to sleep before getting up from her chair.

"Thanks," he said, flashing that devastating smile that sent a bolt of heat straight to her stomach—and elsewhere.

Brother, she reminded herself. "Come on." Snatching up her car keys, she headed for the garage. "And whatever you do, don't speak to me while I'm talking to the police. Everyone around here already thinks I'm crazy. If I start answering you back, it'll just make it worse."

She didn't look to see if he followed as she opened the garage door and got in her car. The little red Fiat had been a gift from David the first year they were married. She loved everything about it, from the tan leather-trimmed seats to the upgraded radio.

"This?" Tyler said, the disbelief in his voice making her smile. "You expect me to ride in this? There's not enough room."

"You'll manage," she replied. "If not, then I guess you can wait here." As she slid behind the wheel, he materialized in the passenger seat, legs folded almost up to his chest. She nearly laughed out loud.

Instead she masked her amusement with irritation. "Quit doing that too," she ordered. "When you're with me, you don't need to act so ghostly."

"Ghostly?" His rich laugh struck a chord low in her belly. "I am a ghost. That's what we do. But for your sake, I promise to try and pretend I'm human."

She shuddered at the word. "You never were just human, I can tell. Before you died, you were Pack. Like me."

Regarding her curiously as she backed out of her driveway, he finally nodded. "How did you know? I'm told the dead no longer have the aura."

Anabel couldn't keep from snorting out loud. "Maybe not to each other. But you do to me. I can see it just as clearly as the aura from any living shifter."

And then she turned up the radio to discourage further discussion.

The winding, tree-lined roads were beautiful in summer and in autumn. Right now, with the leaves beginning to turn, she felt as if she lived in a postcard. She knew other people who'd lived here all of their lives as she had became so used to the natural beauty that they rarely even noticed it. Not Anabel. She appreciated and marveled at her surroundings every day.

As she drove to downtown Leaning Tree, she tried to think how to best approach this. Turning the radio down slightly, she glanced at him. "Any ideas on what I should say? I mean, I can't just walk into the police station and demand information on the search for the missing girls. That would make them really suspicious."

"I see what you mean," he replied, frowning. "You'd become an immediate suspect, especially since you believe everyone considers you off your rocker anyway."

His words stung. "Hey," she protested. "It's fine for me to say stuff like that. Not so much for you."

Again the deep-throated laugh. "Of course," he said, shaking his head in mock chagrin. "I should have understood."

Shocked, she realized he was teasing her. No one had joked with her in any way since David died. Probably because everyone at first felt bad for her and then later, after her breakdown, most folks acted afraid of her.

This used to hurt and baffle her, before she'd given in and decided to embrace her own semiscary weirdness. She'd started dressing in black after David was killed anyway. With a little embellishment using Stevie Nicks for inspiration, she'd taken black to a whole new level. And the funny thing was, she loved wearing one of her flowing outfits and seeing the way everyone eyed her. She thought she looked pretty. Who cared if everyone else disagreed?

Another sideways look at her ghostly companion, steeling herself against his masculine beauty, confirmed her suspicion.

"For someone who's worried about his sister, you're a bit of a jokester, aren't you?"

Just like that, his half smile vanished, replaced by a steely expression. Instantly, she regretted her comment.

"Are you always so serious?" he asked, faint mockery in his voice.

She decided to answer honestly. "Yes. Especially when dealing with something like this. I don't find serial killers or women being held prisoner amusing."

"Neither do I," he shot back. "But I have found making a joke or two can help relieve some of the pressure."

Since she didn't have a response for that, she kept quiet.

"I do have a question." Clearing his throat, he eyed her. "Exactly how powerful are you?"

So intent had she been on focusing on thinking of him like a brother, the question didn't immediately register. She blinked, frowning, as she met his gaze. "I'm sorry—what?"

"How much power do you have?"

"That's what I thought you said. I don't understand what you mean. If you're talking about firepower, yes, I do own a gun. I've even taken classes to learn how to handle it. For my own protection, of course."

Now he frowned. "I'm not talking about a weapon, though that may come in handy, and I think you know it. I'm asking about your powers. You know, your magic. How strong is it?"

"Magic?" Then she remembered she was talking to a ghost. "Tyler, the only magic I possess is the ability to see and hear spirits. Most times it's more like a curse than magic."

His gaze slid over her, the assessing look in his eyes saying he wasn't sure if she was serious. And then he grimaced and shook his head. "I understand. Good one.

You've proved your point. I shouldn't have accused you of being too serious."

"But—"

He waved away her protests. "You almost had me fooled for a moment. You must be a very powerful witch indeed, if you're trying to hide it."

More oddness. A powerful witch, huh? Maybe he thought she dressed like this because she had magic. Or something. Who knew? Every second she spent with him kept getting weirder and weirder. "I'm just a regular person who happens to see ghosts." And had already had one mental breakdown. She fervently hoped this wasn't another. "I thought you ghostly beings knew everything."

One dark eyebrow arched, his face showing an uncanny awareness of how uneasy she was becoming.

"What makes you think that? If we knew everything, I'd know exactly where to find my sister." He turned away, staring out at the road ahead of them. "And I wouldn't need you."

Good point. Somewhat relieved, she decided to keep on trying to help. "Let's head to the police station. I'll figure out something to say that won't get me thrown in jail." She hoped.

Tyler rode in the passenger seat of her car as if he were alive, just because he wanted to study this Anabel Lee a bit more closely. When he'd received Dena's frantic pleas for help, he'd searched for the most powerful witch he could find. He'd been drawn to the energy radiated from Anabel, just like all the other ghosts, apparently. He'd immediately realized he'd made the right choice when she not only looked at him, but could hear him when he spoke.

One thing that had taken him by surprise was her beauty. Tall and graceful, slender and shapely, and her delicate features left him momentarily speechless. Her midnight hair tumbled carelessly down her back, adding to her attraction. But her copper eyes fringed in long, sooty lashes had done him in. He'd never seen anything like her. Exquisite, enchanting and sexy as hell. The instant he'd met her, he'd felt the impact of her femininity like a sucker punch to the gut.

Which pissed him off royally. After all, he'd come back as a ghost to save his sister, not fight an overwhelming attraction to a witch. Which, despite Anabel's claims to the contrary, she most definitely was.

He didn't understand why she insisted on lying about her magical ability. Maybe if he told her they were most likely dealing with not only a serial-killer psychopath, but a powerful warlock, she'd come clean. Because everyone knew to fight magic with magic, didn't they?

Or maybe, maybe she just didn't know.

The instant that idea occurred to him, he discounted it. How could she radiate power and not understand who and what she was?

For now, he decided to let that topic rest.

"So," she asked, shooting him a sidelong glance that told him she felt nervous, "in the afterlife, do you still shift into a wolf?"

"Of course," he answered, playing along. "We are what we are. Dying doesn't change that." He thought for a moment and then completed his statement. "At least, until we're reborn into a new body."

"Of course." And she laughed, as if he'd made a joke. "Reincarnation too? Why not."

Not sure what to think about this, he decided not to pursue this topic either. Things were confusing enough, what with warlocks and serial killers and ghosts. What choice did he have but to let it go? For all he knew, powerful witches thought differently from everyone else.

And, he reminded himself, Anabel Lee had to be a witch with very strong powers. She had to be, if they were to have a prayer in defeating the man who'd captured and enslaved his sister. If it turned out she wasn't, then he'd chosen wrong and Dena would die.

Contenting himself with looking out the window, though Leaning Tree looked exactly as he remembered, he was struck anew by the rustic beauty. Right now the green leaves flirted with shades of yellow, red and orange. In a few weeks, they'd blaze with color, as soon as the first crispness started to creep into the air. Autumn had always been his favorite time of year.

A moment later, they pulled up at the police station. The one-story, redbrick building looked the same. Again, memories surfaced. He'd spent a fair amount of time here as a kid, when his father was arrested for whaling on his mother.

"Wait here," she ordered, shooting him a stern look as she got out of her car.

"Right." He did exactly as she said, for maybe ten seconds. And then he materialized inside the station, waiting for her by the battle-scarred counter of the front desk as she walked in.

The dirty look she gave him made him smile.

"Anabel Lee." The frizzy-haired woman behind the counter sounded less than thrilled. "What do you want?"

To her credit, Anabel didn't react to the overt hostility in the receptionist's tone. "I'd like to see Captain Harper, please."

The other woman, whose name tag read Brenda Winder, appeared unmoved, squinting at Anabel through thick glasses. "Of course you would. Why don't you tell me what it is you need, and I'll see if I can find someone to help you? Since I am, you know, the dispatcher. That's what we do." Her unkind smile had Tyler clenching his fists.

He glanced at Anabel, to see what she would do. To his surprise, she'd assumed a deferential posture. "I'd prefer to discuss it with him, thanks."

Pursing her mouth, the other woman glared at her. "Have a seat. I'll let him know you're here."

Without commenting, Anabel found a metal folding chair and lowered herself into it.

Enraged, he went to her. "What was that? Why do you let that person talk to you that way?"

Her sigh sounded more weary than exasperated. She kept her voice down, since to anyone else it would appear she was carrying on a one-sided conversation with herself. "I tried to tell you. Most of the people around this town consider me crazy, an unwelcome nuisance at best. No one in Leaning Tree wants to have anything to do with me, never mind talk to me."

"Because of your power?"

She moved her hand in a chopping motion. "Enough about the power. I don't have any, so stop pretending I do."

Before he could respond, Anabel looked up. Her entire body stiffened. "Now look what you made me do," she hissed, her porcelain skin turning tomato red.

Brenda Winder stood back behind the desk, staring at Anabel with a horrified and smug expression on her meaty face. "Talking to yourself again?" she drawled. "Crazy is as crazy does."

Stone-faced, Anabel kept staring straight ahead and didn't bother to reply. Finally, Brenda tired of tormenting someone who wouldn't respond and went back to reading something on her computer.

A few minutes later, a stocky man with wide shoulders and an even wider belly stomped into the room. His bushy

gray eyebrows lowered in a frown, and he eyed Anabel
as if he expected her to present him with something dis-
gusting and distasteful. "You wanted to talk to me?" he
asked, sounding anything but accommodating.

"I did." Smiling, Anabel got to her feet gracefully.
"Good to see you, Captain Harper. Could we please talk
in your office?"

"Out here will do just fine."

"No." Anabel straightened her shoulders, her smile
fading and her gaze direct. "It won't. I need a little privacy, please."

The captain sighed, stopping just short of rolling his
eyes. "Sure. Why not? Come on back. I'm sure you know
the way."

Another puzzle. Resolving to try to find out from Anabel what all this meant, Tyler glided along after them as
they walked through the crowded open area buzzing with
activity. They passed several uniformed officers, a few
criminals or complainants, and not a single person ac-
knowledged or greeted Anabel. She made a beeline toward a small office in the back corner.

Most of the police officers were busy, which might
excuse them. Some were on the phone, others talking to
people sitting in their desk chairs. Suspects? Tyler looked
for handcuffs, noting two people at opposite ends of the
room who wore them.

Despite that, the instant they realized who had just
walked into the room, every single person stopped what
he or she was doing and stared.

Tyler would have liked to believe this was due respect
for her power, but some of the officers seemed disgusted.
A few others exchanged glances with their coworkers,
even going so far as to shake their heads or roll their eyes.

Not respect, then. Eyeing Anabel's slender form as she

marched across the room, head held high, ignoring them all, for the first time he wondered what her story might be.

Truth be told, until now he hadn't wondered about her story. He'd gone to her simply because he'd heard she could see and hear him and she'd radiated amazingly great power. They'd come to an arrangement. He'd help her get what she wanted if she'd help him save his baby sister.

End of story. Except it wasn't.

Even though he'd been a shape-shifter, able to change into a ferocious wolf, wizards, warlocks and witches generally creeped him out. Any shifter with a lick of sense tended to avoid magical beings, since they were powerless against them. Even the vampires were careful to avoid them.

But now one had Dena. And if Tyler wanted to save her, he had no choice but to take on a warlock. At least he had a powerful witch at his side.

Once again he eyed Anabel, who'd finally reached the captain's office and had taken a seat, crossing her gorgeous long legs and tilting her head as she waited for the captain to work himself down into his own chair and work his enormous stomach behind his desk.

Finally, he grunted and got himself settled. "All right, Anabel. Since Lilly and all the rest of the McGraws refused to press charges against you, I'm guessing you haven't come here to talk about any of that."

Anabel shook her head rapidly, sending her long, dark hair whipping around her face. Tyler caught himself aching to wrap a strand of it around his finger and pull her to him.

"Of course not," she said. "That's history. They've moved forward, as have I."

"Then what can I do for you?"

She took a deep breath, her jaw tightening. "A friend

of David's wrote me from Afghanistan. He wanted me to check on his sister. She lives here in Leaning Tree. According to him, she's gone missing."

Brilliant. Tyler wanted to hug her. He restrained himself, not wanting to startle her. Besides, without a corporeal body, she wouldn't be able to feel it.

"Really?" The captain's gaze sharpened. "What's her name?"

"Dena Rogers," Anabel answered. "Her brother, Tyler, is really worried."

"Let me see what I can find out." Using his computer, Captain Harper tapped in some information. "Ah, yes. Here we are. Two weeks ago one of her coworkers asked us to do a welfare check when Ms. Rogers didn't show up for her shift at the junior-college cafeteria. We checked but found nothing. Her house was empty, but there were no signs she'd met with foul play or anything. My officer determined she must have left willingly."

"I don't think so—" Anabel began.

"Ms. Lee." Speaking sternly, Captain Harper interrupted. "It's entirely possible she went on vacation."

"Not without telling her brother," Anabel shot back, her spine straight. "That's why he got in touch with me."

"I see." Steepling his fingers, the older man sighed. "Then why don't you tell me what it is you want me to do?"

"Find out what happened to her. Her brother told me she'd been talking about several other missing girls. Has anyone in your office put together information linking them?"

To give him credit, Captain Harper's expression remained unchanged. Except for his eyes. Those appeared about to bug out of his head. "I don't have any idea what you're talking about."

"That's sad."

The captain narrowed his eyes but didn't respond.

"I would appreciate it if you would look into it," Anabel continued with a quiet dignity. "As soon as possible. It's not enough that Tyler Rogers is over there serving our country. I don't want him worrying needlessly about his sister."

"I'm sure there's no need to worry. She'll turn up eventually. Young people frequently disappear on some crazy adventure."

The man's patronizing tone set Tyler's teeth on edge. "If you won't at least do your job—" Anabel stood, the movement graceful "—I'm going to have to investigate on my own."

To Tyler's disbelief, the police captain winced. "No need to do anything rash."

"Twenty-four hours." Anabel looked him right in the eye. "I want you to investigate the disappearance of several young women in the area around Leaning Tree over the past few months. I'd like to know what you've learned by this time tomorrow. If I don't hear from you, I'll consider that notice that you want me to take matters into my own hands."

From the tight set of Captain Harper's jaw, he wasn't happy at all about her proclamation, but he nodded. "I'll see what I can find out."

"You do that." With that, she turned to go.

Following her out the door, Tyler marveled at the powerful energy radiating from her. How was it possible she didn't realize her own strength? It wasn't. Therefore, he had to believe she simply didn't want him to know.

She sailed through the outer room and past the startled receptionist without a word. Outside, she rushed over to her little car, opening the door and climbing inside.

Only once she was there did Tyler realize her hands were shaking too hard to fit the key in the ignition.

"Deep breaths," he told her as he folded himself up into the small passenger seat. He wasn't sure what he could do to help. "Do you want to talk about it?" In his admittedly limited experience, most women welcomed the opportunity to discuss their feelings.

But Anabel was not most women. "No," she said, averting her profile. "I'm fine." A moment later, she managed to start the car and put it in Drive.

"What was that, back there?"

Not looking at him, she lifted one delicate shoulder in a shrug. "I already told you, people in this town think I'm crazy."

"But you didn't tell me why."

She shot him a sideways glance, her eyes shuttered. "Does it really matter?"

"I guess not. But I'd still like to know."

"I talk to ghosts. Think about it."

He couldn't help laughing at the sour note in her voice. "They see you walking around talking to air. Is that what you're telling me?"

"Exactly. And I dress the part. Plus, I did something I shouldn't have and almost cost a really sweet woman her life. I don't think anyone will ever forgive me for that."

Thus the captain's reference to the McGraws. He, like just about everyone in Leaning Tree, knew the family. Since they'd declined to press charges, whatever Anabel had done couldn't have been too bad. Tyler wondered if he should ask, but the raw agony in her expression made him decide not to. Whatever she'd done, it seemed clear she felt bad about that now.

Neither spoke as she drove slowly down Main Street. He took his time admiring the huge leafy oak and maple trees, the restored old buildings and the bustling shops. "It still looks the same," he mused. "I see the small Dutch Reform church is now fully restored. And the shops and restaurants appear to be doing a booming business."

"We get a lot more tourists than we used to," she grudgingly admitted. "It's really busy in the fall when all the city people take drives to see the foliage." Again she looked sideways at him, almost as if it hurt her eyes to meet his gaze dead-on.

"I remember," he said.

"How long have you been gone from here, anyway?"

"That's a good question." He tried to calculate, failing miserably.

"A reply like that means you aren't really going to answer."

He laughed. "Give me a minute. I'm trying. Like I said, time passes differently in the hereafter."

"What's the last year you remember? Let's start with your last tour of duty in Afghanistan."

Flashes of light, an explosion, red and yellow and orange. Screams of pain. Wincing, he tried to block the random sights and sounds from his memory.

When he finally found his voice again, he sounded hoarse. "Not there. Too intense. Let's start with something better, more pleasant."

"Okay. When did you graduate from high school?"

Now, that he could answer. "Nineteen ninety-seven." Thinking about that, he couldn't help smiling. "Leaning Tree High. Did you go there?"

"I did, but I graduated in 2001. I was just starting high school the year you finished."

"Which would explain why we never met," he said.

"How do you know we didn't?" Though her question was casual, for some reason it sent a chill up his spine.

He decided to keep his answer light. "Because I'd remember." The rest of it, what he didn't say, was that she, with her long midnight hair and exotic bronze eyes, was the loveliest woman he'd ever seen. He had to believe his younger self would have recognized that too, even back then.

Chapter 3

Apparently oblivious of his chaotic thoughts, Anabel continued to question him. "And then after high school, what did you do? Did you enlist right away?"

His head had begun to hurt. "My turn. I get to ask you something next."

"Really? I had no idea we were playing some sort of game." Since her dry tone contained a thread of amusement, he decided to take that as encouragement.

"What did you do after high school?" he asked.

"I went to college. Columbia, to be exact. Three months in, I loved life and the city. Then I met David Lee. From Tennessee. He was in New York on leave."

Though he hated the dark sadness that crept over her lovely face, he wanted to know more. Before he could speak, she forestalled him by making a chopping motion with her hand.

"My turn," she said, earning a reluctant smile from him.

"Go ahead."

"Remember, we're trying to get a rough idea of how long you've been a ghost," she said.

Though he didn't know why that mattered, he decided to play along. "Okay."

"When did you enlist?"

He sighed. "About two months after graduating from high school."

"No college?"

"Nope. Not only did I not have the money or the grades, but I didn't have the inclination. I was working a dead-end job, learning how to do bodywork at a Chevy dealership. I woke up one morning, decided I wanted to be a soldier and drove to the army recruiter's office."

"And then—"

"My turn." He softened his tone to lessen the sting. "How long were you married?"

"Nope," she said, turning away, but not before he saw the hurt flash across her face. "My marriage is off-limits. Ask something else."

Thinking quickly, he spoke. "What about friends? Surely you must have some friends in this town."

She gave him a look designed to stop a charging leopard in its tracks. "You're going to keep pushing this, are you?"

"I'm just trying to figure out what makes you tick, that's all."

"Well, don't. There's not a reason in the world you would need to know."

"Actually, there is." He gave her what he hoped was an unguarded smile. "If we're going to be working together, I should at least learn a few things about you."

"I talk to ghosts," she said, her voice curt. "Isn't that enough?"

"Not really." Equally blunt, he rubbed the back of his neck. One thing that always startled him was how he occasionally still had human aches and pains and itches, even in ethereal form.

"What?" Staring at him, she frowned. "Explain yourself."

"You talk to ghosts. I get that. It's great, and that particular talent is what enabled me to get you to see and hear me. But how is the ability to view spirits going to assist you in freeing my sister?"

She looked thoroughly annoyed. "Maybe I should remind you that you asked me to help you with this, not the other way around."

"I did. But I was under the impression you had some form of magical ability, as well."

Now. Now he expected she would finally admit the truth.

"Well, you were wrong."

His heart sank. "It's more likely you just don't know your own powers."

"Really?" Shaking her head, she snorted. "I know myself better than you think. And to answer your other question, I do have a few friends. They're all sort of fringe people like me."

"Fringe people?"

"Yeah." Expression carefully blank, she smiled at him. "As a matter of fact, you need to meet one of them. My friend Juliet. She owns the yoga studio and metaphysical bookstore downtown and calls herself a medium."

"And you don't believe her?"

"I have no opinion either way. She's my friend and whatever she wants to accept as true is fine with me." A hint of mischief sparked in her amazing eyes as she widened her smile, which made him catch his breath.

"That's why I want you to meet her. I'm curious to see if she senses your presence."

"Has she ever sensed one of your other ghostly visitors?"

"No, but I've never brought one into her studio. I usually get rid of them as soon as they appear."

Curious, he nodded. "Do they appear often?"

Instantly, her smile vanished. "Too much," she said grimly. "There are an awful lot of dead people trying to communicate with the living."

"You know, you could make money if you had a TV show and traveled around the country like the *Long Island Medium*. Why don't you?"

Clearly, his attempt at a joke fell flat. She looked at him as if he'd grown two ghostly heads. "That's not for me. All I want is for the specters to leave me alone. Which, thanks to you, they are."

When he was in the afterlife, Anabel's energy had pulled him to her. He'd been seeking, and then the blaze of energy she gave off shone like a beacon, cutting through gray. The fact that she'd been able to see and hear him had been a welcome bonus.

"You draw them to you," he said slowly.

"How? And why? Surely there must be a way to turn it off."

He debated the best way to tell her. Finally, he decided to just say it. "Anabel, I believe you have magic inside you. Untapped, but powerful. We're going to need to figure out how to bring it to the surface."

"Bring it to…" They stopped at a red light and she turned to face him. "Why would I want to do something like that?"

If her crossed arms were any indication, she definitely wasn't going to like what he had to say next. "Because whoever has my sister is a warlock. And you're going to need your magic to defeat him."

"A warlock?" Repeating Tyler's words, Anabel sucked in her breath. As a shape-shifter, she knew there were all kinds of other supernatural beings out there, like vampires and mer-people, but as far as she knew, no one had any special powers, except for the fae. Even as a child in school, when they'd learned the history of the Pack along with all the other supernatural, witches and warlocks had never been mentioned. Not once.

While she—and others of her kind—could change form, as far as she knew, no one could fly. Or start fires with a look or a wave of their hand. Magic didn't exist.

Yet Tyler talked as if it did. There were certainly insane living people; therefore, it followed that there could be crazy dead people, as well. "Look, Tyler. I agreed to help try and find your sister. You didn't say anything about having to defeat some sort of magical being."

"I believed—believe you have magic too."

She waited, in case there was more, but he didn't elaborate.

"Well, if you need somebody who can fight magic with magic, you've picked the wrong person," she said. "I'll assist in every way I can, but you'll need to find another witch or warlock to help get her out once we find her."

"Deal," he said promptly, which sort of annoyed her. "Do you know any witches?"

Fine. He wanted a witch, she'd get him one. "My friend the yoga instructor is not only a medium but a witch." Okay, technically Juliet was Wiccan, but Tyler was a ghost and Juliet wouldn't be able to see him.

Tyler's ghostly form briefly solidified, which she was

beginning to realize meant excitement. "Do you think she'll help us?"

Immediately, she regretted saying anything. "Tyler, she's Wiccan. She runs a yoga studio and metaphysical bookstore, like I said. If she practices any magic, which I doubt, it's not powerful."

"How do you know?" His husky voice vibrated with enthusiasm. "She might hide it from you. Most magical beings don't go around advertising their power, you know."

"No, I don't know." Apparently, he was serious. She sighed. Maybe new insights into the world were learned in the afterlife.

"When can we meet her?" Tyler asked, his hazel eyes glowing.

Fine. She gave in. "How about now? We're already in town."

Again his form appeared solid. "Sounds great."

Mentally shaking her head, she took the next left onto Third Street. Juliet's bright green VW bug was parked in front of the small white-frame corner building, with a bookstore on one side and a yoga studio on the other.

"You're in luck. She's here."

Pulling up next to her friend's car, Anabel parked and got out. As she headed toward the yoga-studio door, she glanced at Tyler's strikingly handsome form, floating a few feet off the ground. "Remember, Juliet won't be able to see you."

"You never know," he said agreeably. "She might have a few secrets from you, the same way you keep things from her."

Resisting the urge to grumble under her breath, she inhaled deeply and opened the door. The set of tiny bells chirped and chimed their usual muted happy sound. The air smelled like spearmint and rosemary. This never failed to make Anabel smile.

At the sound, Juliet glided from the back room, her unlined face serene. "Anabel!" Moving forward, she hugged Anabel and kissed her cheek. "Class was over an hour ago."

"I know. We came because…" Crap. Not only had she said *we*, as in plural, but she really didn't have a good reason for being there.

"We?" Juliet's perfectly arched eyebrows rose. She peered behind Anabel. "Is someone else with you?"

"No. Sorry." Ignoring Tyler, who now hovered over Anabel with a look of intense concentration on his face, she swallowed.

"What's wrong?" Juliet placed a soothing hand on Anabel's shoulder. "Something is troubling you. I can sense it."

"Aha!" Tyler crowed. "See? She has powers. I knew it."

Anabel could have sworn Juliet glanced at Tyler, though she didn't acknowledge his presence. Of course she didn't. She wasn't crazy, like Anabel.

Doing her best to ignore Tyler's outburst, Anabel nodded. "Do you have a moment to talk?"

"Of course." Turning, Juliet pushed through the row of beads making a curtain in the doorway and led the way back to her office.

Once inside, Anabel took the second chair, since Tyler had materialized in the first one.

"Now tell me what's bothering you." Juliet's dulcet tones were, as far as Anabel was concerned, one of her best assets.

"Um, okay." Might as well just blurt it out. "I hope I'm not being offensive, but as a Wiccan, do you happen to practice…magic?"

To Anabel's relief, Juliet smiled. "We do practice some small, white magic." She leaned closer. "Anabel, have you come because of your power?"

Stunned, Anabel gaped at her friend and tried to ignore Tyler's smug smile. "Power?"

"Yes. You have an aura of power surrounding you. More than just your shifter aura. I thought perhaps something had happened to make you realize this, so you'd come to me for help."

"Power." Aware she was repeating the word yet again, Anabel shook her head. "You do realize my life is already strange enough, don't you?"

Smile widening, Juliet leaned over and patted her arm. "No rush. When the time is right and you have questions, please come to me. I'm not an expert by any means, but I can enlist the help of my coven to teach you. It's far better to use such power for light rather than dark."

Despite herself, Anabel shivered. "Dark magic." Her throat felt dry. "You're telling me that such a thing is real?"

"Unfortunately, very real." And then, while Anabel was trying to digest all this, she swore her friend cut her eyes and looked right at Tyler. As if she too could see him.

"I think she can see me," Tyler said, confirming her thought.

"I can," Juliet admitted, making Anabel gasp. "And hear you too. However, I only see a blaze of energy, not a physical body. Is that what you see, Anabel?"

"No." Still in shock, Anabel looked from Juliet to Tyler and back again. "I see him like he must have looked when he was alive."

Tyler flashed a cocky grin. "Of course you do," he said. "You have way more power than she does."

"I need to go home." Anabel stood, suppressing a flash of panic. "I need to go home right now."

Knowing her friend would understand, Anabel rushed outside and got into her car. She managed to get the key in the ignition, start the engine and put the car in Drive before she realized Tyler wasn't there.

Fine. He was a ghost. He'd show up eventually. Right now she needed to be alone.

Tyler remained seated, though with every fiber of his being he wanted to rush after Anabel. Instead he studied Anabel's friend, taking comfort in the aura of peace and tranquility radiating from her.

"Why are you here?" Juliet asked, apparently having no issues with conversing with a ghost. "Many others have tried to contact her and she's sent every single entity away. What's different about you?"

"I don't know. Maybe it's because I really need Anabel's help," he answered. "I was drawn to her, by her power."

"A lot of spirits are. I get the odd few myself, every now and then, but not nearly as many as she." She leaned forward, her faded blue eyes twinkling. "She thinks I don't know."

"Why?" he asked. "What is it about her? Is she a witch? How is it possible she isn't aware of her power?"

"Anabel is descended from a long line of powerful witches. Unfortunately, her mother died when she was young. There was no one else to teach her. My coven and I have been waiting for the right time." Cocking her head, she studied him. "It would appear your arrival has signaled that the time has come."

"Why wouldn't you have taught her before now? It seems to me she could have used an advantage."

The other woman shook her head. "Anabel has been very unsettled since losing her husband. There were instances when she might have chosen to use her power for bad rather than good."

"How do you know all this?"

"I've been tasked with helping guide her. My coven has long been aware of her and her family, and we watch to make certain she continues to walk within the light." Juliet looked pensive. "Of course, she's given me a few scares a couple of times. Like when she almost caused that poor girl, Lilly McGraw, to get recaptured by that cult. You might know the McGraws, if you're from around here. They own and operate Wolf Hollow Motor Court Resort."

"I know the McGraws, but I don't know Lilly."

Juliet nodded. "Lilly was here with Kane McGraw. She'd been held captive by some crazy cult, and they were hunting her down even after she was freed," she continued. "For whatever reason, Anabel helped this cult. Maybe out of jealousy, as she apparently once had a thing for Kane."

"Helped them?" Tyler wasn't sure he understood. "Anabel helped cult members locate Lilly?"

"Yes. She led Lilly into a trap. Both Lilly and Anabel almost lost their lives with that one."

"Why? Why would she do such a thing?"

"She was confused." Juliet sighed. "And hurting. After David died, Anabel became convinced that Kane McGraw was her mate. She wrote him letters. He never responded. When Anabel learned Kane and Lilly were true mates, she went a little…crazy."

Now everything fell into place. "That explains the way everyone at the—" about to say *police station*, he caught himself "—in town treated her. Like she was dirt."

Expression sad, Juliet nodded. "Folks have long memories around here."

He shook his head. "I'm sure she had her reasons. Anabel's energy shows she's a good person. Did she say why?"

"Maybe if you ask her, she'll tell you," Juliet said gently. "It's her story to share or not. Meanwhile, I'd like to know what you need someone with power for."

Eyeing her, he made a split-second decision and decided to trust her. "A powerful warlock has taken my sister—and maybe a couple of others—captive. I need power to locate them."

"And fight him," she finished. "I see. I'm not sure Anabel is your best bet. She's powerful but completely untrained."

"What about you?" he asked.

But the older woman had already begun shaking her head. "I am not nearly powerful enough. In fact, Anabel is the most powerful witch I've ever known. It's in her blood."

"Then I have no choice," he said. "Maybe you can train her, if you can do it quickly. There's not a lot of time. My sister's life is in danger."

She blinked up at him. "You're a ghost. You should be able to find your sister."

"Yes, that would be true. If a powerful warlock wasn't shielding himself and her."

"Oh." Juliet still sounded stunned. Shell-shocked, even. "Do you know who this warlock is?"

"No." Tyler glided toward the doorway. "Thank you for visiting with me," he said.

"You're welcome." Her wide smile attested to the truth of her words. "If there's anything I can do to help you and Anabel, let me know."

"I will." And he winked out, reappearing in Anabel's living room. She hadn't arrived home yet, which was probably a good thing. She'd seemed pretty freaked out, and the last thing he needed was for her to make a panic-fueled decision to try to send him away again.

Her cat hissed and puffed up his fur immediately upon seeing Tyler. The long-haired black beast had been enjoying a sunny spot on the carpet near the front window. As cats went, this one was large and appeared powerful.

"It's okay, cat," Tyler said, lowering his voice and trying to sound friendly. "I'm not here to do any harm."

Apparently, the feline believed him, as he settled back down, turning his head and pretending to ignore Tyler while grooming his fur and stretching, all at the same time.

Tyler guessed this was a good thing. He'd never had much to do with cats, like most shifters. The two species—wolf and feline—were natural enemies. Tyler supposed it was a measure of Anabel's uniqueness—or maybe her power—that she had a cat as a pet.

The sound of a car pulling into the driveway heralded Anabel's arrival. She slammed into the house, looking around wildly until she saw him.

"You are trouble. Nothing but trouble," she cried. "My life was already messed up before you arrived, but you're making it even worse."

He grimaced. "I'm sorry. I have no choice."

"How?" she demanded. "How do you even know your sister's in danger? You're dead. How the heck would she be able to contact you?"

"Her energy reached out to me. She asked me to save her from him. She's pretty desperate. Who wouldn't be, in her situation?"

"I want no part of it. I'm done." Straightening, she waved her hand, giving him a flat, cold stare. "I want you to leave."

Though he knew she couldn't see it, her power flared,

radiating from the edges of her fingertips as she pointed at him.

This time, he had no choice but to do as she commanded. As the compulsion filled him, he felt himself being pulled away, as if a giant vortex had opened to suck him right back out of this world.

"Wait," he shouted, desperation fueling his words. "You can't let my sister die. This is your chance to atone for what you did to that Lilly girl."

Instantly, the energy sending him away faltered and then dissipated. Relieved, he wiped his hands down the front of his pants.

Anabel sighed, looking down before meeting his gaze. "Juliet told you about that?"

Glad now that he'd stayed and talked to the other woman, Tyler nodded. "She did." Impulsively, he moved forward and put his hand on her shoulder. Of course, she couldn't feel his ghostly touch—heck, he could see through his own fingers—but the gesture made him feel better. "My sister is only twenty-five years old. She doesn't deserve to suffer like this."

After a moment, she nodded. "I'll try my best. I can promise you that. As to this mysterious power I supposedly have, I don't know what to tell you about that."

He took a deep breath, deciding to bulldoze ahead since he really had no choice. "Juliet said she could train you."

Her beautiful bronze eyes narrowed. "Oh, she did, did she?"

Might as well tell her the rest of it. "She told me you're descended from a long line of powerful witches. Your mother died before she could train you."

"Or even tell me." Moving away from him, she sighed. "My mom was killed in a fire when I was three. My dad got me out and went back for her. He died too."

"I'm sorry." He considered and then decided, why not? "If you'd like, when this is over, I can try to find their spirits too."

"We'll see." Spinning around, sending her gauzy black skirt flaring out around her like a flamenco dancer's, she headed into the kitchen. "I'm starving. It's long past the time I normally eat lunch. I hope you don't mind if I eat."

"Why would I mind?" he asked, genuinely curious.

"I guess I assumed eating was something you missed," she said, flashing a tentative smile. The power of that smile almost brought him to his knees.

Stunned, chest tight, he wondered if all the men in Leaning Tree were blind. Anabel was the most beautiful woman he'd ever met. And eighteen months of being a widow was long enough for every red-blooded man to make a move. How was it that they weren't beating a path to her door? That was something he'd never understand.

If he'd been alive… As soon as he had the thought, he pushed it away. He wasn't alive, hadn't been for a long time. No point in tormenting himself with what-might-have-beens.

Oblivious, she'd turned away and had already started sautéing something in a cast-iron skillet. Curious, he moved closer, frowning slightly when he realized the thing was full of vegetables.

"Where's the meat?" he asked. "That's the one thing I do miss. As a carnivore, I liked a nice rare steak."

"Eww." She actually shuddered. "I'm a vegetarian." Then she watched him, apparently waiting for him to react to her joke.

Laughing, he obliged her. "Good one."

She shook her head, turning back to the skillet. "I'm serious. When I need protein, I turn to other sources like beans, nuts, soy and grains."

Horrified, he eyed her. "It's a wonder you're not sick. Shifters need meat. End of story."

"Really? You're entitled to your opinion, but I haven't had meat in over a year. And I've never felt better."

Her black cat leaped up onto the counter, eyeing the sizzling food. Anabel shooed him off. "Get down, Leroy."

Immediately, the feline obeyed, twining around her ankles and mewing.

"He's hungry," she said. "Just a minute, baby."

Eyeing the cat, Tyler shook his head. "Please tell me he's not a vegetarian too."

"Of course not. He eats high-quality dry cat food. Tuna flavored, I think."

Finished cooking, she turned off the burner and transferred her meal to a plate. Then she went to the cabinet and poured her pet a bowl full of kibble, placing it on the floor for him to eat.

She carried her plate to the table, sat and dug in. Even watching her eat was an act of sensuality. "Now, if we're done discussing my diet, let's get back to our plan of action. I was thinking about talking to some of your sister's friends."

"Since the police won't?"

"Have they? Do you even know?"

"Since they've been treating her disappearance like she left voluntarily, I'm guessing no."

She finished chewing before responding. He watched as she blotted one corner of her full mouth with a napkin, aching to put his tongue there instead. "I'll find out. I'll need a bit more information, like where she worked and lived. How about we start this afternoon?"

Gratified, he nodded. "I like that you don't waste time."

"Might as well do it on my day off. I have to go back to work tomorrow. On workdays, my time is limited."

"Work?" He said the word as if it were foreign. "What do you do, exactly?"

"I used to be an executive secretary to the president of Leaning Tree Bank. I was well regarded and made good money. Best of all, I was respected, the competent wife of a military man. But that had been in another life, before David died and my entire world had been turned apart."

Heart aching for her, he instinctively realized the last thing she'd want would be his pity. "What do you do now?"

"I cook," she answered, lifting her chin. "In the diner. I'm on the morning shift. I have to be there at six a.m. I work until two." She didn't mention that the pay was minimal. If not for the life-insurance policy that David had taken out when they were first married, she'd have had to take a second job.

"Leaving your afternoons free."

She shook her head. "I do have errands to run too, you know. But I'll work on your sister's case each day."

"Each day?" Horrified, he stared. "Don't you understand? She doesn't have that much time. We need to find her now."

Chapter 4

Now. If only she really did possess some magical power that would enable her to help him. Anabel hated the idea of a young girl, trapped in some dark place, subject to the whims of a cruel and probably psychotic man.

"Tell me how," she entreated. "I'll do whatever I can. But I don't know what else to do."

"Find the warlock."

"Okay." She waited for him to say more, but apparently he thought that was enough. "And how do I do that?" she finally asked. "And don't say 'use your power,' because I have no idea how."

And furthermore, she wasn't entirely sure she even had power to begin with. And if by some miracle she succeeded in finding the warlock, then what? Call the police? She doubted they'd even help. They'd already made it clear they regarded her as a dangerous eccentric.

He thought for a moment. "Maybe Juliet can give you a crash course in magic. She did offer."

"Maybe. Though I have a feeling something like what you're talking about isn't simple."

"Probably not." He straightened, meeting and holding her gaze. "But we're talking about my sister's life. I'd hope you'd do whatever it takes to save her. We're about out of time."

Telling him she'd think about it, she finished eating her meal, concentrating on the food while trying to puzzle out some sort of solution. She wanted to help him find his sister; she really did. She just had no idea how.

When she looked up, her ghostly visitor had vanished.

Blinking, she looked around. Tyler was gone.

He didn't reappear that afternoon, though when her phone rang shortly before five and it was her boss, Jeb, calling to tell her she wasn't needed tomorrow and, in fact, could have a few more days off, she knew somehow Tyler had been working behind the scenes to clear the time she needed to help him.

Though she wouldn't like the lost wages, she thanked Jeb and agreed, promising to be back by the end of the week. She hoped she wasn't losing her job. While Jeb had never seemed to mind what the townspeople thought of Anabel, especially since she'd worked out of sight in the kitchen, she wouldn't put it past some uptight haters to try to cause her to lose her employment. There were a few small-minded people mean enough to do something like that.

She kept waiting for Tyler to reappear, though she knew she should have been relieved at his absence. He fascinated her, though, and she was honest enough with herself to know part of that was because he was so ruggedly masculine. If he hadn't been a spirit, she imagined her skin would sizzle if he were to touch her. Even the thought sent a bolt of heat through her.

Pushing the thought away, she occupied herself with weeding her garden and trying to gather up the nerve to call Juliet and ask her to help. But she couldn't even imagine the conversation. How did you ask someone, even your best friend, to teach you how to use your magic like a witch?

At dinnertime, she took to the internet and tried to find information about magic. But the general weirdness put her off, and she stopped before she felt too alienated from herself. If the townspeople thought she was strange now, imagine if they learned she supposedly was a witch with magical abilities.

For a few minutes, she sat in her living-room chair, eyes closed, trying to concentrate. "Magic," she whispered, feeling slightly foolish but going ahead anyway. "If you're there, help me out. Show me where to find Tyler's sister."

But nothing happened. To be honest, she wasn't sure how she would have reacted if something had.

Absurdly lonely—odd because she'd gotten used to being by herself—and sort of missing Tyler, she puttered around the house until her normal bedtime.

Since she didn't have to be up at four thirty, she didn't have to turn in early. But old habits died hard and Anabel had always taken comfort in a routine. So she got herself ready to turn in.

Tyler didn't return, not even when she turned out the lights and climbed into bed. Counting her blessings, she closed her eyes with a smile on her face, waiting to fall asleep.

That night, he invaded her dreams. The instant Anabel realized it was his arms holding her close rather than David's, she struggled, trying to wake herself up. But sleep gripped her tightly, refusing to release her. So she settled for pushing Tyler away.

But her body, so long untouched and alone, craved his, and every touch brought a thrill of electric longing pulsing through her. And truthfully, when she pretended to twist away, and he came in for the kiss, molten fire seared her lips as his mouth claimed hers.

Deep within her, desire flared, tugging at her, turning her inside and out. But she'd pledged herself to one mate and had sworn not to ever betray him. Not even in death.

"No." Meaning it, she broke the embrace and pushed Tyler away. The hurt look on his handsome face gave her pause. But then, it was her dream and she had the right to control it.

Except…a little voice whispered in her mind. It *was* only a dream. And more than eighteen months had passed since she'd allowed her body to experience the thrum of physical need, the heady thrill of desire. Only a dream. Not really betrayal.

So she let herself flow forward, back into his strong arms. In her dream, Tyler was no longer ghostly. No, he was a man and had substance. She ran her fingers over corded muscle, her breathing hitching, while her lips ached to kiss him again.

And so they did. Kissing and touching, nothing more. No sin, this. Her clothes stayed on, even if it seemed the heat blazing through her veins might melt them off. And so it went, endless in the way of dreams. Until she woke and the dream vanished like a puff of smoke.

The guilt struck her the instant she opened her eyes. Unreasonable, unfathomable, but there nonetheless. The tangled sheets looked as though someone had actually been there, and her body ached with a heaviness that had nothing to do with reality.

She told herself it had been only a dream, that she hadn't

really been unfaithful to David, as if you could be with a ghost anyway.

Still, first thing after getting up, she reached into the nightstand drawer and pulled out the photo of her deceased husband she'd always kept there. Once, she'd kept it right beside her bed so it would be the first thing she saw in the morning and the last at night. A year after his death, she'd finally put it away, finding the pain still too unbearable. Now she needed to gaze at David's beloved face, as if doing so could erase her memory of her sinfully sensual dream.

"Is that a picture of your husband?" Tyler's deep voice made her jump. And blush, instantly hot all over, as if he might somehow know about her nighttime subconsciously lustful thoughts.

"Yes." Short answer, while she stared at the photograph and waited for the familiar grief and agony to consume her. When it didn't immediately slam into her, she nearly panicked.

"I miss him so much," she whispered. And then, with the words, came the familiar throat ache. "We loved each other, you know. He was a great husband."

"Let me see."

Heaven help her, she started again. While she'd been intent on her former husband's face, Tyler had glided so close he was looking over her shoulder.

Wordlessly, she held up the frame. "This was right before he left for his last tour."

Tyler swore, shocking her. "I know that guy. Or knew him, I should say."

"What?" Not sure she'd heard correctly, Anabel spun around to face him. She felt numb, except for the slow, insistent beat of her heart in her chest. "You knew David? Are you sure?"

"Let me see the picture again."

Slowly, she turned the frame around. "Where were you stationed?" Her voice seemed to come from a distance.

"That's classified." Grimacing, he shook his head at what had apparently been an automatic response. "Sorry. It doesn't matter now, of course. I was stationed at Tangi Valley, Maidan Wardak Province. As was your husband."

"Eighty klicks from Kabul. He told me that, even if he couldn't tell me the exact name of the place." Hearing the defeat in her tone, she sighed. "David said the troops called it Death Valley."

"It wasn't a pleasant area. Lots of Taliban." He winced, as if the memory was unpleasant. "It's where I died."

"David too."

"Roadside bomb?" He sighed, not waiting for an answer. "We dealt with that a lot. Our presence has always been a bone of contention among the locals."

She nodded, unable to think past one thing. He'd known David. Finally. Someone who could speak of her husband as a living, breathing person rather than a mere statistic. Desperate to hear more, she sat down on the edge of her bed, still clutching the frame. "How well did you know my husband?"

"Dave?" He scratched his head. "Not all that well. We were on different shifts, so I didn't see him all that often. But we played cards a couple of times."

"He didn't like being called that," she said. "Dave. He always made everyone use his full name, David."

"Really?" He shrugged. "Out there in hell, formality and civility die with every explosion. We called him Dave. Everyone did. Heck, my name is Tyler and everyone referred to me as Ty."

That made sense. "I wish you'd known him better. In the last month or so before he died, I hardly heard from him. What few letters he was able to get out didn't even arrive until after he'd been killed." She swallowed to get past the lump in her throat. "I'd love it if you could share some stories about him."

"I'm sorry. I wish I could too."

Almost afraid to ask, she did anyway. For months she'd been plagued by nightmares, picturing various scenarios in which her mate had been killed. "Were you there when he…died?" Her voice came out a whisper. "All I know was that it was a bomb. They—the military—told me there was nothing left of his body to send back. So I didn't even have that."

For once, Tyler went silent. She watched him, praying with every fiber of her being that he would be able to tell her something. Anything. When she'd pressed for more information, all the military did was give her their apparently standard line: "killed in the line of duty."

"No," Tyler finally answered, crushing her hopes. "I was not there when he died. At least, not that I know of. When I try to reflect on my last memory of that place, I'm pretty sure he was still alive. So I must have died before him. How long did you say he's been gone?"

"A little over eighteen months." Which meant Tyler had been dead longer than that.

"I see." He nodded. "Again, I'm sorry I can't tell you more. From what I knew of him, he seemed like a nice guy."

"Thank you for that." She put the photograph back inside the drawer. Though it wasn't much, actually hearing something, anything, about David, helped ease the edge of the constant ache she always carried inside her. Lately, though, she'd noticed it had lessened. There were actually larger and larger patches of time when she didn't think about David at all. Guilt stabbed her as she realized this. She'd promised herself never to forget him.

Looking up, she met Tyler's gaze. Something in his tortured expression made her stomach lurch. For a ghost, his features were really well-defined. "What is it? You're not telling me everything, are you?"

With a shrug, he nodded. "Nothing bad, so don't worry. Just something else I remembered. I think I know how I died."

She waited, bracing herself.

"There had been a few of the guys, including me and your David, who'd skirted the edge of danger working to help some of the locals, most particularly the children," he continued. "Our superiors had reprimanded us once, turning a blind eye after that."

"That's good, isn't it?"

"Yes. Of course. But dangerous."

"Yet you and David still did it," she marveled.

"It was impossible not to. The locals were starving. We smuggled rations to the women, brought the children trinkets and treats sent from home and did our best to ease the damage."

She waited, aware there were often two sides to every story.

"The Taliban sympathizers hated this. That's how I was killed."

Though she detected a tinge of shame in his voice, she saw none in his expression.

"They watched and the next time we snuck out to deliver goodies, they'd set up a trap."

Bracing herself, she nodded. When he didn't speak again, she sighed. "Let me guess. The suicide bomb you'd mentioned before?"

"Yes. Took out at least two of us, and some women and

children too." Rugged features expressionless, he stared off into the distance, as if remembering the sound of the gunfire and explosions, the screaming and shouting. All the pain.

His next words confirmed this. "Anabel, they didn't even care that they'd killed themselves or their own people."

Aching, she wished she knew a way to comfort him. "I'm sorry," she said, aware her words couldn't possibly be adequate. Then, because he was a ghost and she really wanted to know, she went ahead and asked. "What was it like to die?"

Lost in his thoughts, he didn't at first respond. When he raised his head to look at her, all emotion had been erased from his handsome face. "A sharp flash of pain. And then…nothing."

"Nothing?" She frowned. "I was hoping for something more inspiring. Like you could say you found yourself in a tunnel, moving toward a bright light, all that. You know?"

"I do know."

Was he laughing at her? She squinted at him, not sure. "And?" she finally prodded. "Are you going to tell me what it's like?"

"It was liberating," he said. "Once I'd shed that ruined body, joy filled me. I went to another place. Another plane. I knew I'd come home."

Nothing but contentment and happiness filled his voice now. "But because of the violent manner of my death, my spirit went into shock. It was all too traumatic, and they took me to a healing place."

"A healing place?"

He waved his ghostly hand, about to say more, and then didn't. "That's all I can tell you."

"But…why are you here? Why didn't you move on?"

"Because somehow I heard my sister's cries. Her prayers for help. So instead of moving forward as I should have, I was allowed to remain tethered to earth."

"I'm not sure I understand. You're a ghost."

"Yes." He smiled, and the beauty of him struck her deep inside her heart. "I was permitted to come back as an ethereal being in the hopes of saving my sister. She's being tortured, and while death would be a release from the pain, it's not her time to die. Still, I fear he will kill her. And if he doesn't, her suffering is terrible. We've got to get her out of there."

"We'll figure out a way," she promised, reacting to the sheer desperation in his voice.

Apparently overcome, he turned away. For a moment, his ghostly form flickered and vanished, before solidifying once more.

"Thank you." When he met her gaze, his hazel eyes glowed with determination. "Meanwhile, have I answered all your questions?"

She thought of her dead husband, the man she'd mourned for so long. "Since you said David was still alive when you died, I take it he wasn't with you that night?"

"I don't actually know. If he was there, I don't remember him. But I'm guessing he was killed doing something similar."

Miraculously, this helped ease her heart more than anything she'd heard or read about the troops in Afghanistan. "He died helping women and children," she whispered, marveling again that war hadn't changed her husband's generous heart.

"Most likely." Tyler shrugged. "Though I wasn't there, so I can't know for sure."

"I do. I know inside me." Turning, she headed toward

her bathroom. "I'll be out in a little while. You can wait in the kitchen, if you'd like."

His wry grimace made her smile. "Sure. I'll go in there and inhale the aroma of the coffee brewing. I used to enjoy my first cup in the morning." With that, he drifted away, his broad shoulders and narrow waist drawing her eye until she could no longer see him.

Shutting the door, she couldn't help feeling sorry for him. He'd died a noble death too. Had he no one to mourn him? She realized she'd never asked about his family. Surely he must have had parents, maybe even other siblings, someone to mark his passing. She'd ask him later.

She knew only of the one sister, Dena, who'd surely mourned her brother. So much so that she'd cried out to his spirit in her pain and terror. Their tie had been so great that he'd come back from wherever he'd been to try to save her from a fate worse than death.

Again, a noble man. One with a generous spirit, like David.

She glanced at herself in the mirror and paused. A woman of purpose stared back at her, brown eyes blazing, expression resolute and determined. And resilient. Somehow, after all she'd been through, she realized she'd emerged stronger for it.

Fine. Decision made, she turned the shower on and, as soon as the water got hot, stepped inside. If she had magic power inside her, she'd learn how to use it to locate Tyler's sister. As for doing battle with the warlock person, well, she'd have to deal with that when it happened.

As Tyler drifted into the colorful kitchen, he took in the green cabinets, orange walls and colorful paintings. More of Anabel's personality. How strange that it happened that the woman he'd sought help from had been married to one of the guys in his former unit. He was pretty sure it wasn't a fluke. One thing life after death had taught him was that there were very few real coincidences. Things happened for a purpose, and while he might temporarily be blinded to what that might be, he knew to keep an eye out.

While he and Dena were growing up with a drug-addicted father, his mother had shielded them as best she could. Older by ten years, Tyler had tried to be the man in the family, but as a kid, he hadn't fully realized that his father might kill him rather than hurt him. His mother had, always stepping in front of the blows, taking the brunt of his father's drug-fueled wrath.

Desperately wanting to defend his mother, despite her strict orders not to intervene, Tyler had helped in every way he could besides beating the man to a bloody pulp, which he fully planned to do once he was older and stronger. In the meantime, he'd taken care of his mother when her bruises and broken bones incapacitated her. He'd cooked and done laundry and watched after his baby sister. He'd learned to change her diapers and mix her formula, sleeping on the floor by her crib in case his doped-up father got any stupid ideas. When his mother had found out about this, she'd put a stop to it, promising Tyler she'd make sure nothing happened to the baby.

And she had. She'd always made sure to be in the way of her husband's fists and vitriolic bile. Despite her petite stature, she'd displayed enormous courage, though Tyler had never understood why she wouldn't leave. All she'd say when he asked was that he was too young to understand. Eventually, he'd figured out that his father had sworn to hunt her down and kill her and his children should she ever try to run.

Finally, their father had disappeared. Tyler had heard the man now lived on the streets, a slave to his own demons. Periodically, he'd show up at the house, but only to take money, which he used to buy more drugs.

Tyler had never understood why his mother gave the man anything at all.

As soon as he'd graduated from high school, Tyler had enlisted in the army. For him, the military was not only an escape, but a chance to make something of himself, to make sure he didn't end up like his father.

Their father had overdosed when Dena was seventeen. Tyler had been stationed at Fort Bliss in El Paso, Texas. He'd been granted leave and had hurried home to help out.

He hadn't been sure what to expect. A celebration, perhaps? Instead he found his mother insensible with grief and his baby sister angry at the woman who'd raised them.

"What's wrong with her?" Dena had asked. "He spent his life making her miserable, and all she can do is cry."

"I don't understand either," he said, putting his arm around her shoulders. "But I do know Mom needs us. Let her grieve, and be there for her, the way she always was for us."

"She should have left him" had been Dena's response. Since Tyler tended to agree, he didn't reply.

After the funeral, he'd gone back to base and kept in touch with his sister. He'd celebrated with her long-distance when she got a job at the junior college. Sure, it was in the cafeteria, but she'd had plans, she told him. She wanted to take some classes, with an eye on earning her degree. He'd been proud.

What Dena hadn't told him was that their mother had started using the very same drugs that had killed their father. Heroin, mostly. Sometimes meth. Their mom had died right after Tyler was sent to Afghanistan, though he hadn't learned about it for two weeks. He'd raged and grieved and worried that his sister might follow this horrible fam-

ily pattern. Dena had assured him that she wouldn't. He'd
believed her. Neither of them had wanted anything to do
with that lifestyle.

After that, he and his sister had been on their own. And
then Tyler had gone and gotten himself killed. And Dena
had gotten into a bigger mess than he ever would have
thought possible. If he didn't get her out, she was going to
die too young, just as he had. Even though it wasn't her
time to go.

Anabel had to help him save her. She had to. He would
accept nothing else, even if it cost him his own movement into eternity.

Being a ghost felt more like being alive than he'd expected. Sure, he couldn't eat or drink, didn't have to elimi-
nate bodily waste or sleep, but he felt all the same human
emotions he'd experienced when he was alive.

Including desire. That one had surprised the hell out of
him. Every time he got close to Anabel, his entire body
tightened in places that shouldn't have been possible for a
ghost. At first, he'd tried to keep telling himself that it was
due to her beauty and the power that radiated from her.

But after the first night, when he'd found himself watching her sleep, aching with the kind of physical need he
couldn't possibly satisfy without a flesh-and-blood body,
he'd known it was more. Much, much more.

He wanted her. Desired her. In all the ways a man
wanted a woman. Except he wasn't a man. He was a ghost.

This had to be his own personal form of hell. Because
there was absolutely nothing he could do to ease the craving.

When Anabel finally emerged from her morning preparations, showered and dressed in a pair of faded black
jeans that hugged her curves, with her dark hair in a jaunty
ponytail, he couldn't make himself stop staring. She was

the sexiest woman he'd ever seen, bar none. Again, that lust stabbed through what once had been his body.

"You look…glowing," he said. He really sucked at compliments.

"Thank you. I guess." Her smile made her aura illuminate even brighter, making a glowing halo around her head.

For whatever reason, he felt the need to elaborate. "I don't just mean your aura, though yours is spectacular. But your human form is beautiful."

Her smile widened, making her whiskey eyes sparkle. "Wow. Thanks. You kind of made my day."

He found himself smiling back. Maybe he wasn't so bad at this complimenting thing after all.

He let his gaze drink her up, his entire body burning. Funny how he still felt as if he had a body, even though he didn't. Even when she turned away, completely unaware of his desire, he tracked her with his gaze.

Focus, he reminded himself. He'd come back for a reason—to save Dena, not ache for a woman he could never have.

Pouring herself a cup of coffee, she added cream and sugar before taking a deep sip. "Ah," she sighed. "That's good."

"Torturing me now?"

For an instant, she looked stricken, and then she shrugged. "Not my intention at all. But I apologize nonetheless."

He gave a quick dip of his head to show the apology had been accepted. "What's on the agenda for today?"

"I'm going up to the college where your sister works. I want to talk to some of her friends."

"Sounds good." Action, finally. He approved. "What about?"

She gave him a long look, clearly debating what she had to say. "I need to find out about her boyfriend."

"I can save you some time on that. Dena didn't have one," he answered, confident.

One eyebrow raised, she nodded. "Okay, then I need to find out about anyone she might have dated or slept with."

"No need." He shook his head. "Between work and school, she didn't have time. She would have told me if there was anyone special."

Making an exasperated sound, she grimaced. "Tyler, I hate to be the one to break it to you, but I'm pretty sure your sister isn't a saint. This man who has her had to have met her somehow. I'm going to try and gather information to see if we can figure out who he is."

Chapter 5

Tyler started to speak, then thought better of it. No doubt she was right. Not only was she pretty and socially active, but Dena was a healthy twenty-five-year-old. He shouldn't be acting like the overprotective big brother, not now. Not only had he managed to get himself killed and leave her without any family, but clearly he hadn't succeeded in teaching her to be careful.

Unless, as Anabel said, the man who'd grabbed her had been someone she'd trusted.

"You're right," he admitted. "But you have to consider that it could be a teacher, or a janitor, or even one of her coworkers."

"Or some guy she'd dated," Anabel pointed out. "There are a lot of crazies masquerading as normal in the dating scene, let me tell you."

He cocked his head. "You've been dating?"

"I tried. Once or twice—that was it. Just a month ago. I thought it might help me to, you know, get over David.

After that, I gave up and deleted my profile from all the dating sites."

Jealousy stabbed him, completely unwarranted.

"Good for you for trying," he said, aware of the lie and feeling like a fool. "I think after eighteen months, Dave would approve of you getting back out there."

"No," she said softly, her expression shutting down. "He wouldn't. David was my mate. You were Pack. You know what that means. He's the only one I will ever love."

Slowly, he nodded. "I do, though I'm not sure I believe in that particular myth."

"Myth?"

"Yes. I honestly don't know anyone who actually met their mate."

She pointed to her chest. "Now you do. Me."

Ignoring the emotions swirling inside him, he eyed her. "How did you know? I mean, we all have people we're attracted to, even people we love. What made you think Dave was actually your mate?"

"I didn't just think it. I knew, the instant he kissed me."

He thought of what he'd learned from Juliet. "And Kane McGraw? Did you also *know* he was your mate?"

At his words, her eyes filled with tears. "I had a breakdown, Tyler. I wasn't myself." Holding herself stiffly, she turned away from him.

Clearly, he'd gone too far. He'd realized it the instant he finished speaking. "I'm sorry," he said. "I just wanted to point out to you that it was possible for you to find love again."

Like with me. More foolishness, as he was nothing but a shade of a man. He waited for Anabel to shoot him down.

But she didn't respond. Instead she hurried away. A minute later, he heard the sound of her bedroom door closing.

* * *

Though initially she'd been hurt by Tyler's words, the more she considered them, the more Anabel understood his thought process. Of course he'd doubt her conviction once he learned she'd erroneously dubbed a second man her true mate. As if she'd ever been unsure about David, or he about her.

No, she'd been lonely, stumbling around close to the end of a ledge, and when she learned Kane McGraw had come back to town, she'd sought a way to end the dark cloud of loneliness. Back in school, she'd always had a crush on Kane, even dated him a few times despite his being several years older than her, and with the twisted logic of depression, she'd managed to convince herself that the impossible was real.

When he rejected her, saying he loved another, it had been the final shove and she'd gone under. Her bewildered pain and her burning desire for vengeance had blinded her to the truth and to the light. In a moment of weakness, she'd let the darkness in and had nearly caused a good woman to lose her life. Worse, she'd later learned that Lilly Gideon, the woman Kane loved, had spent fifteen years imprisoned by her own father and his religious cult. She shuddered to think she'd nearly sent Lilly back to that awful life.

After that, she'd lain low. Gradually recovering, aware no one in town would ever look at her the same way again.

She'd made several clumsy attempts to make it up to Lilly McGraw, until finally the other woman had hugged her and told her to stop, that she forgave her. For that, Anabel had been grateful.

Now, for the first time in a long while, Anabel had hope. Never once had she imagined she'd be given the chance to atone by saving Dena Rogers.

While she didn't personally know Tyler's sister, she could only imagine what kind of hell the younger woman now faced. Similar, she thought, to what Lilly Gideon had once faced. The parallels of the two women's predicaments didn't escape her.

Once she freed Dena, she would have wiped her own slate clean once more.

And Tyler could... She couldn't help wondering what would happen to Tyler once they'd succeeded in freeing his sister. He'd go back into wherever ghosts went when it came time to move on. The light, she assumed. At least she hoped so. The alternative would be very bleak.

Glancing at her watch, she saw it was nearly nine. If she wanted to get her day started, she couldn't hide out in her bedroom forever. One thing she'd learned since her meltdown was she had a lot more inner strength than she'd ever suspected. Magic would be a definite bonus.

So she straightened her shoulders, took a deep breath and opened the door. When she walked back into the kitchen, Tyler's ghostly form hovered exactly where she'd left him.

Again struck by his large, masculine frame, she sucked in a breath. How he, even though a ghost, could practically radiate virility stunned her. Though this time, she noticed an air of isolation around his tall, broad-shouldered figure.

The question in his hazel eyes made her heart skip a beat.

"I'll do it," she said, not giving him a chance to speak. "I need to see if I can take a crash course in learning how to access my magic. Once I have some sort of grip on that, I can seriously hunt for whoever abducted your sister."

He bowed his head, a swath of dark hair falling onto his forehead. "Thank you."

Uncomfortable with her visceral reaction to so much

male beauty, she nodded. Keeping busy would be the best distraction from those kinds of crazy thoughts. "Let's go." Snatching up her car keys, she headed toward the door. "We'll stop and talk to Juliet. I think her first yoga class of the day just finished up. I'm hoping she'll have some pointers for me."

Trying not to smile as Tyler crammed his long legs in the passenger seat of her Fiat, she sang along to the radio during the short drive downtown.

As it turned out, Juliet had a lot more than pointers to help Anabel. "You'll need to read these," she said, grabbing a short stack of books from a bookcase behind her desk. "This will be a good starting place. Once you have, come back to me with questions."

Anabel glanced at the books, then at Tyler, who gave an almost imperceptible shake of his head. "Juliet, I'd love to read them—and I will, eventually—but right now I'm short on time. Tyler's sister's life is in danger, and I'm afraid I'm going to need a crash course in magic in order to save her."

Appearing nonplussed, Juliet swallowed and slowly put the books down on top of her desk. "It's not that simple," she began.

"Make it as simple as possible, please." Though she hated to interrupt her kind friend, Anabel knew every second must be an eternity to the poor woman being held prisoner.

Eyeing her, Juliet appeared to consider. "All right," she finally said. "But you need to know, magic can be dangerous without knowledge. Extremely dangerous."

Anabel locked eyes with her friend. With her smooth face and long gray braid, Juliet always radiated peace and tranquility. And strength, Anabel thought. "Teach me how to protect myself."

"I'll do my best. But understand, you could still be killed. I don't know how powerful this warlock is."

Tyler began to flicker, his form wavering in and out of view. Anabel glanced once at him, bracing herself for the swooping of her stomach as she did. Their gazes locked and held as he slowly solidified. *I'm okay,* he mouthed.

Once she knew he was all right, she refocused all her attention on Juliet. "Teach me as much as you can in as short a time as possible."

Juliet nodded. "How long do I have?"

"A woman's life is at stake, so I don't have long." Anabel glanced again at Tyler. "A day?"

Frowning, he shook his head.

"How about twelve hours?"

This time, Tyler reluctantly nodded.

"Twelve hours?" Eyebrows raised, Juliet glanced at her wrist even though she wasn't wearing a watch. "Sorry. What time is it now?"

"Nine thirty. That gives us until tonight."

"It'll have to do, I guess." Juliet sighed, her soft blue eyes sharpening. "It's not nearly long enough, but let's get started on some basics."

After a quick explanation of what magic was—not so much an external thing, but part of Anabel's inner spirit—Juliet told her it was time to see if Anabel could feel her power deep inside herself.

Anabel didn't even have to think. "No."

"Well, then we're going to try and feel it."

"I already tried last night. Nothing happened."

"We'll try again."

"How?"

"Take a deep breath," Juliet advised. "First, you need to slow down your pulse. Your heart is beating so fast I can see the fluttering in the hollow of your throat."

Self-consciously, Anabel raised her hand to her neck. "Sorry. I'm a little nervous."

"Deep breath."

Obediently, Anabel inhaled. "I can't help it," she said, fidgeting in her chair. "This is all very odd."

"Then we'll wait until you're tranquil." Rising, Juliet lit a candle, moving it over so the scent was close to Anabel. "We may have to do some yoga if this doesn't help. Breathe. It's eucalyptus. Very calming."

Desperate, Anabel inhaled the scent, trying to think calming thoughts, using the same mantra she used when meditating. A moment or two later, she blinked. Darned if she didn't feel better. More confident and stronger.

"Now we'll talk about power," Juliet said, smiling slightly as if she knew Anabel's thoughts. "Everyone has a spark of magic inside. Some just have more than others."

Anabel nodded, the fear trying to creep back in. She couldn't really explain her intense nervousness, but for some reason the entire idea of having magical powers scared her.

If Tyler's sister hadn't needed her help, Anabel figured she would just have let the so-called magic stay locked up inside her. If she'd even ever learned of its existence, that was.

"That you are able to see ghosts as more than energy speaks to your level of power. That's one of the ways it manifests itself." Juliet grinned. "And the fact that your ability to see and hear spirits didn't make you go stark, raving crazy is another testament to your strength."

Strength. "I rarely feel strong, though I've realized what I've been through and overcome has given me strength. But that doesn't matter. Tell me what else I should be able to do. Most important, I need the ability to track this creep who has Dena."

"And fight him," Tyler chimed in, making Juliet jump.

"I forgot about you," Juliet said, shooting a stern glance in his general direction. "Fighting won't be possible, not without a lot of practice. But I can teach Anabel to protect herself."

"That will have to do," Anabel said grimly. "As long as I can hold him off long enough to get his captive—or captives—out."

"And then what?" Juliet asked, her sharp voice telling Anabel what she thought of that idea. "He'll likely be furious. You won't be able to hold him off forever."

Again Anabel and Tyler exchanged a glance. Again, her heart turned over in response. Tearing her gaze away, she focused on Juliet. "Then you'd better do your best to teach me as much as you can. It's not like I even have a choice."

Tyler didn't know what it was about Anabel—other than her beauty—but every time their eyes met, he found himself entranced. His fascination deepened the more time he spent with her, which was not only impossible, but an unnecessary distraction. He'd come back to the earthly plane with one objective—to save his sister— and he couldn't let this compelling attraction detour him.

So he decided to leave the two women alone. There wasn't much he could do anyway, other than be a disruption. Anabel had asked Juliet for twelve hours—an eternity for his sister, trapped and tortured. But this was only the second day since he'd appeared and begged Anabel for help. She needed to learn how to tap into her power if she wanted to have a prayer of finding Dena. He had to allow himself to trust and to hope.

He left the human plane and went to the gray area he privately thought of as the in-between place. Not earth, but not the afterlife either. Once there, he made himself still and then sent himself out. Seeking, searching, for the spark of life force that belonged to his sister.

There. Faint, but still burning. He zoomed to it, passing through nothing and everything, clouds and earth and night sky. When he reached her, in that damp, dank place where she was being held, he once again tried to communicate with her and comfort her.

But Dena had no power and couldn't sense his presence. In fact, he realized she'd sunk into a state of consciousness where she couldn't sense much of anything at all.

Horrified, he took stock of her condition. Her once slender body had become emaciated, and even though she lay curled in a corner in the fetal position, he could see the sharpness of her bones. Her labored breathing attested to her general state of unhealthiness, as did her lank and tangled hair. Even her aura had changed, becoming speckled with brown and black, as if a rotting poison festered inside her system.

She didn't have much longer. Tyler wanted to weep. And rage and storm. Most of all, he wished he had substance, so he could free her from the metal shackles tethering her bony ankles to the concrete wall.

As his emotions roiled inside his spirit, he felt the approaching force of a heavy blackness descending on him. On them. Not just dark, but…evil.

Which meant the warlock had sensed his presence. Magic, reaching even into the realm of spirit. Dangerous. Deadly, even.

Tyler tried to retreat but found he could not. Invisible chains bound him, as surely as if a giant arm had reached out and held him against the concrete.

Shocked, horrified, he made his form as ethereal as he could. Still, he could not escape the grip of the other.

How powerful was this man, that he could not only sense a ghost, but also hold him down without saying a word?

Magic. Something inside him stirred in response.

Again, he eyed Dena, aching at the palpable pain radiating from her. Even in her comatose state, his sister must have sensed the presence, as well. She began to shake, making faint sounds—protests or pleas for help.

Tyler concentrated on her. With every bit of energy he possessed, he willed her to lift her head, to realize he'd come in answer to her entreaties. From the light, bringing a small illumination to the shadows.

The instant the thought occurred to him, the dark energy coalesced into a black flame of energy. And laughed, a chilling sound that echoed in the concrete chamber. Whatever part of the warlock that held Tyler became a fist. And the fist began to squeeze.

Despite the fact that none of this should have been able to happen, Tyler felt the tightening grip crush the spark out of him. He stifled panic, struggling to fight. Another few seconds, and he didn't doubt it would be snuffed out permanently.

How was it possible for someone—anyone—to have this much dark power?

Anabel. He called out her name with every fiber of his being, hoping against hope that she'd somehow hear him. And that she'd be able to save him.

Tired, Anabel once again allowed Juliet to put her through the paces. "Focus, concentrate and expand," she chanted obediently, trying like heck to send her energy outward. She felt extremely foolish that after three hours of trying, she still had not succeeded even once.

This time, she did. Something pulled her, tugged at the edges of her consciousness, and she allowed herself to follow the shining threat tethering her to him. To Tyler. Shocked, she realized he was in some sort of trouble.

The instant she reached him, she understood. She felt the dark oppression of the other's magic like a heavy weight on her physical chest, even though her actual body still sat in a chair in Juliet's office.

With her heart beating a rapid tattoo, she tried to do as Juliet had instructed. Focus and concentrate. Tyler was a ghost. While it shouldn't be possible to trap an ethereal spirit, the other had done so, using magic.

Therefore, it followed that Anabel could use her magic to free him. "Come to me, Tyler," she ordered. "Come to me now."

Air whooshed—physical or otherwise—and Tyler came to her. All at once, she found herself back in her body in Juliet's office. The impact of what she'd done knocked her from the chair to the floor. She felt dizzy and weak, as though her legs might not be able to stand. Taking a shaky breath, she held on to the back of her chair as she slowly climbed to her feet.

"Are you all right?" Juliet rushed around the desk to help her up.

Anabel waved her away, searching for Tyler. "I'm fine."

"What happened?"

Spotting Tyler, nearly incandescent, in the doorway, Anabel smiled. "I just freed Tyler, my ghostly friend. It looks like the warlock had trapped his spirit. Such a thing shouldn't be possible, should it?"

"No." Juliet gaped at her, her faded blue eyes wide. "You seriously went up against this evil psycho and won?"

Dropping into the chair, Anabel put her head between her knees, willing the vertigo to stop. "Whatever I did seriously zapped my strength."

"But you succeeded?"

"Apparently so." Anabel gestured at Tyler. "Maybe I do have a prayer of saving your sister after all."

"Maybe so." Tyler drifted closer, flickering in and out of existence. Even so, the maddening hint of arrogance about him made Anabel smile.

Rather than smile back, Tyler shook his head. "We need to be careful. He wasn't aware of us before. Now he most certainly is."

Then, before Anabel could react or respond, Tyler vanished in a tendril of smoke.

"Ask him what happened," Juliet urged. "How'd the warlock get him?"

"He's gone." Anabel rubbed her aching temples, missing Tyler more than she should. "I'll ask him later, when I see him again. In the meantime, let's work some more. If that warlock does come looking for me, I want to be as prepared to face him as I possibly can be."

Eyes bright, Juliet nodded.

They practiced drills over and over until Anabel could barely see straight. Eventually, she was able to focus her concentration enough to light a wadded-up piece of paper on fire. Juliet clapped. "Very good!"

"That's something, right?" Anabel asked, desperately in need of an encouraging word. "I'd hate to think we've spent all this time for nothing."

"It is something," Juliet responded, her smile slowly fading. "And that shows your potential. But if you really want to win against a warlock, it's not nearly enough."

Anabel groaned. "I'm exhausted. I think I'm finished for today. I have no more energy. Let me sleep on this tonight and I'll practice in the morning."

Something in her tone made Juliet lean closer, concern in her eyes. "Practice what? Promise me you only mean to try these simple exercises like we've been working on."

Anabel didn't even have to think. "I need to do more. And to do it better. The clock is ticking and I must find where Tyler's sister is being held. First thing in the morning, I'm going to try to locate her."

"How?"

"I'm not sure. But if Tyler could use her energy to find her, surely I can do the same. And since I'm alive and can't float through the air, I'm hoping I can trace her that way."

"It's not much of a plan." Arms crossed, Juliet sighed. "And since the bad guy now knows someone with magic is looking for him, it could put you at risk, as well."

Frustrated, Anabel pushed to her feet, stumbling slightly. "If you have a better idea, please let me know."

"I don't," Juliet admitted. "But still…"

Anabel hugged her friend. "I know you're worried, but I'll be fine. I've got to pick up the pace. Tomorrow will be the third day since Tyler came to me asking for help. That's entirely unacceptable. His sister has been held prisoner for way too long."

Juliet opened and then closed her mouth. Looking nearly as exhausted as Anabel felt, she nodded. "Fine. Practice. Read the books. And call me if you have any questions."

Driving home, Anabel kept expecting Tyler to pop into her car. When he didn't, the disappointment felt way deeper than it should have. After all, he'd been in her life for only two days. Had she really gotten used to having him around that quickly? If so, her loneliness had made her more vulnerable than she'd realized.

Despite giving herself a stern talking-to all the way home, she felt a sense of urgency in her need to see him. When she got home, it was all she could do not to run into her house, looking for him.

But he wasn't there. Stopping short of calling his name, she felt the emptiness of the place in a way she hadn't since

David's death. Just great. Despite her self-imposed isolation and her confidence that she'd become self-reliant, put
a sexy man in her path for a few days and she'd already
become—not dependent, but intertwined with him somehow. Not fair. She of all people didn't deserve the ache of
missing someone again. Especially someone she barely
knew. Who happened to be a ghost.

Putting him from her mind, she fixed herself a bowl of
cereal for her dinner and then got ready for bed.

After crawling beneath the covers, she must have fallen
instantly asleep. Because when she came awake again,
startled, her nightstand clock showed it was almost three
in the morning.

What had awakened her? Sitting up, she peered around
the pitch-dark room, trying to get her bearings. Had Tyler
returned?

But no, she saw no ghostly presence, no shimmer of
energy either. Since the sun hadn't yet risen, she assumed
that he'd retreated to whatever place ghosts came from.

Something else, then. Something inside her…

The urge came upon her suddenly, like a match lit to
dry timber. She needed to shape-shift. More than a need—
a visceral command that she do so immediately. Right
now. The instant she realized, she tried to think back, to
remember when she'd last changed into wolf.

Too long. More than a month, actually. Which explained
the fierceness of her urgency to comply this instant.

Which was good, since shape-shifters who didn't change
walked a slippery slope into madness. Again, she found
herself wishing for Tyler. It would be exhilarating to have
another wolf to run with. That was, if he could still change.
Even though her kind was meant to run in packs, lately
Anabel had done all her shape-shifting alone. She liked

it that way, really. She'd told herself that so often that she almost believed it.

Slipping from the house into the cool, predawn breeze, she let the light of the three-quarter moon pull her toward the woods. Since she wore only the large T-shirt she slept in, as soon as she'd stepped into lush undergrowth below the towering oaks and pines, she pulled it over her head and draped it across a stack of large rocks. She always used them for the same purpose when she changed.

Then she smiled and turned around in a complete circle, lifting her arms high to the forest and the night sky. This ritual wasn't necessary, of course, but it made her happy, so she always did it.

Beneath her skin, her wolf rippled with impatience, wanting out. For a moment, she held her inner beast at bay and then dropped to all fours to begin the process.

Chapter 6

As Anabel initiated the change, the shifting tore through her, swift and vicious, almost as if the beast feared she'd change her mind. Pain mingled with pleasure, a peculiar combination. And then she was wolf.

Lifting her head, she sniffed the air, amazed as always by how different the wolf viewed the world. Her beast used smell first, then sight and sound.

And tonight, as usual, the forest was a feast for the senses. She tried to start off at a walk, but the joy to be wolf filled her and made her run. She crashed through the underbrush, feet drumming into fertile earth, rustling through long-fallen leaves.

Smaller animals bolted ahead, terrified by her passage. Even though they were prey, she wasn't hunting. At least not yet.

When she burst upon a clearing, she slowed to a trot, then a walk. Finally, she stopped and inhaled deeply. The human part of her regretted that she'd gone so long without letting her wolf run free. As wolf, she lived in the here and now, without worries or guilt or stress. In the days after David had been killed, she'd taken to spending days as wolf, the sorrow too deep to face as human.

Of course, like all shifters, she'd had no choice but to eventually change back to her human form.

Now, though, as wolf, she refused to think of those things any further. At this moment, she thrilled to the power in her muscular, lean form.

A flash of movement to the right caught her eyes. Sniffing, she smelled nothing, no other animal's telltale scent. Which wasn't good. At all.

Dropping into a hunting crouch, she began to approach the area where she'd seen the movement. Her nighttime vision was good, and as wolf, she never imagined things that weren't real.

A moment later, she had her answer. There, near the dense underbrush near a towering oak, sat another wolf. One whose form shimmered in and out of existence with each wisp of wind and who bore no scent. Like Tyler.

A ghost wolf? Mystified, she continued to study the other animal. Previously, all her ghostly encounters had been as human. She'd never before seen the specter of a wolf. Like Tyler, this one was big and gave off the aura of a male.

And then, as she drew closer, the other wolf cocked his head. Something in the glimmer of his eyes gave her the answer.

It was Tyler! Her ghostly companion must have finally shown up at her house and found her gone. So he'd followed her wolf, wearing the form of his own beast.

She hadn't known ghosts could do that.

She also hadn't known how happy she'd be to see him

once more. Especially now, since she was running without a pack.

Heart singing with joy, she panted at him. And then, because she was wolf, she spun and took off running again. Delight pulsed through her with the pounding of every paw on the earth.

Wolf Tyler kept pace, his shimmering ghostly form beautiful. He ran full out, making her think he had difficulty matching her pace, which only had her increasing her effort to see if she could outrun him.

Tongue lolling, grinning a wolf's grin, she ran and ran until she could run no more. Even a lope or a jog failed her. Sides heaving, she let herself crash to the ground. Lying there, panting and trying to catch her breath, she refused to even glance at the shade of her visitor.

Because she knew what came next. Shifters always became aroused when they changed back to human. Most times, unless they were with an agreeable party, they ignored it. Usually when a male and female shape-shifted alone, consent and desire were implied.

Shock rippled through her as she realized what she wanted. She wondered if he felt the same. But if he did, how would that even work with a ghost?

There, on the rock where she'd left it, her nightshirt. She'd run full circle. The time had come.

With a groan, she initiated the change back to human. This time, the shift went slowly, as her beast felt reluctant to relinquish the form. It hurt. A lot. Yet even so, her body tingled with pleasure.

And desire.

Foolish, foolish girl. Always wanting something she couldn't have. And even if she somehow, miraculously, could, doing so would be too dangerous.

Ignoring Tyler for her own peace of mind, not wanting

to see if he'd remained wolf or changed back too, she got up slowly, wincing at her sore muscles and aching bones. Snagging her oversize T-shirt off the rock, she dropped it over her head. The soft material rubbed against her pebbled nipples, making her bite her lip.

Despite her exhaustion, her entire body buzzed with want. She knew if she turned and faced him, she'd lose what little control she had and make a fool of herself.

Frustrated, she kept her eyes straight ahead, praying he didn't decide to materialize in front of her, and plodded back to the house. Once inside, she headed straight back to her bedroom. A quick glance at the clock showed she still had over an hour until sunrise, so she crawled beneath the sheets and hoped for sleep.

Instead she lay there burning.

At some point, she must have drifted off. When she next opened her eyes, yellow sunlight streamed through her window. A quick glance around her bedroom revealed she was alone, so she stretched and smiled. She'd done it. Resisted temptation and spent time in her lupine shape.

Being wolf had been good for her. More than that. Freeing her wolf brought perspective to the craziness that had been her life for the past two—now three—days since Tyler had shown up.

Now she felt as though she could accomplish anything. She could do this. Not only that, but she would succeed.

As if thinking of him had summoned him, Tyler appeared in the doorway. Still as wolf, his ghostly fur shimmering in the lemonade light of morning.

Studying him, she realized he was beautiful. Large and strong and powerful, his silver fur gleaming. He padded closer, and she noted his eyes still looked the same, shining with intelligence and humor. Awed, her chest tight, she thought he might have been the most beautiful wolf she'd ever seen, bar none.

At the thought, guilt hit her hard. She shouldn't think that, couldn't. David also had been a striking wolf, with his glossy black pelt and compact, muscular body. David should always have been the perfect wolf to her. Not Tyler, a man she barely knew.

While she watched, the ghostly wolf shimmered and faded away. A second later, a man stood in its place. A naked man, fully aroused.

Heat shot through her. She dragged her gaze away, but not before she noticed the size of his massive arousal. She'd only thought she'd faced temptation the night before. Desire consumed her. She felt it coursing through her blood like an electrifying drug. Her harsh, uneven breathing testified to how turned on he made her. One look from his smoldering eyes, and she nearly came. As she bit back a groan, her body tingled in response.

So did her guilt. Again. She shouldn't be fighting the urge to climb all over him, but she was. Worse, she could barely restrain herself from taking the hard length of him into her— No.

"Put some clothes on," she barked, her voice raspy and wobbly. "You're a ghost, so make some material-ize. Now."

He knew, damn him. He raked his eyes over her, slowly, seductively, making her clench. Then, as she continued to glare at him, he slanted a look at her, part mischief, part smoldering, before waving his hands. A second later and he was back in his military fatigues. Still as handsome, still as sexy, but no longer naked.

Damned if she didn't feel a twinge of regret. Though she could still see the bulge from his still-aroused body.

"What was all that?" she lashed out, furious with herself as much as or more than him. "Didn't I ask you to stop just appearing? You don't have to shadow me every step of the way."

Was that hurt flashing across his chiseled features?

As he drifted closer, she saw the way his hands were clenched into fists.

"Anabel," he said, the hoarse tone almost a plea. When he reached for her, she didn't try to dodge him, well aware a ghost couldn't connect by touch.

But somehow Tyler did. Not a ghost, but a man, strong and solid, pulled her against his muscular chest. A shudder of raw desire immobilized her. Shocked, she froze. Unable to resist or move.

Tyler was real. She could feel his uneven breathing, as rough as hers, and his heart pounding under his skin. While she tried to process this, he cupped her face in his large hands and covered her mouth with his.

The strong hardness of the kiss burned her like fire, searing her to the core. This…wasn't real, couldn't be real, and yet as pleasure made waves inside her, she realized she could no longer fight. As his mouth ravished hers and she felt his arousal swell against her, a hot ache grew inside her, making her dizzy. Her body throbbed with passion, with desire, disbelief, a potent combination of wonder and lust.

Heart hammering foolishly, and an undeniable web of attraction building between them, she knew this couldn't be happening. If it did, she might have finally crossed the line between reality and insanity.

Finally, that realization gave her the strength to resist, despite her inner protests. "No," she said. Throat aching, she pushed against him, both with her physical body and her inner strength.

This time, her hands went right through him, exactly as they should.

She gaped at him, once again a ghost. "How did you...?" she asked faintly.

To his credit, he appeared as stunned as she. "I don't know." His hazel eyes smoldered and blazed, pinning her. The rasp in his voice matched hers. "That shouldn't have been possible. Unless..."

"Unless what?" But she knew. Somehow she knew. She'd wanted him so badly she'd willed him to change from ghost to man.

"Unless your magic made it happen." As if he'd read her mind.

"I didn't do anything." Defensive, she shook her head. Conflicting emotions roiled inside her. Longing—yes, still that—and amazement, mingled with a healthy dose of terror.

What had almost just occurred? She didn't understand and, apparently, neither did Tyler.

Even worse, her entire body still sang with desire for him. She craved him. Someone who not only definitely was not David, but was a ghost.

Body still throbbing, she took a minute to try to gather up her shredded composure. "You're here to save your sister," she reminded him firmly.

"Yes."

"Nothing more."

"No." He sounded certain.

"Good." They could do this. If she simply didn't think about how Tyler made her feel, she could focus. Dena Rogers was in big trouble. And the evil warlock who had her had become aware of both Tyler's and Anabel's presence.

Tyler stayed in the other room as Anabel hurried through her morning rituals. She needed to learn, to cram as much information into her brain as she could by study-ing the books Juliet had given her to read.

After a quick shower, she blow-dried her hair and pulled on jeans and a T-shirt before heading to the kitchen, again forgoing her normal witchy attire. The irony wasn't lost on her either, though for now she figured it would be best to dress like everyone else if she wanted to roam around unobtrusively and ask questions.

Tyler waited at the kitchen table, appearing as his usual ghostly self. He watched as she approached, unsmiling, a serious look in his hazel eyes.

Her cat, Leroy, groomed himself on the counter behind the ghost, appearing completely at ease while waiting to be fed. Contrary to his past behavior, which had involved arching his back, whipping his tail and a lot of hissing and snarling, he no longer appeared bothered by Tyler's ghostly presence. Great. Even her own cat had become a traitor.

Leroy blinked at her, meowing once, asking for his morning meal. Which she gave him, filling his bowl with tuna-shaped kibble before turning to attend to her own breakfast.

A bowl of cereal, a mug of coffee and she settled in to scan through the first book while she ate. She flipped through the pages rapidly, seeing more of what Juliet had told her. *Focus, focus, focus.* A lot of practice exercises involving the inner self and chanting, and more talk about focus.

Finally, bored and feeling a bit cranky, she closed the book and eyed Tyler. "Today, I'm definitely going over to the college since we never made it there yesterday. I need to talk to as many people as possible who might have been friends with your sister. Someone has to know something."

This time, Tyler didn't speak. Nodding, he simply hovered a few feet off her floor, looking more ruggedly masculine than any ghost had a right to.

She ignored her body's twinging and aching and forced an impersonal smile. "Go ahead," she said. "Ask. Whatever it is, let's get it out of the way so we can start the day."

"Okay. First question. Do you always shift alone?" Tyler asked her.

Whatever she'd expected him to say, that hadn't been even close. "Yes. Oh, I didn't used to. Back when David was alive, I did like everyone else and changed in a big pack of shifters. No one minded. But these days, they've made it clear I'm not welcome."

"Who?" He sounded outraged, making her smile.

"It doesn't matter." Carrying her bowl to the sink, she rinsed it and placed it inside the dishwasher. "I'm running late. If you're coming with me, since it's my turn to ask a question, I'll want an explanation of where you disappeared to yesterday after I pulled you from the darkness."

As they buzzed along the road in the impossibly tiny car, while sitting next to the most beautiful woman he'd ever met—alive or dead—Tyler wished she would mention the kiss. The soul-shattering, gut-wrenching, incredibly arousing, *real* kiss. Impossible as that sounded. Anabel must have a great deal more magic than anyone realized to do something like that.

"Well?" she demanded, barely a moment after backing out of her driveway. "Where'd you go?"

Deliberating, he sighed. There were things he could talk about and others he wasn't allowed to. If he even tried to put voice to the something forbidden, he knew from experience that he'd find himself unable to speak.

Where he'd retreated yesterday was one of those sacred and thus secret things.

"I can't," he finally said. "Maybe it's enough to say I went back to rejuvenate my energy."

She shot him a look from under her lashes, her bronze-colored eyes gleaming. "Like a heavenly spa?"

Throat as tight as his chest, he gathered himself enough to respond to her deliberately light tone. "Sort of."

"That warlock who tried to crush you. I don't suppose you happened to get a look at his face, did you?"

"No. He was pure energy. Black, oppressive darkness. And very powerful."

Her sigh echoed his feelings. "I gathered as much."

Once they exited the main road, as they pulled onto the college campus, he directed her to the area where his sister had always parked when she went to work. "It's close to the cafeteria," he explained, pointing at the neatly land-scaped beige brick building. "All the buildings with red roofs are part of the college."

"Good to know." Pulling the key from the ignition, she dropped it in her purse. "I need to remind you again to do me a favor. Please don't talk to me when I'm asking other people questions. Not only is it confusing, but if I forget and speak to you, everyone thinks I'm nuts."

"I promise," he said, meaning it. Not for anything would he cause her the kind of hurt she'd suffered the last time they went to town. At least he didn't think anyone in this part of town knew much about her. This area had a younger demographic, and the kids rarely went to the older part of downtown, preferring to hang out in the immediate area.

Or at least that was what he'd gathered from the few times he'd visited Dena when he was home on leave.

With a nod, Anabel got out of the car and began to walk briskly up the sidewalk toward the building. Her jeans fit her well and she looked young enough to be a student here. He followed, unable to keep from admiring the utterly feminine sway of her hips and the perfect heart shape of her rear.

Pulling open one side of the heavy metal door, she glanced at him quickly before stepping inside.

The smells were a powerful combination of wonderful and confusing. He thought he could identify bacon and toast (mouthwatering) and cleaning detergent and cigarettes (nauseating).

The interior of the cafeteria appeared pretty much deserted. Of course, they were too late for breakfast and just a bit early for them to start serving lunch. Most of the kids inside were either studying or hanging out, waiting for the workers to put the food out.

Anabel eyed the room and then apparently made a decision. She went to the clean and empty counter and stood. "Excuse me."

Busy cooking or preparing or talking, most of the people working in the back ignored her. Only one person, a slender girl with straight dark hair and huge brown eyeglasses, looked up.

"I'm sorry. We're not open yet," she said, smiling politely at Anabel.

"I understand." Anabel smiled back. "I'm looking for Dena Rogers."

That brought the girl over. "I'm sorry. She quit. Or something. It was really unlike her, to just not show up for work like that. We were friends, but she won't answer her phone." She shrugged, her expressive face unable to hide her hurt. "I'm hoping she's all right."

"Well, that explains that," Anabel muttered, managing to sound both shocked and disappointed. "I wanted to surprise her. I am—or was—a good friend of her brother's. Before he died, he asked me to give her something of his."

"Oh no." Brushing her hair away from her face, the younger woman grimaced. "She loved her brother. She was devastated when he was killed. I think that's why she joined that church."

Church? Tyler barely restrained himself from demanding Anabel get more info. His sister had never been all that interested in religion.

"Do you know the name of the church?" Anabel asked, smiling sweetly. "Maybe they'll know how I can find her."

"Sure." Turning, the girl grabbed a receipt book and a pen. "It's called Everlasting Faith. It's a nondenominational church in the old shopping center by the train tracks." Handing the paper to Anabel, she pushed her glasses back up on her nose. "Do me a favor, will you? When you find Dena, ask her to call Lola. Tell her I've been worried about her."

"I will." Anabel folded the paper and put it in her purse. "Thank you so much."

Once they were back outside, Tyler could barely contain himself. "She has to be wrong. Anabel wasn't the type to go to church."

"Maybe not. But maybe after you died… Grief makes people act in strange ways," she said, sounding unperturbed. "Let's go check this place out and see if we can learn anything more."

A few minutes later, they pulled up in front of a shopping center that had been converted into a church. The sandstone-colored brick gave the place a mellow appearance, though if not for the sign out front, Tyler would have no idea it had become a house of worship.

"I swear this used to be a grocery store," he said, following Anabel as she headed to the smudged glass front door.

"Shhh." Finger to her lips, she glared at him. "Remember, no talking to me once I'm in there."

Inside, the place appeared deserted. It had been sparsely decorated, an inexpensive oak table with a vase, a mirror and a few chairs. A vibrant blue area rug was the only color in the monochrome room. Tyler supposed that since it wasn't a Sunday, the church ran on a skeleton crew, but the pastor should be around here somewhere.

"Can I help you?" A pleasant-faced, older woman with curly gray hair approached. She wore what looked like a seventies housedress and white Keds.

"Yes, ma'am." Anabel's pleasant smile didn't reach her eyes. "I'm looking for the pastor."

The older woman drew herself up, narrowing her eyes as she studied Anabel. "Don't I know you? Weren't you on the news? You're the one—"

"Is the pastor here or not?" Anabel cut her off.

"He's here." Still staring at Anabel as if she'd brought the plague into the sanctuary, the woman—apparently the church secretary—spun around to go and then stopped. "His schedule is pretty busy, so I'm not sure he'll be able to see you," she said. "You might need to make an appointment and come back another time."

Clearly, the place wasn't exactly a beehive of activity.

From the rigid line of Anabel's back, Tyler knew she had to be biting her tongue. "Tell him it's an urgent matter concerning one of his church members and her deceased brother."

Deceased. Tyler suddenly realized he despised that word.

Though she had to have heard, the secretary hurried off without responding.

"Nice, wasn't she?" Tyler commented. "So much for treating others like one wants to be treated."

"Shhh." Anabel shot him a quelling look before turning to eye the hallway.

A moment later, a tall, barrel-chested man with wire-rimmed glasses and a shiny bald head appeared.

"Hello," he said, his voice friendly as he held out his hand. "I'm Pastor Tom Jones. And you are?"

"Anabel Lee."

He laughed as he shook her hand. "It's great to finally meet someone who's been burdened with a name as famous as mine. Do you get a lot of people mentioning the raven saying 'Nevermore' to you?"

She grinned back. "Probably as often as you get people singing songs their grandmothers danced to, like 'Delilah.'"

"I'm surprised you know it." He looked thoughtful. "Though you're right. A lot of our mothers and their mothers loved that guy. Me, not so much."

Still smiling, she nodded. "I can imagine."

"Now, what can I do for you?" he asked.

Her expression stilled and grew serious. "I'm trying to locate Dena Rogers. I went by the college cafeteria and was told she'd quit. Someone mentioned she regularly attended this church. I'm hoping you know where I can find her."

The pastor studied her, his expression unchanging. "Do you mind telling me what this is about? Lola—the young lady you talked to earlier in the cafeteria—called me. She said you'd brought Dena something from her deceased brother?"

"Yes." Anabel nodded. "I did. But that, I'm afraid, is private, for Dena only. Can you tell me where I might find her? Or, if you can't do that, could you call her and ask her to meet me here?"

Appearing lost in thought, he finally dipped his chin. "I would if I could, but Dena hasn't been to church at all the last few Sundays. I can call the number I have on file for her, if you'd like."

"Yes, please. If you don't mind, that would be very helpful."

"Wait here," he said. "I'll just be a moment."

The instant Pastor Tom left the room, Tyler crossed over to stand in front of Anabel. "All we've been able to establish is that Dena's disappeared. We already knew that."

"Give it a minute," she hissed back. "The more people we talk to, the more information we might learn about where she went. I do find it interesting that Lola found it necessary to phone the pastor warning him we might come by."

Giving a slow shake of his head, Tyler crossed his arms and moved away to wait. A moment later, the pastor returned. "I called." He grimaced and spread his hands. "The call went straight to voice mail, like she had her cell turned off. I'm sorry I couldn't be more helpful."

Tyler didn't think he sounded all that sorry. He reached out, trying to unobtrusively test the limits of the man's power. The pastor must have sensed something, because he swatted at the air near his face, as though a mosquito or fly circled him.

"I'm really sorry," he repeated.

Anabel made a sound of disappointment. "That's too bad. It's not often I get to deliver something to someone from a relative who died serving our country."

"Ouch." He grimaced again. Glancing at Anabel, he

then looked past her. Tyler could have sworn the other man stared directly at him.

Could Pastor Tom have magical ability? And if he did, could he be the man who'd captured Dena and even now held her hostage?

Chapter 7

Trying not to show her frustration, Anabel gave the pastor her number in case anything else turned up, and they left the church. Once in the car, she followed Tyler's directions and drove to the apartment complex where Dena had lived. Her ghostly companion had gone oddly silent, probably because he found this painful.

The apartment building, though older, appeared well taken care of. The brick had been painted a bright white, and the blue trim gave it a cheerful appearance. There were two floors, with all the doorways on the outside, and a set of steps at each end. In addition, each unit had one floor-to-ceiling window next to the blue front door.

"Not too bad," Anabel said out loud.

"Yeah, if you don't mind the lack of landscaping."

After Tyler's comment, she realized he was right. There were a few scraggly shrubs and no trees until the edge of the half-dead grassy area. Just parking lot and building. "I wonder what happened."

He shrugged. "As far as I can remember, it's been like this ever since the place was built."

As they crossed the parking lot on the way to the stairs, Anabel stopped. An icy chill spread over her, originating in her solar plexus and radiating from there to the tips of her fingers. It wasn't painful, more like uncomfortable. "Wow." Placing her hand on her stomach, she took a deep breath. "Do you feel that?"

Tyler frowned. From the perplexed look on his face, he didn't. "Feel what?"

She shook her head, unable to articulate. They continued on, and she'd just about begun to wonder if she'd imagined things when she felt it again. "There," she gasped. This time, the cold felt like a fist aimed at her stomach. She nearly doubled over, trying not to panic. Dimly, she knew she needed to remember to breathe.

"Anabel!" Tyler's voice, sharp and decisive. The sound of him caught her, pulling her back from whatever edge she'd been about to tumble from.

"That's not good," she said, her breath coming shallow and fast.

"Do you think it's the warlock?" Fist clenched, he appeared ready to do battle.

"I don't know." She inhaled, forcing out the breath. "It could be. Probably is. But why here? You don't think he's keeping her prisoner in her own apartment?"

"No. I've checked the place out thoroughly." Tyler floated ahead of her. "Come on. It's this way, up the stairs."

The energy's icy grip on her dissipated after she reached the top of the concrete stairs. Following Tyler to unit 205, she paused in front of the door and tentatively reached out, using the method she'd been taught by Juliet. *Focus, focus, focus.*

And nothing.

Relieved, she exhaled. "Whatever it was, it's gone now."

Unable to tell if Tyler appeared disappointed or glad, she raised her fist and knocked on the door.

A moment later, she knocked again. "Well, that was a waste of time. But then, since we both knew she wasn't here—"

She cut off as the door opened. A tall, slender girl with long, blond hair and heavily mascaraed eyelashes peered out at her. "Can I help you?"

Stunned, Anabel closed her mouth. "Yes. I'm looking for Dena Rogers."

Affecting a bored look, the young lady began to close the door. "She's not here."

Anabel thought quickly and stuck her foot in to keep the door from closing. "And you are?"

After a yawn, which she didn't bother to cover with her hand, the girl sighed. "Tammy. Dena's friend. Roommate, even. She's been letting me crash here."

"For how long?" Tyler demanded, forgetting she couldn't hear him.

Anabel glared at him. "Really?" Directing her attention back to Tammy, she narrowed her eyes. "How long has it been since you even saw Dena?"

Tammy shrugged. "I don't know. A week. Two weeks. It's been a while."

"Did she tell you where she was going?"

"No. I'm not her mother." Scrunching up her freckled face, she grimaced. Despite this, she still managed to look pretty, fresh and innocent. An all-American girl next door, heavily made up. "Are you a cop or something?"

"No. I'm—I was—a friend of Dena's brother. He sent something to me and asked me to give it to her."

Interest flickered in Tammy's bright blue eyes for the

first time. "The guy who was killed in Afghanistan? I saw pictures of him. He was pretty hot."

Unable to help it, Anabel glanced up at Tyler to catch his reaction. To her surprise, he appeared unamused and unimpressed, still eyeing Tammy with apparent distrust.

"Ask her how she knows my sister," he demanded.

"Did you work with Dena?" Anabel asked.

"No. We both go to the same church."

"Everlasting Faith?"

Surprise registered on Tammy's face. "Yes."

"We just spoke to Pastor Tom before coming here. He didn't seem to know where Dena was either."

"Look." Tammy shifted her weight from foot to foot, clearly done with the conversation. "I don't know what you want. I can't help you." Then, nudging Anabel's foot out of the way with her own, Tammy closed the door. A second later, they could hear the sound of the dead bolt turning.

Anabel sighed. "Another dead end."

"For you," Tyler said. "Wait here." And he swirled into mist, through the door and into the apartment.

Great. Damned if she was going to lurk outside someone else's apartment door while he did who knew what inside. Anabel headed back toward the stairs, bracing herself in case the chill came on. But she made it all the way to her car without reexperiencing anything and she got inside to wait for Tyler.

A moment later, she shook her head. Tyler was a ghost. He could appear wherever he wanted. Since there clearly wasn't any danger, he could just meet her at the house.

She drove away. Still, misgivings plagued her. What had been that negative energy back at the apartment? Should she have waited, just in case whatever it had been attacked Tyler?

Considering, she almost went back. But her misgivings also directed her to study her own house.

Everything seemed exactly the same as when she'd left earlier. No open doors, broken windows or signs of forced entry. Outside her own entrance, she stopped, using the focusing techniques she'd learned to see if she could sense any dark energy.

Nothing came up and hit her in the face.

Relieved, yet still hesitant, she unlocked the door and went inside. The instant she stepped into her foyer, Anabel knew something was wrong. Off. Her first clue was the way Leroy stood, backed into a corner of her living room, all puffed up and hissing. At nothing.

In the past, this had meant they had a ghostly visitor, which Anabel could always see, just as well as her cat.

Not this time. She squinted, peering around the room. Nothing. She could feel the faint tingle of some sort of leftover energy, residue but nothing more.

Most perplexing. But hopefully not dangerous. Whatever or whoever had been must have gone.

"It's all right," she told her cat, going to comfort him. Leroy was having none of that. He yowled and hissed and took off as if the hounds of hell were nipping at his heels. Anabel stared after him, debating if she should catch him, put him in his carrier and go somewhere else.

But surely if she were in danger, she'd sense something.

Leroy reappeared, leaping sideways, the way he did when he'd indulged in too much catnip. Keeping close to the wall, he moved right behind Anabel, still eyeing something only he could see.

A heartbeat later, Tyler appeared. Anabel glanced at her cat, who continued to stare in a completely different direction.

"I thought I asked you to wait," he began. "I checked out the apartment and—"

"Not now." She gestured toward Leroy. "Look at him. I don't see anything, but clearly he does. Can you tell if there's another ghost here?"

Frowning, Tyler drifted around the room, sniffing as if he wore his wolf form. Finally, he looked at her and shrugged. "I've got nothing. The protective circle is still in place."

Leroy didn't think so. Back arched and black fur fluffed up so much he looked as if he'd touched a live electrical wire, the cat hissed again and jumped sideways. He took off running, disappearing down the hall.

"Leroy thinks differently."

Lazily appraising her with his gaze, Tyler shrugged. "I don't know. You're the one with all the power. Did you sense anything?"

"I tried. I found nothing." She took a shaky breath, frustrated at the way his nearness got her all hot and bothered. "I'll try again." And once more, she followed the same steps she'd used to find Tyler before and pull him free. *Focus. Focus. Focus.* Fully expecting to find absolutely nothing.

This time, she felt a rush of darkness, as deadly icy as the feeling that had stabbed her earlier. But as quickly as she felt it, the dark energy cut off, like an iron wall slamming down, blocking Anabel.

Dizzy, she opened her eyes. "I felt the same thing earlier, at Dena's apartment. Dark and heavy, just like the force that had you trapped." Suddenly, she realized what she'd said. "He was here," she gasped. "I felt the lingering traces of his magic."

Hurrying over to the coffee table, she grabbed one of the books and began flipping through it. "I know I read something about the tracks magic leaves in the atmosphere. Here it is."

Looking up at Tyler, she read the passage out loud. "Both good and bad magic leave trails of pure energy for an adept to read. They are easily distinguishable." The rest went on to describe something similar to what she'd experienced. Icy cold and pain for dark magic, and warmth and goodwill for bright.

"That's all very interesting." Tyler sounded frustrated. "But yet another day is nearly over and we're no closer to finding my sister than we were before."

"Yes, we are," Anabel insisted. "At least now we have some suspects. There's Pastor Tom and that Tammy person, who's taken over Dena's apartment." She couldn't quite keep her dislike from her voice. She couldn't pinpoint exactly why, but Tammy had gotten on her last nerve. That in itself could be a clue.

"True, but I think you can scratch Tammy from your list. Whoever has Dena is clearly male."

"Really?" Tilting her head, she regarded him. Every time she looked at him, she ached for his touch. "And you know this how?"

"I saw him when my sister first reached out to me. And her voice, calling out to me to save her from him. Him."

"Okay." Anabel dropped into a chair. "Though I'm still not willing to give up on Tammy yet. She could be a helper or something."

He shrugged. Eyeing him, sexy as hell, even standing at attention with his entire posture ramrod straight, she wondered why he never let himself be off duty and relax. Maybe even wear something else besides the uniform, especially since it made him look even more ruggedly virile. Each time she saw him, the pull grew stronger.

Maybe the uniform and military posture were his way

of dealing with that tug. It was entirely possible he was having the same problems dealing with this attraction as she was. Heat shot through her at the thought.

Focus, she reminded herself, deliberately shutting out any awareness of him. They needed to work together to find Tyler's sister. "Do you think there's any possibility it could be the preacher?"

His look felt so galvanizing that her mouth went dry. "It could be. But I thought you could sense the darkness. Did you get anything like that from him?"

"No," she admitted. "Though if he is the warlock and really is that powerful, maybe he can cloak it."

"Maybe." He narrowed his eyes. "One thing I could tell about Tammy is that she's not powerful at all."

His insistence on defending Dena's roommate gave her pause. But for now, she decided to give him the benefit of the doubt.

"Okay, so we can probably cross Tammy off our list, then." She couldn't explain her reluctance to admit this. "Even though my gut instinct says she knows more than she admits."

"Well, leave her on our short list, then," he said, one corner of his mouth curling up in a slight smile. "Though personally, I think this church has something to do with Dena's disappearance. Something about that pastor rubbed me the wrong way."

She couldn't help smiling back. "Not religious, are you?"

"Not particularly. I've never been one for organized religion. I always had my own relationship with the divine, though."

Gaze locked on his, she admired the certainty in his voice. Of course he was certain—he'd actually died.

"You know, I've talked to a lot of ghosts since David died. But I never had an in-depth conversation with one."

One eyebrow arched, he gave a slow nod.

"Do you mind if I ask you a few questions?"

"Go ahead." He sounded resigned.

"After you, um, passed, did you know everything right away? Was it really like coming home?"

Moving closer, he continued to hold her gaze, making her pulse speed up. "It was," he said. "And that's about all I can tell you right now."

Slightly disappointed, she nodded. The message was loud and clear. No more questions about the afterlife.

Unwilling to let him see how his closeness affected her, she stood her ground. "Okay, then. Back to the church. If you really think they were involved with Dena's disappearance, you must have some theories as to why."

Was it her imagination, or did he seem relieved?

"There could be any number of reasons. Power, sex and money usually are involved somewhere. For all we know, Pastor Jones could be a power-hungry, sex-crazed megalomaniac."

Though she nodded, because, after all, anything was possible, she seriously doubted it. "I didn't get that vibe from him at all."

"So maybe I'm wrong." Tyler sounded glum. "Because if he was sex-crazed, he definitely would have reacted to a woman as beautiful as you."

Beautiful? Stunned, she froze. Even David, who'd loved her, had called her only pretty. She'd never in her life been told she was beautiful. Even though she knew she wasn't, she felt a flush of pleasure that Tyler found her so.

Focus, she reminded herself. She couldn't keep letting her ultraconsciousness of his appeal distract her.

"Do you think he's the one who grabbed your sister?"

Though she didn't like to consider the idea, it certainly wasn't beyond the realm of possibility. It wouldn't be the first time that a so-called man of God had hidden behind his religion to do awful things.

"I don't know," he admitted.

Her stomach growled, reminding her she needed to make something to eat. Wishing she could get herself to think of Tyler as a buddy or a brother or something, she bustled around the kitchen and put together a quick evening meal.

The doorbell rang just as Anabel finished making her dinner salad. With a sigh, she looked at Tyler, who shrugged.

"Make sure you check through the peephole," he cautioned her, sounding unruffled.

"Of course," she responded, slightly miffed that her meal had been interrupted.

When she looked out to her doorstep and saw who was standing there, she gasped. "It's Pastor Jones."

Instantly, Tyler dropped his carefree attitude. "Don't let him in. The fact that he came here proves I was right about him."

"He could have a valid reason to pay me a visit," she pointed out, whispering. "Maybe he has some new information about your sister."

Finally, Tyler nodded. "Fine. I hope he does."

Taking a deep breath, she squared her shoulders, opened the door slightly and stared at the preacher.

"Good evening, Ms. Lee." His smile seemed friendly enough.

Still, she continued to stand in the doorway, blocking entrance into her house. "Pastor Jones. I have to say, I'm surprised to see you here. How'd you find out where I live?"

"My dear, it's very easy to look anyone up on the internet," he gently pointed out.

Since he had a point, she nodded. His appearance still felt wrong, a bit like stalking. "You could have called. Especially since I gave you my number."

He lifted one shoulder. "I wanted to have a face-to-face conversation."

This was kind of creepy. She tried not to show her unease. "All right, then. What can I do for you?"

Looking pointedly past her, he pushed his glasses up on his nose and sighed. "May I come in?"

"I'd rather talk out here."

This surprised him. Appearing slightly hurt, he cocked his shiny bald head. "You don't trust me."

"I don't know you," she countered. "And I'm not in the habit of letting strange men into my house. Once again, why are you here?"

"You said to contact you if I had any news of Dena Rogers." Pushing his glasses up his nose again, he appeared frustrated. "I am the pastor of a very respectable church. I can assure you, I have no ill designs on your well-being."

She had to give him props for effort, even if his overly white smile reminded her of a television preacher, which increased her nervousness. Still, he *was* a pastor and she didn't have any bad vibes from him.

Finally, she went ahead and stepped aside. "I'm sorry. Please. Come on in."

His barrel chest led the way as he entered. "What a lovely home you have," he said, his tone gentle and respectful. She supposed he often visited with shut-ins or members of his congregation. Which would explain why he believed he was so good at making people feel at ease.

Except he wasn't. Not with her, at least. She wasn't

worried or stressed, just watchful. Something about the man got her hackles up, but she also supposed that might be due to her past negative experiences with zealously religious people.

Meanwhile, Tyler stood in the entrance to the kitchen, massive arms crossed, shaking his head. She was actually glad the preacher couldn't see him.

"What did you find out?" she asked, turning back to Pastor Jones. His blank look made her instantly suspicious. "About Dena," she clarified.

"Oh yes." His self-depreciating laugh made her want to cross her own arms. "I don't actually have anything concrete to report. But when I put the email request out for any information about her disappearance, one of her girlfriends contacted me."

Now, this could be helpful. Anabel kept her expression blank, not wanting to show too much eagerness. "And?"

Instead of answering, he looked pointedly at her couch. "May I sit?"

Pushy, wasn't he? Hating to be rude, Anabel nevertheless shook her head. "I'd rather stand. I was just about to eat my dinner when you rang my bell."

Of course, he apologized profusely.

Waving this away, she finally did cross her arms. "Are you going to tell me what Dena's friend told you?"

"Oh yes." Yet he didn't say anything else.

One of her books on magic was open on the coffee table. The pastor wandered over to it and began flipping through the pages. The instant he realized what kind of book it was, he recoiled.

"Magic?" Frowning, he glared at her. "Are you a devil worshipper?"

Though she wanted to laugh, Anabel knew to do so might be dangerous, so she shook her head instead. "Not at all. I'm doing some research. Now seriously, I'm hungry and I'd like to get back to my meal. Do you have some information to give me or not?"

If the older man took umbrage at her rudeness, he didn't react. Instead he studied her intensely, making her feel as if she were under a microscope. This was getting stranger and stranger. She actually began to think Tyler might have been right. The pastor might have been the one to abduct Dena.

Which would mean she'd just placed herself in grave danger by letting him into her house.

Tyler moved closer, standing by her side as though he considered himself reinforcement. Even though only she could see him, she gathered strength from his presence.

The pastor continued to study her, his expression kindly. "Do you attend church?" he finally asked, managing to sound both sad and confrontational all at once.

"Not that it's any of your business, but no. I don't. Now please, Pastor Jones. What did Dena's friend tell you?"

Still eyeing her as if he expected horns to pop out of her head at any moment, he finally sighed. "She came to tell me she thought Dena's new boyfriend must have done something to her. Since I never met the young man, and can't vouch for him either way, I thought I'd simply pass the information on to you."

Finally. A real, live, genuine clue. Careful not to show her eagerness, Anabel nodded. "May I have her name and number so we can contact her?"

"We?" His puzzled frown and the way he peered around her, as though trying to see someone else in the room, made her wonder if the pastor could actually see Tyler but wasn't letting on.

Cursing her careless slip of the tongue, Anabel gave him a sheepish smile. Tempted to pass it off as a joke and say she'd used the royal "we," she wondered if the pastor would even get it. "Sorry. I meant so I can contact her, not we."

Which she supposed was better than some lame non-explanation. Or the truth, which would make her sound even crazier. She could picture Pastor Jones's reaction if she told him she'd meant herself and a ghost, who happened to be present in the room at that very second. No, that wouldn't go over well at all.

The older man's face grew troubled. "I don't have her phone number on me, though I can check the church directory when I get back. I know she's attended services in the past, several times with Dena. The two of them used to hang around together a lot."

Anabel nodded, unable to resist glancing at Tyler. "Can you describe her?" Maybe if they got a description, Tyler might recognize her.

"Sure. She's tall, slender and blonde. She does wear too much makeup. Cute girl."

A sneaking suspicion made Anabel ask, "Does she have freckles and blue eyes? And look like she could be a cheerleader for a professional football team or something?"

The pastor's face relaxed. "Yes, that's her," he said happily. "Tamara, I think her name is."

Tammy. The girl who'd been staying in Dena's apartment. She'd made no mention of Dena having a boyfriend.

"Thank you so much, Pastor Jones," Anabel said, crossing to the door and reaching for the handle. "I really appreciate you stopping by." Which she did, sort of. Mostly she still felt a bit creeped out, as if he might be a potential stalker.

"It's my pleasure. Please call me Tom," he said, apparently not getting the hint as he made no move to leave. Clearly, he was too well mannered to simply take a chair since she hadn't invited him to sit. She supposed she ought to be grateful for the small blessing.

"Uh, okay. Well, thanks again for coming by." Maybe if she actually opened the door?

Still oblivious, he nodded. "You're welcome. Since I'm already here, how about we talk about you paying a visit to one of our services? We have four on Sundays, starting at eight in the morning."

"No, thank you," she said, as politely as she could while reining in her impatience. "Now if you don't mind, I've got to eat since I have somewhere I need to be. If I don't leave soon, I'm going to be really late. And hungry." Behind her back, she childishly crossed her fingers at the tiny white lie.

Finally, he got the not-so-subtle hint. He nodded. "All right, I understand. Please, if you change your mind, just stop by. Anytime, all right?"

As she opened the door, she nodded and forced a smile. All she could think of was how badly she needed to jump in her car and drive over to the apartment to confront Tammy.

As he passed her, the pastor stopped and bent down, giving her a fatherly kiss on the top of her head. So help her, she was so startled she jumped, bumping his wire-rimmed glasses and sending them flying from his head.

"I'm s-so sorry," she stammered, reaching to pick up the glasses before something worse happened.

Unfortunately, Pastor Jones reached for them at the same time, nearly causing them to bump heads. With his face mere inches from hers, he mouthed two words. *Be careful.*

Chapter 8

Stunned, Anabel handed the pastor his glasses and got to her feet. He left in a hurry, without saying anything else. Immediately, she rushed over and closed and locked her front door, heart racing.

"Dena didn't have a boyfriend," Tyler said, clearly having missed the last exchange. "If Tammy is saying so, then she's lying."

"Um, Pastor Jones just told me to be careful." She scratched the back of her head. "A second ago, when we were face-to-face."

Moving closer, Tyler stared. "What? When? I didn't hear him."

"Right when we were both trying to retrieve his eyeglasses. He mouthed it at me, almost as if he thought someone might be listening."

Their gazes locked. Once again, she felt that irresistible lure of him. She thought he must have felt it too, as he broke eye contact. "That's weird. I wonder what he's not telling us."

"Exactly."

He began to pace the room, looking more like a man and less like a ghost. His long-legged stride captivated her. "Of course, we already know to be careful. We're dealing with a warlock, after all. I'm more worried about what this Tammy is trying to do."

"Good point. Let's go ask her right now." Anabel reached for her car keys.

"Let's not," Tyler countered, surprising her. "How about we just call her instead? Since she and my sister still have a house phone, I have the number memorized."

Disappointed, Anabel considered. "I really want to see her face when we ask her why she didn't mention her worry about Dena's boyfriend."

"Maybe because you had a ten-second conversation with her. You were a total stranger, showing up at her front door and demanding to know about her friend. Of course she got defensive. She was so worried she went to talk to her pastor instead."

Anabel eyed him. "Why are you defending her? Again?"

Something flickered in his hazel eyes. "I'm not. I'm just saying it's logical that she'd say more to the leader of her church than to a random stranger."

He had a point. Mulling this over, Anabel finally decided he was right. "Fine. Let's give her a call."

Dialing the numbers as he gave them to her, Anabel listened to the phone ring on the other end, aware her name would display if the other woman had caller ID. When Tammy finally picked up, Anabel was so surprised she almost couldn't speak.

After she'd identified herself and told Tammy why she was calling, Tammy murmured her okay. At first, she didn't say anything, and Anabel got a sinking feeling as she wondered if this call had been a colossal waste of time. Anabel reiterated that the pastor had told her about Tammy's concern, hoping this would reassure the other woman.

"I'm worried about Dena," Tammy finally said, her voice shaky. "We both go to the same church, and I'm afraid her disappearance has something to do with them."

"Not her boyfriend?"

"Boyfriend?" Tammy's shock didn't sound contrived. "Dena didn't have a boyfriend. At least not that I know of."

Anabel's stomach lurched. "That's really strange," she said. "Pastor Jones just left here. He told us you'd come to him to discuss how worried you were about Anabel and how concerned you were that her boyfriend had done something to her."

"He did?" Tammy sounded shocked. "But that's a complete and outright lie. I did talk to Pastor Tom—I called him—but I never said any of that. Not that I'm not worried about Dena, because I am. But I've never discussed anything about boyfriends with the pastor."

At a loss for words, Anabel looked back at Tyler, wondering if he could hear the other side of the conversation. Apparently not, as his impatient expression told her he was waiting for her to finish the call.

"Is there anything else you might be able to tell me, Tammy?" Anabel said, hoping against hope that Dena's roommate would trust her enough to share.

"Yes, there is." Voice stronger, Tammy sounded determined. "I'm concerned about the church. Everlasting Faith. I think there's something weird going on with them, and Pastor Tom is in the middle of it."

Anabel opened her mouth to reply, but Tammy hadn't

finished. "My suggestion to you, if you're really investigating Dena's disappearance, is that you should investigate that church. I've quit going. Being around those people is not a safe place to be."

With that, Tammy muttered a quick goodbye and hung up.

"Wow." Speaking fast, Anabel repeated everything to Tyler.

"One of them is clearly lying," Tyler mused. "But who?"

"And why?" While Anabel didn't entirely trust the pastor, she trusted Tammy even less. "One of those two knows something about why your sister is missing. We need to figure out which one, and maybe that will help us find her."

Leroy yowled from the kitchen, reminding her it was past his mealtime.

"I need to feed my cat. And..." She eyed her salad longingly. "...eat my own meal."

As she headed to get the cat food, Tyler followed, studying her pet. "I wish there was a way to talk to him."

Startled, she looked up at him. "Talk to who? Leroy?"

"Yes. Obviously he sensed something when we did not."

Reaching for the container of cat food, she shrugged. "Cats are sort of known for stuff like that. And I did feel something, though it was just a slight tingle of energy."

The instant she spoke, she felt it again. Even worse, Leroy, who'd never missed a meal in his life, let out a screeching yowl and turned tail and ran.

One minute Tyler had been standing there talking to Anabel, eyeing her cat in order to refrain from admiring Anabel's lush body, and the next, he found himself surrounded by complete and utter darkness.

Meanwhile, he had no idea what might have happened to Anabel.

Tyler swore. He might be dead, he might be a ghost, but he had been a soldier. And he was damn tired of getting pushed around.

"Show yourself," he shouted, clenching his teeth as he spun in the mind-numbing absence of light. "If you're so all-fired powerful, why are you afraid to show yourself?"

Lightning struck, a maelstrom of overbright flashes, painful even to ghostly eyes. And then nothing. Not even a rumble of thunder.

"The hell with you," he shouted, beyond caring if anyone even heard him. He was sick of being powerless and having to rely on someone else to do things he wanted to do himself.

A thought occurred to him. While he knew nothing about the man who'd imprisoned Dena—other than the fact that he was a warlock—he knew men. Most men could not resist a challenge.

"You know, I don't think you're so powerful," he shouted into the void. "You have to pick on weak, defenseless young women. Why don't you take on someone your own size, someone like me? I think I know why. It's because you're afraid."

Nothing. Tyler's heart sank. For all he knew, the warlock had already departed, leaving nothing but his dark magic behind.

A yowl had him spinning around. A second later, he relaxed, realizing that it sounded like Leroy. Which meant, despite the inability to see, he might actually have remained in Anabel's kitchen. This also might have something to do with the warlock's refusal to show himself.

For whatever reason, apparently the warlock didn't want Anabel to see his face.

Right now Tyler had had enough of being blind and powerless. Even though he knew he'd never had Anabel's kind of magic, he gathered his frustration, his rage and his worry for Dena, gathered all of it into a roiling mass of emotion. And then, opening his arms wide, he flung it into the universe. With a grunt and a heartfelt desire that the warlock would take the brunt of it like a fist to the stomach.

Instantly, the darkness vanished, as though Tyler had simply snapped his fingers and made it disappear.

And, as he'd suspected, he'd remained in Anabel's kitchen. "How about that?" he marveled, turning to see Anabel minus her cat, still standing exactly where she'd been. As if time had stopped, freezing her in place.

"Anabel?" While he stared, Anabel blinked and slowly came back to life. Leroy sauntered into the room and began grooming himself.

Tyler felt a flash of fear.

"What just happened?" Anabel asked quietly, her amber eyes wide with fear, her expression puzzled. "I couldn't see you, but yet I felt your presence."

"What about him? Could you tell the warlock was here?"

Her frown told him she couldn't, even before she gave a slow shake of her head.

"He's learned how to shield himself from you or something," he said.

"Maybe." She eyed him. "But what I want to know is, how did you send him away? You had to have used magic. Why didn't you tell me you had magical ability?"

"I don't. At least, not that I'm aware of." He paused, collecting his thoughts.

"Well, if that wasn't magic, I don't know what it was."

She had a point.

"Tell me exactly what you did," she ordered, pushing a strand of her midnight hair behind her ear and then putting the bowl of cat food in front of Leroy. Keeping her gaze on him, she then reached for her salad and began eating.

He wondered if she could see the sensual light that passed between them.

"Tyler?"

Collecting himself, he nodded. "I gathered my emotions and sent them out like a bullet toward the darkness. And bam. Just like that, everything went back to normal."

"That's magic. Of course, my understanding is a bit limited. I'm learning, though, and what you just described sounds a lot like what Juliet told me to do. Focus, concentrate and then…magic."

The idea that he, a ghost, had any magic should have been laughable. But the desperate need to save his sister had Tyler grasping at straws. "Maybe we need to talk to Juliet. I'm thinking if I do have magic, and you and I put ours together, we might be invincible."

Anabel nodded, clearly not convinced. She continued eating, clearly trying to get her salad down before something else happened.

"It's worth a shot," he persisted. "Call her and ask her."

"Fine." She glanced at her watch. "But it'll have to wait. Her next yoga class just started."

Antsy, Tyler nodded. What had happened earlier with him and the dark magic felt as though it had energized him. While Anabel finished her dinner, he left her house, floating high above the neighborhood, heading downtown and gazing down at the town where he'd grown up. Leaning Tree, New York.

He'd missed it while stationed in Afghanistan. But places and things were transitory. People were not. Most of all, he'd missed his baby sister. Knowing she was in trouble and being powerless to help her was awful, as bad as or even worse than dying.

Thinking back to the way he'd been able to gather up energy, he wondered. Maybe he wasn't nearly as power-less as he'd thought. And if he and Anabel put their re-sources together, they might have a shot at beating this warlock.

By the time he returned to Anabel, night had fallen. In the middle of her bedtime preparations, she greeted him with a sleepy smile. "I wasn't able to reach Juliet," she said. "But I left her a message. I'm sure she'll call me in the morning."

Stunned, his chest tight, he managed to nod back, even though he had his heart in his throat. He wondered how she could be so unaware that her smile was a thing of great beauty. "Sleep well," he murmured. "I'll catch you in the morning."

With a casual wave, he drifted into the other room. He knew she'd think he'd left, retreating to whatever place spirits went. Instead he waited, knowing she'd drift off in a few minutes. Then he'd go into her room and spend the night guarding over her.

He found he enjoyed watching her sleep, taking care that she didn't know. The instant her breathing would change, indicating she'd soon wake, he'd retreat, taking himself into another room. She would have been horri-fied to find him there, no doubt citing her sleep-ruffled hair and drowsy eyes. Again, he marveled how it could be possible she had no idea how beautiful she was. Or how sexy and full of life.

Thinking back to his too-short life, he knew if he'd met Anabel while he was alive, he'd never have let her go. No wonder Dave had married her. He actually found himself jealous of the other man.

Dave had been one lucky guy. Tyler couldn't believe they'd been in the same unit. While he was thinking of that, one small thing in the back of Tyler's memory had been bothering him. At base, it had been common practice for the men to flash photos of their girlfriends or wives and family. Tyler couldn't remember one single instance of Dave ever doing this.

Heck, Tyler would have been showing Anabel's picture to anyone who'd look at it.

Which, when he thought about it, sort of blew his mind. Why on earth any man, married to a woman as special as Anabel, wouldn't want to show her off was beyond him.

Anabel stirred, drawing his attention back to her. Watching her like this felt like torture, an addictive combination of pleasure and pain. He burned for her, the irony of that longing striking him as retribution. Before his tour in Afghanistan, he'd never been a monk. In fact, he'd been far from it. His friends had always joked about that, claiming he'd dated 75 percent of the women in the county. And while he'd never made promises, he was under no illusions that he might have broken a heart or two. Maybe this was payback.

Throw in his worry over his sister, and he might as well have entered the first or second layer of hell.

Dena no longer called out to him or even tried to reach him. He could no longer even detect the slightest spark, which made his stomach turn and his chest hurt. He could only hope the bastard hadn't killed her. Surely not. Not in the short number of hours that had passed since Tyler saw her, huddled in that dank and foul room.

"A dragon," Anabel said clearly, startling him as he realized she'd come awake suddenly, without any warning.

She sat up in bed, her dark hair cascading wildly over her alabaster shoulders, her bronze eyes gleaming in the shadowy room. The pull of attraction was so strong he had to clench his hands into fists to keep from reaching for her.

"What?" he managed to say, swallowing hard as he fought to remain unaffected by her lush beauty.

She blinked as she realized he was there. "How did you— Never mind. It's not important. I saw him. The man who has your sister."

Stunned, he stared. "You saw him? You saw his face?"

"No. Not that." Rubbing her eyes, she winced. "But I came up on him from behind. And then he shape-shifted, right before I reached him." She began speaking faster, her words all running together, almost as if she feared he wouldn't believe her. "And when he changed, he wasn't a wolf."

Tyler waited. The Pack wasn't the only shape-shifting species. There were bears and leopards too. Such a thing wasn't that unusual. "What did he become?" he finally asked, when she didn't continue.

"A dragon. Like the ones in medieval tapestries or myths. The beast was huge, with iridescent scales and wings twice as long as a man."

He relaxed. Not that he didn't believe her, but clearly what she thought she'd seen had been only a dream. "Dragons are the stuff of ancient legends," he said carefully, admiring her imagination. "Maybe since it was only a dream, you should consider the possibility that it wasn't reality."

Those marvelous eyes sparked defiance. "Oh, it was real." The certainty in her voice still didn't sway him. "I went there, followed him to his lair. It's underground, like a tornado shelter or bunker. In the woods, like maybe a remote part of the Catskill Forest Preserve or something."

Taking a deep breath, she rushed on. "I saw Dena, as well. She's still alive. Barely, but her heart still beats and she still breathes."

Relief flooded him, even though he still wasn't sure whether or not to believe her. "That's good. I haven't been able to feel her at all."

"He's cloaked her. And himself, which is why I couldn't sense his presence here."

He thought about it for a moment and then decided he had to ask. "Are you sure?"

She didn't even hesitate. "Yes. This was not a dream."

Right then he knew he had to choose. "I believe you," he finally said.

Excitement made her copper eyes shine. "We finally know what we're dealing with. Now we just need to make a plan and free your sister."

A plan. Dealing with a mythical beast no one thought still lived. "How do you know all this? You're just learning about magic."

A quizzical smile spread over her face. "Good point. I don't know. I just do. I've never been more certain of anything in my life."

"A dragon, huh?" Still trying to process the idea.

"Yes." Her voice went dreamy. "He was beautiful, in a frightening sort of way. All glistening scales, blue and green, the colors of a stormy sea. And when he unfurled his wings and launched himself into the sky, I ran after him. I don't think he ever saw me."

From what he remembered reading about dragons, she was lucky the beast hadn't noticed her.

"Even better," Anabel continued, "when he took off and I ran after him, I couldn't help checking out the surrounding area. I saw a few landmarks that might give us some indication of where he's keeping your sister."

Now, *this* was progress. "Tell me," he ordered. "I know this area like the back of my hand."

Jumping up from her bed, she crossed to the dresser,

her long legs flashing ivory. She grabbed a pad of paper and a pen and began to make notes. "I have to get this down before I forget," she explained. "I'll let you look at them once I'm finished."

Too impatient to wait, he drifted slightly above her and watched as she sketched out what she'd seen. To his dismay and disbelief, he didn't recognize a single landmark. "What's this? A windmill?"

"Yes," she said, putting the finishing touches on her sketch. "One of those decorative ones, though larger than normal. Something like this should be unusual enough that even if you don't know where it is, someone will."

He nodded. "What about this?" She'd drawn something that looked like the shell of a concrete building, without windows or doors, except for a single metal door in the middle. "A bomb shelter?"

"Maybe." With a sheepish expression, she shrugged. "I have no idea what it is, but that's where the dragon lives and where he's keeping Dena. I drew it exactly like I saw it. I take it you don't know either?"

"No. Sorry." At her crestfallen expression, he actually reached for her, wincing as his hand passed right through her shoulder and then hoping she hadn't noticed. "It's okay. These landmarks are better than nothing. If we start asking around, maybe we can locate them."

Exhaling, she nodded. "Now what do we do?"

A quick glance at the clock revealed it was just after 4:00 a.m. "I think you should try and go back to sleep. We can work on this again in the morning."

"Sleep?" She sounded affronted. "There's no way I can sleep now."

"Well, you can't call Juliet," he said. "Can you?"

She laughed. "Not at this hour of the morning. How about I look in these books for now?" she said in a reasonable tone of voice. "And see what I can find out about dragons. Maybe there'll be some mention of this sort of thing in there."

"Okay."

She dragged her hand through her hair. "Give me a minute." She padded into the bathroom, closing the door behind her.

He decided to wait in the living room.

A minute later, she reappeared, pushing back strands of midnight hair from her heart-shaped face. Her delicately carved face turned pink with excitement. As he let his gaze rove over her, he saw she'd slipped on a bra and a pair of denim shorts, though she still wore the clingy oversize T-shirt.

A bolt of pure lust rendered him unable to speak. Fortunately for him, Anabel had focused her attention on books.

"Let me see." Eyeing the stack of books, she grabbed the largest one. It had an ornate leather-looking cover, embossed with scrolls and medieval-type writing. "This one seems the oldest."

Carrying it into the kitchen, she pulled out a chair and sat down at the table. She began flipping through the pages.

As soon as he regained his composure, he sat down beside her and read over her shoulder.

They both saw the section on dragons at the same time. "The Drakkor," Anabel breathed. "A breed of shapeshifter so rare it's now believed to be a myth." Raising her head, she met Tyler's eyes. "Except they're not."

"I don't believe this," Tyler said, eyeing the illustration. "Does that look like what you saw?"

"Yes. Exactly, except in real life the colors are much more vibrant."

Crud. Forcing his gaze back to the page, he continued

reading out loud. "'Drakkors were considered the most powerful of all shape-shifters. In addition to their ability to change into a fearsome, fire-breathing beast with the gift of flight, they also have magical talent. It was this same magic that brought about their downfall.'"

Anabel picked up where he left off. "'In medieval times, the Drakkors were as numerous as the Pack. But struggles for power led to war. Two sides were formed—the Drakkor of the Light and the Dark Drakkor. Battles raged, wiping out legions of the beasts. Those few that remained went into hiding. Over the centuries, they began to die out. A sickness attacking only the Drakkors further thinned their numbers.'"

Tyler shook his head. "Wow."

"I know." Eyes glowing like polished bronze, she practically vibrated with excitement. "This is like reading a fairy tale."

"Except for one thing," Tyler pointed out. "If your dream was correct, apparently the warlock is not only a Drakkor, but a dark one. And he has my sister. How do we fight against something like that?"

Once they'd flipped through all the other books, finding only one other reference to the Drakkor, Anabel yawned. Tyler hid a smile. A quick glance at the clock on the microwave revealed that only half an hour had passed.

"You know what?" she said, rubbing her eyes. "I think I am going to go back to bed. Even though I usually get up at four or four thirty when I have to be at work, I've been sleeping until six thirty."

He nodded, wishing more than anything that he could crawl into bed with her.

When she stood, she started to turn to leave and then froze. Wrapping her arms around herself, she tilted her head to look up at Tyler. "I wish you could hold me until

I go to sleep," she said, surprising him. "I confess I'm a bit worried I'll be seeing dragons in my sleep."

The image that came to his mind had nothing to do with sleep. He burned, wondering how even as a ghost, he could still ache with desire and need.

"I can try," he said, remembering the kiss and how he'd managed to become solid that one time. And then, as if he thought she could read his mind, he had to avert his gaze, afraid she'd read the yearning in his eyes.

"Would you?" And because she sounded so damn grateful, he knew he would, even if lying next to her unable to touch her would be akin to lying on hot coals.

Chapter 9

Though she'd worried at first she wouldn't be able to keep her apparently sex-crazed libido from acting up, Anabel felt comforted having Tyler lying in bed with her. Just having him there was nice, even if she couldn't feel the weight of his body on the mattress. When he draped his ghostly arm over hers, she sighed, closing her eyes and pretending to snuggle against him. Aside from a few twinges of lust battling with her exhaustion, she felt better having him close.

Amazingly, she drifted off to sleep.

When she opened her eyes, the nightstand clock said 7:10, which meant she'd overslept slightly. Her heart skipped a beat as she contemplated what would happen if she turned and gave Tyler a good-morning kiss. But rolling over, she realized he'd already vacated the room. Her immediate sense of loss made her chest feel heavy, but she shook it off. If she'd had any dreams, she didn't remember them and woke up remarkably rested.

More than that, actually. Stretching as she got out of bed, she took note of the exhilaration zinging through her veins and glanced at herself in the mirror, unable to keep from smiling. Finally, she had a lead on Tyler's sister. He might not recognize the landmarks she'd sketched, but someone, somewhere, would. The dragon—or Drakkor—had thrown an unexpected wrench in things, but for some reason she felt confident they'd figure out a solution.

Juliet called a few minutes after Anabel finished her breakfast. "I'm so glad you called," Anabel began. "I've got something I need to ask you—"

"First, tell me this," Juliet interrupted. "Who did you piss off now?" She sounded worried and a bit scared.

"No one that I know of. Why?"

"Do you know a Doug Polacek?"

Anabel thought for a minute. "No. I don't. Why do you ask?"

"Think," Juliet insisted, still not answering. "Maybe he was a customer at the diner and didn't like something you cooked?"

"Maybe." Still not too concerned, Anabel sighed. "Those people—who are few and far between, by the way—deal with the waitstaff or the manager. They never make it back to the cook. You still haven't told me what's going on."

"This Doug Polacek has been talking about you, all around town. He's a big guy, at least six-four and three hundred pounds. Pretty intimidating. Even so, he claims you're harassing him. He's hinting you went psycho on him from a love affair gone bad."

Stunned, Anabel gasped. "That's—"

But Juliet hadn't finished. "There's more. From what I hear, he's even gone to the police to get a restraining order against you."

Dumbfounded, Anabel couldn't respond at first. When

she did find her voice, a few heartbeats later, it came out shaky. "I don't understand. I don't even know this person."

"Well, for whatever reason, he's got the entire town stirred up about you again. Almost as bad as last time."

Anabel groaned, her stomach roiling. She remembered how that had been. She'd ended up having to head to the next town over to do her shopping. Between the way everyone had either stared her down without speaking or crossed the street to avoid being near her, she'd felt like a pariah in her own town.

When the harassment started—the eggs on her house and car, the burning bag of poop on her doorstep, her doorbell ringing at all hours of the night and rocks shattering her windows—she'd gotten no help from the police. Though they hadn't come out and actually said so, she'd gotten the impression that they felt as if she deserved such treatment, kind of like making restitution for her sins.

And now some guy whose name she didn't even recognize was starting things up again.

Closing her eyes, she took a deep breath, trying to push away the confusion and fear. *Focus.* When she opened them again, she felt calmer and more centered, as well as resolute. "Juliet, I have no idea why this total stranger has it in for me, but I have enough on my plate. I don't have time to deal with him right now."

Juliet started to argue, but Anabel cut her off. "Listen," she said. "This is way more important. I have a question for you. What do you know about the Drakkors?"

Clearly, she'd stunned her friend into silence.

"The…what? Drakkors, as in mythical dragons?" Juliet's tone made it clear she was worried Anabel had finally stepped off the deep end.

"Not so mythical, as it turns out," Anabel said. "The warlock who has Tyler's sister is a Drakkor."

"Not possible."

The instant denial made Anabel smile. "It is, actually."

"And you know this how?" At least Juliet sounded willing to hear her out.

"I saw the warlock shape-shift. Instead of a wolf, he became a dragon. A huge, monstrous, fire-breathing thing."

"You *saw*?" Juliet practically shouted. "When? Where?"

Now came the hard part. "In a dream."

Silence. When Juliet spoke again, she sounded much calmer. Relieved, even. Clearly, she chose her words carefully. "Hon, you are aware dreams aren't real, right?"

"It's funny how you and Tyler say the same things," Anabel responded. "And both of you know better. Of course I am. But this wasn't an ordinary dream. The warlock had been here. He tried to grab Tyler. Leroy—my cat—sensed him. I think he used a cloaking spell on me."

Another silence.

"You've been reading the books I gave you, haven't you?"

"Studying them," Anabel confirmed. "Believe me. Please. If you learn anything about the Drakkors—anything at all—let me know. I—we—need all the help we can get."

"Wow. I'll see what I can find out. But you also need to deal with this Polacek guy. He's trying really hard to make your life miserable for no reason I can tell. Oh." Juliet's voice changed. "My last morning class is here. I'll talk to you later, okay?" And she ended the call.

Puzzled, Anabel relayed the information about Doug Polacek to Tyler. "I have no idea who he is or why he's trying to turn the town against me." She took a shaky breath. "I'm pretty sure this has something to do with that warlock. I wonder if he's just revealed his identity."

"It wouldn't be that easy."

"Maybe not. Or he might be upping the stakes."

"I hadn't considered that." As the realization dawned on him, horror spread across his face. "You're saying you think it's all a game to him? He's having fun?"

She thought of her dream and the way the warlock had thrown himself into the air after he changed. "Of course he's enjoying himself. What other reason would he have for doing this?"

Ignoring Tyler's frown, she took a deep breath, aware he wouldn't like the next question, but knowing she had to ask it anyway. "Yesterday, I think you showed you have some latent magic ability. Is there any possibility that your sister might have some, as well?"

He frowned, his form once again flickering in and out. "I honestly couldn't tell you that. I'm still trying to figure out if that's really what happened with me. The only thing I can say is if she did she never told me about it. Why?"

"A theory I'm beginning to have. Remember the legends about dragons? They feed off energy. And magic generates a lot of energy."

Hazel eyes dark, he stared at her, so handsome it almost hurt her to look at him. She pushed that thought away, reminding herself that she had to focus if she wanted to continue to learn and grow.

"So you're saying…?"

"He captures those with untapped magic, in order to feed off them."

Expression like a stone mask, he considered. "I don't know. That's a bit far-fetched, don't you think?"

"Maybe. Maybe not."

"If he's capturing people with untapped magic," he said, the concern in his voice telling her he'd realized what this could mean, "then you're also at risk from him."

"True." She knew she sounded unconcerned, but all she

could think about was she might have finally found a way to locate his sister. "Think about it, though. If I can draw him to me, I can reach your sister before it's too late."

"No." Clearly horrified, he began to flicker in and out more rapidly, the way he always did when agitated. His eyes flashed. "That's too dangerous. I don't want you to risk your own life. Then where would we be? Dena would still be his prisoner, and you'd be there along with her. There's no one else I can communicate with except Juliet. I couldn't assist you."

"Juliet knows people who could. She belongs to a pretty tight-knit coven."

He spread his hands. "What does that even mean? How could she—they—help?"

With a shrug, she tried to downplay his concern. "I'm not sure. But surely they could."

"Well, if they can—and we don't have to put you in danger—let's enlist their aid right now."

Though for some reason all her nervousness threatened to come back and grip her, she managed a smile. "She's teaching a yoga class now. I'll call her later. I wish I'd thought of it sooner."

"Me too." He paused, his expression going serious as his form became more solid. "Though I have to say, if Juliet and her coven really can assist us, why didn't Juliet herself mention it sooner?"

He had her there.

"We might not have to stress about that anyway. I can't help feeling as if he's going to continue to attack us to keep us off balance."

Looking decidedly not ghostly, with his muscular legs spread in a warrior's stance, Tyler considered her statement. "He'd only do that if he considered us dangerous."

Though just looking at him made her mouth go dry,

she managed a nod. "You know, I think we just might be. And though I'm just learning, it doesn't seem to matter on the magic thing that you're a ghost and I'm not."

Something flickered in his eyes, reminding her of the amazingly real kiss they'd shared. Her entire body heated at the memory.

It was when she caught herself actually swaying toward him that she snapped out of it. Rushing over to the stack of books, she grabbed one randomly and carried it over to the table. "I don't know about you, but I'm going to try and learn more. Knowledge is power."

To his credit, he met her dramatic—and rather prim, if she did say so herself—proclamation with only a nod.

"While you do that," he said, "I'm going back to the world of the spirit to see what I can find out about the Drakkors."

"Good idea," she began, but he had already gone.

"Whew." Leaning back in the chair, she closed her eyes. Battling an attraction to a ghost. She swore she could feel the sexual magnetism rolling off him in waves—intense and compelling, at times confusing. She didn't understand how she could want him so much.

She stood, alone in her house once more, turning a slow circle. Finally, alone. Even with the urgency of the need to find his sister hanging over her, right now she should have been relishing her time alone. This was how she'd always lived, by herself. At least since David had been deployed. While she'd missed him, especially at night when lying in her empty bed, she was used to it and appreciated the space and the knowledge she could do whatever she wanted, eat whatever she liked and make her own schedule.

Over time, even her bed had come to feel less empty. She'd become accustomed to widowhood. Yes, she often found herself lonely, but she mostly dealt with it by keeping busy. This had worked pretty well. Until now.

Now she missed Tyler. *Tyler*. A man—no, a *ghost*—she'd known only a few days. Not such a long time in the scale of things. Yet she ached for him, craved him as though he were a drug and she an addict. She took comfort in the fact that he didn't know about her constant battle to keep from touching him, caressing him, kissing him. Which, when you considered that their bodies wouldn't be able to actually make contact, felt pretty darn nutty.

Had loneliness driven her to this? Maybe, since his presence was like a bright beacon in thick gray fog, she'd been more lonesome than she'd realized.

Once all this was done, she knew he'd be gone. He couldn't stay. But what he'd given her seemed immeasurable. In a way, a ghost had brought her back to life. Because of him, she now had a purpose. Saving his sister, whose plight had become all too real. Freeing Dena would be more than a way to make retribution to the universe for what she'd almost done to Lilly McGraw. She wanted to save her because no one deserved to suffer like that.

The warlock had to be stopped. She might be new at this magic stuff, but even a novice could sense the breadth of the darkness that consumed this man. Or correction—this dragon.

Her naturally curious mind couldn't help wondering if there were more of his kind out there somewhere. He couldn't be the last one, could he? Maybe there were other Drakkors who'd pledged themselves to the light, who could use their magic to counteract the evil darkness of his. Allies.

As for this Doug Polacek, whoever he was, Anabel decided she had much more important things to do than worry about him and whatever mischief he was trying to cause, though she still needed to investigate whether or not he had any potential ties to the warlock/Drakkor.

Juliet phoned back thirty minutes later, which must have been a few minutes after she got her last client out the door.

"I've called an emergency meeting of my coven," Juliet said, sounding breathless from excitement.

Her coven. For a second, Anabel had forgotten that Juliet was Wiccan. "Do you think they can help?"

"Everyone has magic. Some just have more than others," Juliet said, her positive energy practically crackling across the phone line. "At this point, we might as well try. What have we got to lose?"

"Good point." Anabel sighed. "I hate that I supposedly have so much magic, yet I haven't been able to do much to find Tyler's sister."

"I'm hopeful we can help you with that. We're meeting in the woods near the hill with the changing tree. I'd really like it if you and Tyler could come."

The changing tree. The place where the Pack often met to shape-shift and hunt in small groups. Anabel hadn't been there since David died. Too many memories.

She took a deep breath, pushing away her thoughts. "I don't know. We're not changing or anything, right?"

"No, no. Just meeting." Juliet paused. "Maybe a ritual or two, if it's needed."

"Then why there?"

"It's a place of power and we need all the help we can get. Will you come?"

Willing her heartbeat to slow, Anabel considered. Eighteen months had passed. She'd been gradually trying to move on, to let go of the past. Maybe seeing the changing tree would be another step.

"I can do that," Anabel finally agreed. "We can, I mean.

But will the others be able to interact with Tyler like you and I do?"

"I don't know. We'll find out soon enough. I've asked everyone to be there in thirty minutes or so. See you there." Juliet rang off.

Thirty minutes? Juliet wasn't wasting time. Anabel turned to tell Tyler and then realized he was gone. Not only that, but she had no idea how to summon him back, or even if that was possible.

All she could do was try. If that didn't work, she'd have to go meet Juliet and the coven by herself.

Taking a deep breath, she sat cross-legged in the middle of her floor. Then she closed her eyes, chanting the single word that had become a new mantra of sorts. *Focus.* She pulled inward, shutting down each and every stray thought the instant it occurred.

Finally, she reached that place she considered to be the center of her being, the spot where all her energy lived. Now she must gather and weave, sending tendrils outward, hopefully crossing the barrier between the land of the living and the land of the spirit. To wherever Tyler resided.

She wasn't sure this was the way to do this, nor had she seen anything in any of the books on how to contact a ghost. Just in case, she tried calling his name, raising her volume with each cry.

Tyler. Inhale. Exhale. *Tyler.* Again. And once more. *Tyler.*

Nothing. She didn't sense him or feel him or, when she opened her eyes, see him. It was as if he'd gone so completely into that other dimension that he'd severed all ties to earth and her.

Crud. Disappointment made her throat ache. She got up, dusted her hands off on her jeans. He'd show up when he was ready to. There wasn't a whole lot she could do about that.

"Tyler," she said out loud, speaking to an empty room. "If you can hear me, I'm leaving in a minute to meet with Juliet's coven. They're going to try and help. Juliet said she'd really like it if you could be there."

Again, nothing but silence answered her. She even felt slightly foolish, aware of the fact that if anyone from town were to have seen what she just did, they'd consider her certifiable. Of course, even if Tyler had actually been here, as far as the casual observer would have been concerned, she'd have appeared to be conversing with empty air.

Forget them. She was tired of their condemnation without proof. And the fact that some total stranger had them believing his pack of lies, without them even asking her, made her aware that she needed to take a stand.

Once she saved Tyler's sister, that was. Then she'd deal with the small stuff.

Grabbing her car keys from the counter, she called Tyler once more and then scribbled a quick note before she headed for her car. The changing tree was about fifteen minutes away, but she figured she'd be a few minutes early so she'd have time to collect her thoughts.

And deal with the memories.

She considered those as she drove to the out-of-the-way spot. When she and David had first started dating, they often participated in pack hunts. They both found the mating ritual for wolves much more exciting—and fun—than the long, drawn-out courtship humans endured.

They'd run and played, nipping each other playfully in their wolf form. He'd often brought her his first kill, a particularly juicy rabbit most times. And how great she'd felt the time she beat him and had been the one to gift him with her own small game.

Together as wolves, they'd been quite the hunters. She firmly believed this had strengthened their human relationship.

And the changing tree was where they'd made love for the first time. Where she'd secretly hoped to conceive their baby. Though it hadn't happened, more than ever she wished they'd had a child together. One way to keep a part of him with her always.

David had also proposed here. Right there, kneeling close to one of the giant roots. Anabel had accepted, and once he slipped the ring on her finger, they'd made love in the shade of the old oak.

Sorrow stabbed her. No wonder she'd avoided this place.

As she pulled up in front of the massive oak tree and parked, she closed her eyes. The tree looked exactly the same, just the way the image of it had been burned into her memory. Throat tight, she eyed the twisted branches, the weathered bark and the lush canopy of vibrant green leaves. Juliet was right. It was a place of power. This was the reason the Pack had changed her, going as far back as when the town of Leaning Tree had been established in the 1700s.

Glad hers was the only car in the small parking lot, she got out, last year's dead leaves cracking underfoot as she walked slowly down the winding path toward the huge and ancient tree.

Now that she'd become slightly more attuned to such things, the power radiating from the tree made her skin tingle.

"Wow," a voice said from behind her. "The changing tree. It's been so long, I forgot how much I'd missed this place."

Tyler. Relieved, Anabel turned. "I tried to contact you before I left. I wasn't able to. So I left you a note."

"I'm sorry," he said, his deep voice both soothing and sexy. "I didn't go by the house. I just searched for your energy and came and found you. Why are you here?"

She explained about Juliet and the coven. "They should be here in a few minutes."

Turning back to the tree, she made a slow circle around the massive trunk. With a reverent touch, she laid her hand on the rough bark, feeling the life energy radiating from the oak. "It's so old," she said, her eyes unexpectedly stinging. "I can only imagine what kind of life it's seen."

Tyler watched her rather than the tree, his gaze shuttered. Something in his haunted expression made her shiver. "The Pack has made sure this tree has been taken care of over the years."

She nodded, stopping at the exact spot where David had knelt in the leaves. To her surprise, while she felt the sorrow of an old, precious memory now gone, the crushing pain seemed to have faded.

Life moved on. She'd begun to finally make that journey toward healing.

Another vehicle pulled into the parking lot. Juliet's green Volkswagen. Anabel waved, just as two more cars drove around the corner and parked next to Juliet.

Juliet and another woman got out of the car. Anabel didn't recognize the tall, silver-haired woman, though she admired her grace and the smoothness of her dusky complexion.

Including Anabel, there were seven women in attendance. Most of them wore their hair long. There were only two older women, Juliet and her companion. Anabel waited silently, a bit tense, as they all convened on the changing tree.

"Hello," she ventured, when they were close. "Juliet, I had no idea there would be so many of you."

"Our entire coven," Juliet said, beaming. "Let me introduce you. Everyone, this is Anabel Lee. She's the one I told you about, the one who can talk to ghosts."

Everyone stared at her. Anabel waited for the familiar distrust to cloud the others' expressions. Instead they all murmured serene greetings, dipping their chins as Juliet said each of their names, still smiling. None of them appeared offended by her presence. In fact, they gave off a completely welcoming—even sisterly—vibe.

Stunned, Anabel tried not to show her shock. As she'd realized earlier, she'd grown far too complacent about letting the townspeople of Leaning Tree treat her poorly. Luckily, she didn't have that problem with these women.

"Blessed be," several said at once. Anabel wasn't quite sure how to respond to that, so she simply nodded.

She didn't know what she'd expected with meeting a coven of witches. A group of calm and centered, mostly middle-aged ladies hadn't been exactly the first thing that came to mind.

Granted, she had no experience with this type of thing. Her perceptions were based on what she'd seen on television and in movies or read in books.

Knowing that according to Juliet, Anabel herself was descended from a line of powerful witches didn't help. Actually, she thought, eyeing them as they held their hands out to her so they could make a circle around the tree, she was glad for the complete lack of drama. And if there was one thing she'd come to despise in her life, drama would rank right up there on top.

Still, she mused. They were witches and there was magic involved. She supposed she expected something.

Sliding her hand into Juliet's cool one, she reached out to connect with the woman waiting patiently on her other side.

Chapter 10

A flash of movement caught her attention. Tyler. His set face, clamped mouth and tight jaw showed his irritation at being left out of the circle. She wished he could be included. But then, Anabel didn't think any of the others could see him, except for Juliet.

"An orb," the dusky-skinned woman breathed, pointing directly at Tyler. "I think we're being visited by a spirit."

She sounded so delighted and excited that Anabel couldn't help grinning.

"Didn't you tell them?" she asked Juliet.

"No. Not yet. All in good time," Juliet said, one corner of her mouth lifting as if she tried to hide a smile.

One of the women—Anabel couldn't remember her name but judged her to be the oldest one there—cleared her throat loudly. "Are you ready?" she asked.

A silence fell. One by one, they nodded. Again, the overall mood felt solemn and respectful.

Except for Tyler, glowering at her. Clearly, he hated not being able to participate.

Giving in to impulse, she broke contact with the woman on her right and held out her hand to Tyler. "Come join us," she said, smiling.

One of the women gasped, to be shushed immediately by Juliet. Needing no second urging, Tyler came to stand beside Anabel, gripping her hand with his.

This time, his fingers didn't go through hers. Once again, Anabel could actually feel his touch. As if he were solid. As if he were alive. Just like when he'd kissed her. A thrill ran through her at the notion.

Just as instantly, she squashed it. "Is everyone ready?" she asked, looking pointedly at the woman on her right, who needed to be holding Tyler's other hand.

This woman—called Mary, if Anabel remembered correctly—gave her a perplexed look. "Will you take my hand again?" she asked. Clearly, she could not see or sense Tyler at all.

"Tyler, can you hold her hand?" Anabel wasn't sure how this worked. Was she the only one to whom he could appear solid?

"I can try." Confidence rang in his voice. He reached for Mary's fingers. And his hand went right through hers.

"I feel a chill." Eyes wide, Mary shivered. "Is that orb you guys claimed you could see near me?"

"Tyler is not an orb," Juliet told them, her voice firm. "He's a spirit and he's here with us right now."

Mary gasped, her gaze darting left and then right. "What...what does he want?"

"He needs our help to find his missing sister," Juliet continued. "He is, in fact, the reason we're here. Now please push your fear away and see if you and he can complete the circle. Take his hand."

"You want me to touch a…a ghost?" Mary sounded terrified.

"He won't hurt you, I promise." Anabel gave her a reassuring smile. "I'm holding his hand right now. Won't you please at least try?"

Grimacing, the woman glanced at her friends, maybe hoping for support, maybe for encouragement. No one else spoke, though the other women appeared to wait with an air of calm reassurance.

Finally, Mary took a deep breath and held out her hand. "Go ahead," she said, gazing up at empty air. "Take it." She glanced at Anabel. "Will I be able to feel— Oh!"

Anabel smiled. Apparently, Tyler's strange ability to ground himself more in this world temporarily enabled the other woman to feel his touch, as well.

"Are we ready now?" Juliet asked. Her voice sounded richer and more confident than Anabel had ever heard her. The voice of a woman of power.

Murmurs of assent came from the group. They'd barely died out when Juliet began chanting. The other women picked up the chant with her, making Anabel wonder if they'd memorized the words.

Only Anabel and Tyler remained silent. Beside her, Tyler still felt disturbingly solid, as if she could lean over and lick the corded muscles of his neck.

Shocked, she nearly jerked her hand free. Where had that thought come from? No matter. She had more important things to think about than her totally unrealistic attraction to a ghost.

Focus. Even as she thought the word, Anabel saw the power begin to coalesce in the air. Sparkling, like a braided rope made from lightning, it coiled around the circle of women and then from there, around the massive base of the tree.

Her very skin felt electrified. Sizzling. She fought the urge to break contact with the others, somehow aware if she did, this—whatever this was—would disappear.

Yet while she felt its power, she had no idea of its purpose. Surely Juliet or someone knew. Maybe they'd clue her in soon.

All of the energy vibrating in the air made her dizzy and she briefly closed her eyes. When she did, instead of the blessed cool darkness, the face of the dragon appeared. And his obsidian eyes were fixed directly on her.

She supposed she screamed. At least, she tried to. But when she opened her mouth, no sound came out. Something wrapped around her throat, crushing her breath. Dragon claws, huge filthy talons, tearing into her skin and making her bleed, even as she choked.

Struggling, she tried to fight. As her vision grayed, the notion flashed at her that she was not fighting with her physical self when the attack was in another realm entirely.

Help. She needed help. Yet she couldn't even open her eyes. Tyler still held one hand, one of the witches the other. What was wrong with them? Could they not see she was in trouble?

Focus.

The single word gave clarity to her panicked thoughts. *Focus.* Yet how could she when she could barely breathe?

Power shot through her, almost as if she'd been struck by lightning. She jolted up, conscious that she must not, no matter what, break the circle.

The power sent the Drakkor backward, breaking his death grip on her. She gasped, sucking in air, shaky and grateful and so damn full of energy she thought that if she were to launch herself into the air after her enemy, she could fly.

Who knew? Maybe she could.

The Drakkor roared, a sound of frustration and fury. Any moment she expected fire to shoot from his mouth.

As he retreated, she knew that if she was ever going to locate Tyler's sister, she needed to follow him, somehow.

Taking a leap of faith, she jerked her hands free and jumped into the air. To her relief, she lifted, flying steady and straight, almost as if she had wings or a jet pack on her back.

Ahead of her, the Drakkor flew like lightning. She increased her speed enough to be able to keep him in sight, but not so much that she grew close enough for him to notice. And then what? Once she found his lair—or perfectly ordinary house, which might very well be the case—what did she plan to do?

The safest thing might be to note the location.

Even as she had this thought, the beast turned. Terrible jaws open in a furious roar, it headed straight at her.

Anabel had no weapon with which to fight. Acting on instinct, she stifled a scream and threw up her hands in defense.

Energy whiplashed from her palms, like some fantastical movie special effects. Directing it on her attacker, she bared her teeth. She slammed her power into him, hoping, praying this—whatever this was—would work. And stop him.

Apparently, it did. The Drakkor struggled, roaring in defiance, unable to reach her. Unable, that was, as long as her power held.

Suddenly, she noticed what a drain this took on her energy. The vitality leached from her, more and more with every second that passed. If the Drakkor realized this, all he'd have to do would be to wait her out.

And then what? Most likely she would die here, wherever she was. Alone, taking Dena's last chance at salvation with her.

Decision made, she knew she had to flee, to get back to the safety of the coven, to find Tyler and Juliet and the others.

But how to beat a retreat while holding her enemy at bay?

The Drakkor roared again, launching himself at her. She could feel herself growing weak and knew she wouldn't be able to hold him off too much longer.

She thought of the others, hands linked in a circle around the ancient oak tree. Willed herself there, with every fiber of untapped power that might be left inside of her.

And just like that, she hurtled through space, so quickly even the stars became a blur. Until she found herself lying on the soft earth at the base of the tree, dead leaves crackling under her.

Tyler had sensed something might be wrong with Anabel when her small hand jerked in his. He glanced at her, finding her utterly still, with her eyes closed. Just like, he thought, glancing around the circle, all the others.

He wondered if the others could see the power shimmering like a golden rope made of sparks. As he watched, fascinated, it circled the tree and them. The hair on the women's heads danced with an electrical beat, and their skin seemed to sizzle. Apparently, this didn't hurt. Not one person moved. Yet despite all the stillness, he sensed Anabel had gone a different kind of quiet.

It was dangerous to break the circle. He dared not let go. His own ethereal body appeared unaffected.

The chant ended. Still the women stood, silent and still as statues. Anabel swayed, her mouth opening as if she meant to speak, but no sound came out.

Concerned, he watched her. He felt as if, more than ever, the importance of not breaking the circle overrode everything else.

She began to thrash, side to side, swaying like a hammock between the hands holding on to hers. Tyler remained solid—this was the longest he'd ever been able to do this, which he figured was due to the power generated by their circle and the tree.

Anabel cried out, making his heart leap in his throat. He looked at her friend Juliet, to see what she thought, but she remained standing, eyes still closed.

No one else seemed perturbed. He told himself to relax, that Anabel was right there, her hand securely in his, and nothing could happen to her anyway while she stayed surrounded by all this power.

But he remembered how the Drakkor had taken him unaware and nearly crushed him. Again he eyed Anabel, wondering if she'd give him a sign if she needed some sort of help. She tightened her grip on his hand, which reassured him. As long as her chest continued to rise and fall with her breathing, and she didn't appear threatened, he waited.

Just as he reached this decision, Anabel let out a powerful scream. Jerking her hands free, she jumped forward. And fell, as surely as if struck by a giant, invisible hand.

He ran to her, reaching to cradle her in his arms. But he'd gone back to his ghostly, unsubstantial form, and his hands passed right through her. This made him want to lift his head to the sky and howl with frustration.

The others rushed over, making soft sounds of distress. Juliet and her friend, who appeared to be the leader, gathered Anabel up.

Rage filled Tyler. He hated being a ghost, despised the lack of the ability to help both Anabel and his baby sister.

Once again, he was sick and tired of being insubstantial. Why even allow him to be contacted, if he couldn't even help protect the ones he loved?

Loved.

This should have shocked him, but his anger and frustration eclipsed everything else. That and his concern for Anabel, who hadn't stirred at all since she'd fallen to the ground.

Juliet and her friend were speaking. He moved closer so he could pick up the words.

"Her physical body is fine. The attack was on the other plane."

He shook his head, but no one noticed him. Of course they hadn't. He'd managed to briefly forget that he was a ghost and thus invisible to most of them.

Anabel groaned, her eyelids fluttering. She sat up, moaned in pain and looked around. "What just happened?"

"We don't know," Juliet said. "We were gathering the power, and you just collapsed."

"No." Anabel met Tyler's gaze. "The Drakkor found me."

Several of the women gasped. Juliet, however, remained as calm and coolly collected as ever. "Us," she gently corrected her. "The Drakkor found us."

Anabel nodded, clearly unwilling to battle over semantics.

"And then what happened?" Tyler prodded.

"He attacked me. Wrapped his claws around my throat." Her hand went up, gingerly probing her neck. "He was trying to choke me. His talons tore into my skin and made me bleed."

Tyler nodded, despite the fact that her throat appeared untouched.

"I fought him off," Anabel continued. "And when he flew away, I followed."

Another collective gasp. Only Juliet and the older woman remained silent, their blue eyes watchful.

Anabel kept her gaze locked on Tyler. "I wanted to follow him, to learn where he might be keeping your sister. But this time, I saw nothing I recognized, no landmarks to help guide us." She grimaced. "Maybe because he noticed me after him."

If Tyler had been alive, he would have been holding his breath. "And then what happened?" he asked quietly.

"He came for me." Briefly, she closed her eyes. When she opened them again, they shone like polished copper. "And I fought him off, this time using some sort of magic or energy."

"How?" Juliet asked, sounding unsurprised and intently curious. "What precisely did you do?"

"I used my palms. I'm not sure how exactly, but energy came from them and stopped the Drakkor. I was able to hold him motionless and keep him from reaching me."

Then she told them all how she'd simply decided she needed to come back and she had.

When Anabel finished speaking, the assembled group remained silent. Anabel began shaking, and Tyler once again tried to go to her and offer comfort. But he was not permitted such luxuries. The ache in his chest became a stone.

"Let's go home," he said. "I think we've had enough excitement for one day."

She nodded, saying her goodbyes to the women. Initially, a few of them protested, wanting her to stay longer, but a single look from Juliet quelled their requests.

As she walked to the car, her gait seemed odd, as though her entire body felt sore. Once she unlocked it and got inside, she took a deep breath and grabbed the steering wheel, dropping her head on her hands. "I'm exhausted," she said, her voice husky with weariness. "Even though I didn't physically fight that dragon, my body feels like it did and got its ass kicked."

He waited until she'd started the engine and put the car in Drive before speaking. "We're running out of time," he said. "If we don't get to her soon, my sister will die. I don't know how I know this, but I feel it in my heart."

Straightening, she nodded. "I'm doing the best I can. If you can think of anything else I should try, I'm willing to give it a shot."

Since he had nothing else to offer, he managed a smile and thanked her. Neither spoke for the rest of the short ride home.

As soon as they reached the house, Anabel headed for her bedroom. "I need to sleep," she said, the exhaustion plain on her beautiful face. "Just a couple of hours, and then I'll get up and make myself something to eat."

"Okay," he replied, trying not to sound too worried. "You definitely need to keep up your strength."

The ghost of a smile hovering at the edges of her mouth called him out. Still, he couldn't help smiling back. "I'll wait for you."

The words sounded oddly prophetic.

Tyler checked on Anabel several times during the night. Her even breathing and lack of restlessness told him she slept deeply, healing her body and her spirit. Though he wanted to stay with her while she slept, his attraction had grown so strong it interfered with his thinking. The more distance he maintained between them, the better.

Finally, as the sun began to rise, he retreated to his own corner of the living room and tried again to contact Dena.

The instant he stilled himself, for the first time in far

too long, he was able to feel his sister reaching out to him. This time, he could barely feel the feeble spark of her energy, it had grown so weak.

Unlike before, she didn't speak or even plead for help. He doubted that she could. Nothing but misery and pain radiated from her. Stomach sinking, horrified and afraid, he knew then that they were running out of time to find her. If they didn't locate her soon, the next time he'd see her would be in the misty world of spirit.

He tried to comfort her as much as he could, but he wasn't sure if she even felt his presence. Nevertheless, he remained, trying to transfer some of his energy to her, surrounding her with vibes of healing and strength.

To his relief, some of it must have reached her. She quieted and appeared to breathe better.

Damn, he cursed himself. Here he battled a foolish attraction to a woman he couldn't have when he should have been focusing all his energy on Dena.

The urgency of her situation had never seemed clearer. Now that morning had arrived, it had been five days since he first made contact with Anabel. They had to locate and rescue Dena within the next day or two or she'd die.

They'd learned so much—but not enough.

Having done all he could, he retreated. Back in Anabel's living room, when he came out of his trance, he saw at least an hour had passed, judging by the angle of sun streaming in the window. Great. More time wasted. Exactly what he—and more important, Dena—didn't need.

Anabel had dreamed of landmarks. They needed to go comb the woods, drive around the more remote wooded areas and try to see if they could locate any of the markers she'd seen in her dream.

Fired up, he hurried to find Anabel, figuring she'd still be sleeping. Instead her bed was empty. He rushed past it and found her in her bathroom. She'd just stepped out of the shower. Reaching for a towel, she glanced up and saw him, water drops glistening on her white satin skin. Naked, she was even more alluring, an unwelcome attraction he certainly did not need.

Looking away, he knew the image would forever be burned into his retinas. He clenched his jaw so tightly it hurt. He needed to focus on rescuing his sister, not his mounting attraction for this enigmatic woman.

Eyes wide, Anabel hurriedly wrapped herself in the towel. "Why are you in here?" Her voice came out high and breathless. "What's going on?"

"I need your help," he rasped. "Dena's fading fast."

"I know. We've got to find her." She pointed at the doorway. "But a few minutes isn't going to change anything. Out. Go wait for me in the kitchen. I'll join you once I'm dried off and dressed."

As he backed out of the room, Tyler kept his gaze averted. It was safer that way.

The instant Tyler disappeared, Anabel let out the breath she'd been holding. When he'd walked in on her naked, she'd known an instant's thrill of pleasure. For a moment, she'd wished he wasn't a ghost, but a real, live man, the way he'd been earlier in the circle around the changing tree.

The constant aching of desire never left her. Even when she pushed it away so she could focus, it remained, humming along just under her skin. How ridiculous was that? Bad enough she craved another man's embrace, but how ironic the man wasn't even alive.

Sighing, she toweled herself off and hurried through her normal morning routine. Dressed, she gave a quick glance at herself in her mirror, shaking her head at the woman who stared right back at her. Sometimes she didn't even recognize herself.

Heading to the kitchen, where Tyler waited, she went straight to the coffeemaker and made herself a large mug of coffee. A couple of sips in, she finally felt ready to face her ghostly visitor.

"I'm trying my best to help your sister, Tyler." She let some of her frustration show. "But I don't know what else to do."

"Try again to locate the Drakkor," he said immediately. "He's the only one who knows."

Remorse stabbed her. "I can't," she said. "I'm sorry, but I don't have enough energy still. I need more rest before I try any more magic."

A shadow crossed his face, though he nodded. "How about we take a drive in the countryside? Somewhere in the Catskill Forest Preserve."

She stared at him. "We can do that," she said slowly. "But you do realize that's 287,000 acres and goes through Ulster, Greene, Delaware and Sullivan counties? Where do you propose we start?"

Burying his face in his hands, he cursed. "Damn it. I hate being so freaking powerless."

Stunned, she didn't know what to say. When she finally found the words, she hoped they did her thoughts justice. "Powerless? You are dead, Tyler. Yet somehow you managed to come back as a ghost and do everything you can to help your sister. That sounds pretty damn powerful to me."

He raised his face, staring at her. A spark of some indefinable emotion glowed in his eyes. "Thank you for that," he said quietly.

"You've just got to remember we're doing all we can.

I get frustrated too. I hate the thought of her at the mercy of that Drakkor."

"Me too."

"What I don't understand is why." Anabel rubbed her aching temples. "Nothing I've read about these Drakkors mentions them capturing young women and holding them hostage."

Tyler's grim expression told her he thought he knew the answer. "Well, there's your feeding-off-magic theory."

"I can't find any information to support that. There's got to be another reason."

Mouth twisting bitterly, he looked away. "Sexual deviants aren't particular to any one species."

Though his answer made her feel sick, she kept her voice professional. "True, but I can't help feeling there's more to it than that." She reached for the stack of ever-present books she'd placed on the table and tapped on one particularly thick book. "I keep reading and hoping I'll find it."

Though he appeared skeptical, she chose to believe she saw a glimmer of hope.

"No matter what, fighting that Drakkor almost did me in. I've got to rest up," she said. "I plan to spend that time learning as much as I can about our enemy. I think that's the key. If we can find out why he does what he does, we can figure out a way to beat him."

"Maybe." Tyler didn't sound optimistic. "I can only hope it doesn't take too long, or we'll be too late for my sister."

"You can fly," she pointed out. "While I study, why don't you go and search as much of the preserve as you can, starting with the areas closest to town? You never know—you might see one of the landmarks."

"I think I will."

Though she only nodded, inside she seethed with frustration. Talk about feeling powerless. Supposedly she had been blessed with great magical ability, but because of her lack of training, she had no idea how to utilize it. She'd give anything to be able to zoom to Dena Rogers's side, zap the stupid Drakkor and bring Tyler's sister to safety.

Now she was too darn weak to do anything but rest.

After making some soft-boiled eggs for breakfast, Anabel spent the morning poring over the books. Though Tyler had left, he returned shortly before lunch, brooding and silent, his rugged profile dark and somber. When she asked him if he'd had any luck, he only shook his head, gesturing that she should go back to her reading.

Finally, she closed her book and rubbed her eyes. "I need a break," she announced. "I'll make a quick lunch and then get back to it."

Just as she spoke, she heard the sound of the postal truck delivering the day's mail. "This is really getting to be a habit," she said, half laughing at her own foolishness. "I'll be right back."

Two sales catalogs, one air-conditioning-repair brochure and a letter from a company inviting her to take a competitive look at her home insurance. At least there were no bills.

On her way back in, she realized a piece of paper had been taped to the front door. Curious, she pulled it down and opened it. The black-and-white flyer had been printed on regular paper rather than glossy, so the photograph in the middle looked dull, as if dimmed by the passage of time.

The two faces smiling at the camera made her gasp. The woman, with her long mass of dark hair and exotically tilted eyes, was Dena Rogers in better times, according to the caption. The other, a man with his arms draped casually around her shoulders, was Dena's older brother, Tyler.

Chapter 11

Dumbstruck, she studied the picture, uncomfortably aware that Tyler had not only been alive in this photo, but much more carefree. His ghost self rarely flashed that kind of confident smile, though when he did she felt its impact all the way from her heart to her feet.

Handsome, sexy, masculine—all those adjectives came to mind. How she wished she'd known him then, before she'd met David. Shocked at the wayward thought, she shook her head. What on earth was wrong with her? She'd loved her husband and he'd loved her. They'd been mates, hadn't they?

If so, then why did she feel such an overwhelming attraction to another man? Even worse, to another man's ghost. Mates were just that—one male, one female, for life. Once David had died, she wasn't supposed to ever be able to love another man.

Still she couldn't look away. When she realized she'd been mooning at the photograph long enough, she shook her head at her own foolishness and read the text. And then, disbelieving, read it again to be sure while walking back inside.

"Wow." The sound of his deep voice behind her made her start. Heat flooded her entire body as she met his gaze. Hurriedly, she looked back at the photo, hoping she hadn't inadvertently revealed how he affected her.

"Where did you get that?" he asked, his voice thick with pain.

"It was on my front door. Evidently, Everlasting Faith Church is holding a candlelight prayer vigil for your sister." Composed again, she faced him. "That's pretty awesome, don't you think?"

"Yes," he said thoughtfully, his focus still on the picture. "I find it hard to believe that anybody who can do something so caring could possibly have anything to do with her disappearance."

"Unless that's exactly what they want you to think," she felt compelled to point out.

"Maybe so." When he finally looked up from the flyer, he gave a slow shake of his head. "I haven't seen that photo in a long time."

"When was it taken?"

Glancing quickly at her, he flashed a distracted smile. "Two years ago, when I was home on leave. We'd just come back from a night out eating pizza. We were both so happy to be together again. Family is—was—everything to both of us."

Her throat ached for him. In that moment, she would have given just about anything if she could give him back both his sister and his life.

Of course, she couldn't do the latter, so she'd have to settle for getting Dena free.

"Are you going to go?" He jerked his head at the flyer. "To the candlelight vigil."

Though she hadn't intended to, she gave the idea some serious thought. "Do you think it would help if I did?"

"Maybe. Who knows? But if whoever did this to my sister is there, he might do something to reveal where he's holding her."

"True. I have read that people like that often try to insinuate themselves into the investigation."

He nodded, his chiseled features expressionless. "Then you'll go?"

"Will you come with me?"

The smile that spread across his face had his eyes crinkling and made her catch her breath. "Yes."

Since the candlelight vigil was that night, she wondered if anyone from the church had managed to notify the media. "Media coverage would really help," she mused out loud. "I'm going to call Pastor Tom and see if he's taken care of that."

She had her phone locate and dial the number for her. Pastor Jones sounded surprised to hear from her. When she outlined the reason for her call, he chuckled. "Great minds apparently think alike. I've sent a press release to the local NBC, ABC, CBS and Fox affiliates. Several reporters have already contacted me with requests for interviews at the vigil. So we should have more than adequate media coverage."

"Great." Feeling a bit self-conscious, she glanced at Tyler, who gave her the thumbs-up sign.

"Thanks for checking, Ms. Lee. Are you going to be in attendance, as well?"

Glad she and Tyler had just discussed this, she answered in the affirmative.

"Fantastic." The warmth in his voice made her smile. "I look forward to seeing you there." And he hung up.

Feeling slightly dazed, she put her phone back in her pocket. "I am beginning to see how he has such a high rate of conversions to his church. That man has serious charisma."

Tyler studied her. She didn't know if it was her imagination or not, but he seemed a bit sad. "I think he likes you," he said.

She had to laugh. "No. He merely sees another poor soul whom he hopes to save."

Tyler nodded. "About the vigil. When we're there, try to continually scan the crowd. Look for anyone who seems out of place. I'll do the same."

"Okay." She nodded. "Of course, you have the added benefit of being invisible."

He gave her a fleeting smile. "Fingers crossed we learn something useful."

Though they arrived ten minutes before the scheduled start time, the church parking lot was already packed. "Surely not all of these are members of the congregation?"

Tyler shook his head. "No, I don't think so. This event has been pretty heavily promoted, between the flyers and the TV news and even the newspaper. I bet they did something online too. I'm sure there are a lot of outsiders here, as well."

She thought she could look into his eyes forever. Grimacing at the thought, she parked. "Are you ready?"

"Definitely."

She took a deep breath. "Then let's do this."

One thing Anabel didn't tell Tyler was that she'd always hated crowds. More than that, too many people around her made her feel the panicked urge to flee.

She'd told herself too many times to count not only

that such an irrational fear was ridiculous, but that she couldn't allow such a foolish weakness to get in the way of her search for Tyler's sister. Better to endure the sweaty press of people milling around in the early-evening heat than be held prisoner, trapped in some dark hole.

Thus fortified, she made her way through the crowd, most of them already holding their Dixie cups and candles, though unlit.

She saw Juliet and a few of the other women from the coven. Even her former best friend, Denise Jarvis, had come, waving at her from her position next to her mother and several older women who had to be her mother's friends. Though Anabel hadn't seen Denise in years, she waved back.

Pastor Jones stepped up on a smallish raised platform. A woman seated below him at a small electric keyboard hit a series of notes, and all around, the talking and other noise quieted.

"Let us bow our heads in prayer," the pastor said. All around, everyone did exactly that. Anabel too, though she kept her eyes open and continued to scan the crowd through her lashes. While she didn't know the majority of the people attending, she really didn't see anyone who looked out of place.

Maybe she needed to use more than just her eyes.

As the pastor continued to pray, Anabel focused her attention inward, gathering up her scattered thoughts and silencing them one by one.

Until inside she went quiet.

And then she sent her essence outward, touching the others quietly, seeking what, she wasn't sure. An odd vibration, maybe unquiet tension.

She couldn't read their minds—she wasn't a psychic. But she could feel what kind of heart beat within. Many of the people in attendance were focused on the pastor's words and then on the hymn they'd all begun to sing.

As her essence drifted through the crowd, she found lust and anger, jealousy and irritability. Normal human emotions—nothing on the scale of what she searched for. Nothing like the furious rage consuming the Drakkor.

Finally, the sound of clapping made her blink. Instantly back in her own body, she looked around. Everyone had begun to move, talking to each other.

Juliet made a beeline over. "That was very nice. Did you learn anything?"

"No." With a disappointed—and tired—sigh, Anabel shook her head. "Unfortunately not. If he was here, he's really good at cloaking himself."

"I wouldn't be surprised," Juliet said. "Did you bring your friend?"

"My friend?" Mind blank, Anabel didn't understand at first what the other woman meant. When she realized, she nodded. "You mean Tyler? Yes, he's around here somewhere."

"Good. I talked briefly to Pastor Jones. He seems like a good-hearted man. He's doing everything he can think of to help."

Anabel nodded. "I have to say, I'm sort of surprised to see you here."

"Because we're Wiccan?" Not waiting for Anabel's response, Juliet looked around and shrugged. "There's good energy being generated here. Prayers have power, no matter what religion. This is more like what we do than you realize."

Worried she'd offended her friend, Anabel tried to apologize. Juliet instantly waved her words away. "No worries, hon." She gave Anabel an impulsive hug. "I'm going to run now. If you hear of anything or have any questions, give me a call."

After promising she would, Anabel turned to look for Tyler. As she did, she saw Pastor Jones purposely making his way toward her. Though the last thing she wanted to do was speak with him, she wanted to thank him for putting on the vigil.

Unfortunately, the poor man kept getting sidetracked by members of his own congregation. At this rate, Anabel figured it'd be at least twenty or thirty minutes before he reached her.

Taking matters into her own hands, she expertly weaved through the crowd until she reached his side. "Excuse me," she said, interrupting the ongoing conversation. "Pastor, I just wanted to thank you for putting on this prayer vigil. It was very much appreciated."

"Thank you."

She could tell he wanted to say more but because of his attentive audience, couldn't.

"Time to go," Tyler said, his deep voice so close to her ear she jumped. Which made the pastor and his circle of friends eye her.

"Bug bite," she said, hiding a smile. Then, thanking him again, she took off.

On the drive home, she wondered at the restless feeling making her jittery. Recognizing it, she pushed away the anger. It had been a long time since she'd craved a man this much. Correction—a ghost. All day, the craving had been building inside her, until she felt as if she might explode.

If she'd been a runner, she might have taken off and tried to outrun it. As things stood, she'd simply have to let her desire simmer inside her until it hopefully burned itself out.

Unless… She gasped out loud as a thought occurred

to her. A frightening, yet delightful thought. One that energized her more than a hundred naps. Her heart began pounding as she contemplated whether or not she'd have enough courage to carry it through. Or if such a thing would even work.

Once, just once, she wanted—no, *needed*—to allow herself to feel again. Her husband had died, she was alone and her actions would hurt no one but herself.

"You're in a strange mood," Tyler commented as they pulled up in her driveway.

"Maybe," she allowed, parking and turning off the engine. Now or nothing. "I have a question for you. About that trick you did once before and again during the circle at the changing tree?"

"Trick?"

"Yes," she said, trying to sound casual as she got out of the car and headed toward her front door, despite the fact that she'd begun trembling. "Becoming solid. Any idea how you did that?"

As she put her key in the lock, Tyler materialized next to her. Eyeing her as he followed her inside, he cocked his head. "That? I have no idea how that happened."

Tossing her purse onto the counter, she faced him. Her heart now beat so fast she wondered if he could see it in the hollow of her throat.

"Are you all right?" he asked, eyeing her warily, clearly not understanding. "Why do you want to know how I became solid? All I know is one minute I was a ghost and the next I wasn't. It didn't last long, though."

Again, she wondered if together they could make it last long enough.

"It seems like a form of magic," she prompted. "Surely you must have some idea how you made it happen. Think about it, please. It's important."

Some of the pent-up heat in her tone must have reached him. He eyed her, his gaze going dark. "No, not really. I just was."

"Did you think about it first? Like I have to make myself focus, the way Juliet taught me?"

"Focus." He considered. "Maybe. Part of me wanted it, so I decided to be. And I became flesh, for a short while."

Decided to be. Though she could barely catch her breath, she still tried to sound calm. "I have a question for you. Do you think you can do it again?"

He shrugged. Was he playing with her? Or did he truly not get her feeble innuendo?

"Maybe. Probably. Why?"

Her face heated. She'd always had this unfortunate blushing issue, despite her dark hair. Her pale complexion went from milky white to the color of a ripe tomato.

"I, uh." Deep breath, swallow. Lifting her gaze to his, she managed to push out the words. "I wanted you to be solid because I wondered if you could kiss me again." Even though she ached for more, she'd settle for a kiss. Or so she told herself.

There. She'd said it. She had no idea what she'd do if he said no. Deal with it and move on, as she did with everything else.

In the silence that followed, Anabel panicked. Maybe she'd just made a horrible, awful mistake. Or worse, she didn't want him to think he had to or to feel obligated out of pity. Oh no. "Of course, it's up to you," she began. "Though I think it might somehow help give me back some of my missing energy."

Where had that come from? Maybe it was true. What on earth was the *matter* with her?

"Shhh." Suddenly, Tyler was right there. Eyes glowing, a few inches in front of her, looking handsome and manly and oh so alive.

He kissed her then, before she could even exhale. His mouth—solid and very unghostlike—slanted over hers, making her go weak at the knees.

Tongue mating with his, she deepened the kiss. She knew she shouldn't have, but she had been widowed for so long, and she wanted him with every fiber of her being.

Wanted more than a kiss. Much, much more.

This so shocked her she attempted to back away. But her arms were locked around his neck, her hips molding to his in an invitation that was anything but tentative.

When he kissed her again, she forgot about her hesitation. Heck, she forgot her own name or the fact that he was a ghost. All she could think about was how badly she wanted him inside her.

Energy blazed through her. Whether his or hers or a combination of the two, she had no idea. He moved his mouth from her lips to the hollow of her throat, making her shiver.

"Anabel?" He whispered the question, his breath tickling the edge of her ear. She knew what he asked, without him having to say anything but her name.

Should she? Could she? Throwing out logic and refusing to debate, she took the plunge. "Yes," she said, giving herself permission to let her hands explore. "Definitely yes."

In that moment, and the ones that followed, Tyler ceased to be a ghost. He became real, and Anabel let herself delight in touching every corded muscle, thrilling at his body's response as she skimmed her fingers against his flat stomach.

When she went to tug at his clothes, it occurred to her to simply will them away, and she did. They vanished just like that. Allowing her to feast her eyes on his massive arousal.

"What about yours?" he demanded, his voice like smoke and whiskey. "I want to see you. Every inch of you."

What the heck—why not? Smiling seductively, she blinked and her own clothing vanished. "Here you go," she murmured, groaning as he fastened his mouth over one erect nipple.

"You're absolutely beautiful," he said gruffly.

"So are you," she replied, meaning it. Each touch, every caress and kiss and sigh made her body turn to liquid and fire. When he entered her, she gasped with stunned pleasure as the sheer breadth of him filled her completely.

"Oh," she cried. And then again as he began to move.

Never before had lovemaking felt like this. Carnal and primitive, yet tender and full of emotion. Of love.

No. Shoving that random thought out of her head, she gave herself over to the pleasure building with each thrust of his body.

In a white-hot supernova, she let herself explode. Pulses of pleasure, rocking her body, her world and, ultimately, him.

Tyler followed her into release just as her spasms began to slow down. The brilliant flare of energy, of magic, settled into a steady glow.

As she lay in the circle of his arms, marveling, refusing to feel guilty, she sort of expected him to go all ethereal on her again, back to his ghostly form. But he remained solid, his sweat-slickened body cooling with hers. Nothing had felt as sweet as his embrace, at least not in a long time.

Now what? Deciding to worry about that another time, she let herself relax. To her amazement, she fell asleep.

Leroy's furious yowls woke her. Sitting up, alone once more, she glanced at the clock. She'd managed to sleep past her pet's dinnertime.

Not only that, but Tyler was nowhere in sight. If not for her soreness and the small black-and-blue bite mark just above her boob, she might have thought she'd once again dreamed the entire thing.

Except she felt blissfully, vibrantly, happy. Everything about her—from her skin to her heart to her senses—felt enhanced somehow. She recognized the feeling. After all, she'd felt it once before when she fell for David.

No. She wasn't that stupid. She couldn't be emotionally involved with a man who wasn't even alive.

When her phone rang just as she'd gotten calmed down, Anabel glanced at the caller ID. "Denise Jarvis?" She wasn't sure she wanted to answer. Denise had been her best friend in high school. After Anabel married David, Denise had taken off for parts unknown. She'd always wanted to travel, so Anabel had assumed her former friend let her wanderlust carry her wherever she wanted to go. They'd grown apart organically, leading such different lives.

She'd often wondered why Denise had never tried to keep in touch, and then had put it down to the definite possibility that she'd heard about Anabel's actions from family members still in town and wanted nothing to do with the kind of person everyone believed Anabel had become.

So why call her now?

Deciding she'd welcome the distraction—any distraction—Anabel pressed the button to take the call. "Denise," she said cautiously. "Long time, no see. How on earth are you?"

"I'm okay. Sorry I haven't gotten in touch, but I've been traveling again. I just got back in town a couple of days ago." Denise cleared her throat. "Anyway, I wondered if you wanted to have lunch with me. I'm kind of worried about you."

Resisting the urge to respond truthfully, Anabel sighed. "I promise you, I'm fine. I know you've heard about some of my actions a couple of months past, but I'm trying to move past that."

"Are you?" Denise sounded desperate to believe her. "How do you feel?"

"I'm healing," Anabel said, wondering if she really was. Part of her couldn't help wondering, since apparently she'd become fixated on a dead man, one who was just barely more accessible than her deceased husband.

"I'm glad," Denise said. "Really, really glad. But I've been hearing an awful lot of talk about you and this guy Doug Polacek. Mostly, I'd been putting it down to gossip, but I got a chance to meet him the other day. He's really angry with you. What exactly did you do to him?"

Him again. First Juliet had mentioned him and now Denise. "That's just it. I've never even met him."

Silence. Anabel figured Denise was trying to decide whether or not to believe her. "Look, Denise. I really don't care whether or not you think I'm telling the truth. I don't know Doug Polacek and I have absolutely no idea why he's trying to discredit me."

"Wow." Denise sounded shocked. "Maybe we'd better do some digging and see what we can find out."

Surprised by the *we,* Anabel didn't respond at first.

"How about we get together? We can discuss this at lunch," Denise continued. "Are you free tomorrow?"

Though the idea of meeting an old friend for lunch in a public place made Anabel nervous, she found herself agreeing. Who knew? Maybe it would do her good to get out and get away from Tyler. And she needed to try to find out what this Doug Polacek's problem might be. It might even be tied in to the thing with Tyler's sister.

After lunch, as long as she was in town, she could stop by the police station and see if Captain Harper had dug up any other information.

They decided to meet at Cow Burgers, which had become the carnivorous townspeople of Leaning Tree's favorite burger joint. Anabel's mouth started to water at the thought of one of those thick, juicy hamburger patties, but since she'd given up meat, she'd opt for a vegetarian entrée.

Once she ended the call, she turned to see Tyler watching her, his form much less substantial than usual.

What had she just done? Trying not to panic, she managed a smile. "Are you all right?"

"I think so." His shuttered expression made her wonder if he too was full of regret. Oddly enough, thinking he might be helped. "All that physical manifesting apparently has drained my energy. It's taking every bit of strength I can dredge up to remain here with you."

Now would be the perfect time to tell him to take himself off and get healed, but she couldn't make herself say the words. She both wanted him to leave and wanted him to stay.

Good night, she'd become even more of a mess.

"I'm sorry," she said softly. A quick glance at his still-flickering form revealed he was studying her, a hungry look on his rugged face.

Her stomach lurched. *No, no, no.*

It'd be so much easier if he'd simply pretend nothing had happened, wouldn't it? Or would that hurt even worse?

She no longer knew which end was up. "I'm meeting a friend in town tomorrow. While I'm there, I thought I'd stop at the police station and see if the captain took me seriously."

"Good idea."

"I thought so." She settled on deliberately cheerful, even though her insides were churning.

"I used to love a Triple Cow Burger," he said, still watching her. "Ghosts don't get hungry and we sure don't have to eat, but I'd give a lot if I could just taste a single bite of one right now."

"I haven't been in a long time," she said. "But if I could figure out a way to make you solid again, I'd bring one home for you."

As soon as the words left her mouth, she realized what she'd said. Her entire body blushed. "I mean, so you could eat. But since you can't, I'll just have to enjoy a burger for you—though a veggie burger."

"Oh, I'm going with you." His tone left no room for argument. "There's no way I'm letting you try and face that crazy Doug guy without a little ghostly help."

Still in shock from the sudden onslaught of feelings, she glared at him. Panicked, she wanted to push him away, make him leave, give her time to regain her bearings. "Not this time, okay? I think you should go back out in the forest and search some more. Actually, I need a bit of a break from all this."

Tyler had gone awfully still. "How is confronting Doug Polacek taking a break?"

"It's time," she said firmly. "I don't know what his problem is, nor do I care. But he needs to stop. Besides, if he confronts me, what are you going to do, anyway?"

Tyler's furious expression told her she might have gone a bit too far. "You know what? You're right. I'm nothing more than a spirit, a specter, a shade. I'm absolutely powerless to do anything without your help. And I should let you know how seriously pissed off that makes me feel."

Though she almost reacted in kind, with anger, she reined herself in again. For an instant she wondered if she should say more, like how terrified their burgeoning—and impossible—relationship made her feel. In the end, she decided to simply repeat her earlier apology. "I'm really, really sorry."

"It's not your fault," he said tightly. "Nor mine. Someone up there is playing a giant, cosmic joke on me. All I wanted to do was try and save my sister, not get tangled up emotionally with you."

Before she could even think of a way to reply to that, he winked out and disappeared.

Leaving her aching and confused when she should have been relieved. His words haunted her. Tangled up emotionally? Really? Clearly, she wasn't the only one having feelings she shouldn't be having.

People in town already believed her crazy. Well, she definitely would be if she allowed herself to fall for a ghost.

Tyler had stated the facts very well. They needed to work together to save his sister. Once that had been accomplished, Anabel could go back to her empty, lonely life. And Tyler could return to being…dead.

Chapter 12

Cow Burgers had just begun to fill up when Anabel arrived the next day. It had just turned eleven thirty, so the die-hard lunch rush wouldn't start for another half hour.

Head held high, ignoring the few people who cast her looks, censuring or otherwise, Anabel searched the interior. Hopefully, Denise would already be seated so Anabel could simply slide into a booth and hide behind a menu if she wanted.

Except she didn't. She'd actually begun to grow weary of always hiding. Since she didn't see Denise yet, she approached the front desk and asked for a table for two.

The teenage girl nodded her pink-tipped head, clearly not recognizing her. Laughing at herself—did she really think she was such a celebrity that everyone in town knew her name?—Anabel followed the hostess to a table, rather than a booth. She pulled out her chair, taking a seat facing the entrance. She decided to wait on looking at the menu until her friend had arrived. Since she worked as a cook, she didn't go out to eat much and she decided to enjoy this rare treat.

Instead of hiding away, she kept her head up and gazed around the room. Several people openly stared, though they looked away when she met their gaze. She refused to let them ruin her day. Heart light, she smiled and waved as Denise walked in.

Her friend looked exactly as she had the last time Anabel had seen her. Tall, with an angular prettiness and close-cropped blond hair, the crinkles around her bright blue eyes a testament to her ready smile.

Anabel jumped up and they hugged. Denise still wore the same perfume, a fragrance that smelled faintly of roses. "You look fantastic!" Anabel exclaimed.

Studying her, Denise grinned. "So do you. I can't believe it's been so long since I've seen you."

After they'd taken their seats, Denise pushed the menu away, still smiling. "I don't even have to look. I always get the Fiery Cow Burger. It has pepper jack cheese, guacamole and jalapeño peppers."

Anabel winced. "Ouch. But you know what? That sounds perfect, except I'll have a veggie burger with the same toppings."

When the waiter came, they both ordered. Once he'd left, Anabel leaned forward. "It's really great to see you," she said softly.

"Same here." Denise glanced around. "I have to tell you, I've heard so much bizarre gossip about you, I got concerned. Actually, you're partly the reason for my stop in Leaning Tree. I decided to take a minivacation here and make sure you were okay."

Touched, Anabel swallowed. She didn't want to tell her old best friend how alone she'd felt after David's death. She knew Denise had been busy with her career as a journalist, traveling all over the world reporting for a prestigious magazine.

"I thought of you often," she finally said. "I even bought a subscription to your magazine, just so I could follow your stories."

Pleasure flashed in Denise's eyes. "Thank you," she said softly.

"Was it exciting?" Anabel asked. "Living the kind of life you did?"

Before Denise could answer, the waiter brought their diet colas.

"Sometimes." Denise took a sip from her straw. "I've been all through Europe and most of Asia. Next I'm being sent to check out Australia and New Zealand."

"I used to always want to travel," Anabel admitted. "In fact, until David was killed, we kept a list of places we wanted to go."

"I'm so sorry." Denise covered Anabel's hand. "I wish I could have met him. I couldn't believe it when my mother told me he was killed in Afghanistan."

In the past, Anabel had found discussing David too painful to bear, so she'd always changed the subject. This time, she felt a slight twinge of grief, but nothing she couldn't handle.

"Thank you. After eighteen months, I guess I've gotten used to being a widow," Anabel said, realizing it was true. "At first, it was hard and I briefly came unhinged. I actually believed Kane McGraw and I were meant to be together."

Denise winced. "I heard about that. I take it you're all better now?"

"Yes. I am." And she was. She reached into her purse and pulled out her wallet. "Since you never met my husband, here's a picture of him right before his last tour."

Studying the snapshot, Denise beamed. "Wow. I can see why you fell for him. He looks good in a uniform." She passed the photo back.

Completely relaxed and feeling more confident than she had felt in months, Anabel nearly told her about Tyler. The second she realized her mistake, she closed her mouth. She could imagine how that conversation would go. *And he's a ghost but looks sexy as hell in his uniform...* No. She'd have to let that pass, thank you very much.

Instead Denise started discussing an area in Thailand where she'd spent six months, and the conversation moved on to other things.

Their burgers arrived and they both dug in. "Every bite tastes as good as I remembered it," Denise gushed, rolling her eyes in bliss.

Mouth full, Anabel nodded. Neither woman spoke again until they'd both finished their burgers and half their fries.

"I'm stuffed," Anabel groaned.

"Me too. But there's one other thing I've been missing from this place and I swear I'm going to make room."

As if he'd heard, the waiter appeared and asked about dessert. Anabel and Denise shared a quick look and then both said "cheesecake" at the same time. Just like in the old days. "One slice, two forks," Anabel clarified.

Once the waiter left, Anabel sighed and leaned forward. "Okay, even though I've thoroughly enjoyed this lunch, I think we've beat around the bush long enough. Now tell me, who *is* this Doug Polacek guy, anyway?"

Denise gave her a shocked look. "You really don't know?"

Taking a deep breath while wishing for patience, Anabel shook her head. "I told you, I don't even know him. I couldn't pick him out in a line of men."

"Wow. I thought you were kidding."

"Nope. Not about something like this."

"Ah." Denise gave her the secret smile that—back in high school—Anabel had called her *gossip grin*. "Where do I start? Doug Polacek is single, a lawyer, relatively new in town. He's very handsome—like he could be a TV star. Women are all over him. From what I hear, he's cut a wide swath through most of the women under forty in town."

"Under forty?" Anabel grimaced. "Exactly how old is this guy, anyway?"

"I don't know. My best guess would be right around forty."

Then and there, as the waiter brought out their shared dessert, Anabel knew what she would do. "I want you to take me to meet him," she said, stabbing the cheesecake with her fork. "Right after we finish here."

Denise stared, her fork in hand. "You what?"

Chewing, Anabel swallowed. "That's really delicious. Try it."

"I will. But first I need to know what you've got planned."

"Planned." A second bite met the same fate as the first. War on cheesecake. "I think I've got the right to actually confront the man who's going around town accusing me of everything under the sun."

Denise had finally gotten her own forkful. She chewed it as if it were made of ashes. "Um, I think he might have gotten a restraining order on you. I don't think you can actually meet him."

"Really?" Anabel whipped out her phone. "Let me call the police department and find out."

Since she had the number stored in her contact list, this took only a few seconds. Brenda Winder answered on the second ring.

"Leaning Tree Police Department," she sang cheerily

into the phone. However, as soon as Anabel identified herself, Brenda's pleasant tone changed.

"I'm sorry—he's in a meeting," she said in response to Anabel's request to speak with Captain Harper.

"Fine, then let me speak to someone else. I don't care who, as long as it's someone wearing a badge."

Brenda stuck her on hold without another word. For whatever reason, Barry Manilow played on hold. Halfway through "Copacabana," someone who identified himself as Officer Pitts came on.

"How may I help you?" he drawled. Something in his voice told her Brenda had used the time Anabel had been on hold to fill him in on the nutcase he was about to speak with.

For that reason, and that reason alone, Anabel resisted the urge to make a joke about his name. As in, police work must be the pits for him. She knew he probably got jokes all the time and no doubt didn't appreciate them.

And right now she needed him as much on her side as she could get.

"I need to find out if there's a restraining order against me," she said.

"We don't handle restraining orders, ma'am."

Stunned, she wondered if he might be messing with her, then dismissed the notion. He had no reason to lie. "If you don't, then who does?"

"That would be the court. You'll need to contact Judge McCurdy."

Just perfect. Judge McCurdy wasn't one of Anabel's admirers, to say the least. He'd sat in when the McGraws had debated filing charges against her for what she'd done to Lilly, Kane McGraw's true mate. Lilly herself had talked them out of it. Bad memories from what seemed like another lifetime. Anabel politely thanked the police officer and ended the call.

"Well?" Denise asked. "What did you find out? Do you have a restraining order or not?"

"I don't know. I have to call the judge." Instead of doing so, she put the phone down on the table. "But if he got a restraining order, wouldn't the court have to serve me notice?"

Denise shrugged. "Maybe. I don't know. I have no experience with that sort of thing."

Anabel did a quick search of the internet using her phone. "According to this, he could have gotten an emergency, temporary order if he truly felt his life was in danger." She snorted. "I don't think he could have proved that. For a regular restraining order, the judge has to hold a hearing and both parties have the right to attend and present evidence or offer testimony. And bring witnesses. After all that, the judge has to determine if there really is a threat."

She looked up and grinned at her friend. "So I'm thinking it's safe to say that there is no restraining order against me."

Expression fascinated, Denise nodded. "Well, that's good, then." Her eyes widened as Anabel grabbed the check, glanced at it and then dropped a twenty and a five on the table.

"Lunch is on me," Anabel said. "Now take me to where this Doug Polacek guy works. I need to ask him what his problem is."

Though Denise offered a few token protests, Anabel could tell she was more curious about what might happen than worried.

"His office is downtown," Denise said. "Off Main."

They located the two-story stucco-and-glass building easily. The new construction stood out like a sore thumb.

"Let me guess," Anabel said. "The architect was from California or New Mexico."

"Arizona, I think." Denise grinned. "It's a pretty building, though it's out of place here in upstate New York."

Parking, Anabel shrugged. "I agree," she said. "Are you ready? Let's go."

Denise hung back, her smile fading. "Are you sure we can't get into trouble? The one thing I do know from my job is you don't mess with lawyers. They can sue you."

"For what? He can't sue me for asking him where he gets off dragging my name through the mud. Come on."

Denise groaned, but she got out of the car.

Righteous indignation propelled Anabel through the lobby, where she looked on the signboard to figure out which office housed Polacek. "There. Smith, Howard and Polacek. I guess he's a partner. They're on the second floor."

Denise punched the elevator button, but Anabel decided to take the stairs. "It's only one floor up," she said, sprinting up. Denise followed a bit more slowly.

At the door housing the law firm, Anabel didn't hesitate. She pushed the door open, smiled pleasantly at the young, blonde receptionist. "We're here to see Doug Polacek," she announced.

The young woman tilted her head. "Do you have an appointment?"

"No." Moving closer, Anabel kept her smile in place. "But give him my name. I know he'll want to see me."

When she spoke her name, the receptionist's blue eyes widened. "J-j-just one moment," she stammered. Instead of using the phone to let her boss know of his visitor, she got up and headed back to deliver the news personally.

"I bet they kick us out," Denise pronounced in a gloomy voice. "Or call the police."

"They won't. And they can't call the police. We've done nothing wrong. Since Doug Polacek has gone through such lengths to get my attention, he's going to see me. Just wait and see."

And wait they did. Five minutes, ten. Watching the second hand move on the clock, Anabel refused to fidget. She didn't know why or how she knew, but she had a good idea there might be some sort of concealed camera in the reception area. No doubt this Doug Polacek watched them, hoping for signs of discomfort.

Well, she wouldn't be giving him that much satisfaction. She made poor Denise discuss current fashions and when she'd exhausted that, sports. Denise had begun to eye her as if wondering if she'd lost her mind.

Finally, after they'd been waiting nearly twenty minutes, a tall, muscular man with longish dark hair sauntered into the room. An overabundance of confidence came with him.

"Anabel," he exclaimed, arms opened wide for a hug, as though he already knew her and they were long-lost friends. "You didn't tell me you were coming to see me today. What on earth are you doing here?"

"Cut the crap," Anabel said sternly, ignoring Denise's shocked gasp. "I don't know you and you've never met me. Not even once. So I want to know why you're spreading nonsense about me all around town."

Flashing her a dazzling white smile, he held out his hand. "Why don't you come with me to my office? We need to discuss this privately, don't you think?"

Ignoring his outstretched hand, Anabel nodded. Every single instinct she possessed had gone on high alert.

"Come on, Denise," she said, feeling as if she could use all the help she could get.

"No." He uttered the single word with authority. "You come alone, or I have nothing to discuss with you."

"I'll wait here," Denise piped up, sounding both thrilled and utterly terrified. "Take your time. I'm sure you two have a lot to talk about."

Since she now had no choice, Anabel straightened her spine and nodded. Head held high, she followed Doug Polacek down the hall.

"Here we are." Stepping aside, he gestured toward a large corner office. "Have a seat, please."

Obstinately, she shook her head. "Thanks, but I'd rather stand."

He cocked his head quizzically, then finally nodded and closed the door. When he went around to sit behind his massive mahogany desk, she found herself moving away, instinctively careful not to have her back to the door.

While part of her scoffed at this—what did she really think would happen?—the careful, watchful part of her wholeheartedly approved.

"Well?" she finally asked, since after Doug took a seat in his fancy leather chair, he only placed his hands on the top of his desk and looked at her. "What do you have to say for yourself?"

"I'm not sure I take your meaning." He spoke the lie with a calm casualness that infuriated her.

"I've been told by several people that you've been going around saying horrible things about me. Accusing me of stalking you, when in fact we've never even met. Why are you doing this to me? I don't even know you."

"That's where you're wrong," he replied, his voice changing somehow, from oily pleasantry to sharp, ruthless steel.

"We have met and you have been stalking me. I had to go public, in hopes of getting you to confront me."

Dumbfounded, wondering if he was insane, she stared at him, at a complete loss for words. Then, as her gaze locked on his, she realized he spoke the truth. Her heart froze in her chest.

"You," she whispered, realizing where she'd seen that particular glinting gaze before. "You're the Drakkor."

"I am. I should tell you, it wasn't very difficult for me to learn your identity once you followed me and then paid me that little visit. And now you, my dear, have walked right into my trap."

One of the supernatural abilities Tyler had as a ghost was the ability to make himself invisible. All he had to do was increase his vibratory frequency. Most people couldn't see him anyway, but since Anabel and a few others could, he knew he could keep this ability in reserve.

And today, since his energy level was at an all-time low and Anabel had ordered him to stay away, he knew he'd need to use it. In fact, the instant he'd heard Anabel agree to meet a friend in town for lunch, he had a gut feeling he'd need to watch out for her. Especially since she'd mentioned Doug Polacek.

Not wanting to be a complete stalker, he'd followed her to the restaurant, hovering just far enough away to give her privacy, but close enough that he could zip over if she needed him. The irony of his lack of physical ability to help her didn't escape him.

Still, he knew he'd try whatever he could should the need arise. Even magic.

When she and her friend left the restaurant and headed downtown, he rode along in the car, aware he might need to know where they were going.

The instant he heard Anabel say the name Doug Polacek, he stifled a groan. On the one hand, he admired Anabel for refusing to put up with that guy's verbal abuse any longer; on the other, he thought this might be the worst possible time to stir things up. His sister needed to be Anabel's primary focus right now. This was day six, and he didn't know how much longer Dena could make it.

Still, Tyler knew he had to trust Anabel's instincts. If she thought confronting this Polacek guy was important, then maybe it was.

Hidden, he waited in the reception area with Anabel and her friend, felt a shock of recognition when the attorney presented himself. Recognition, but from where? If he'd met Doug Polacek while in the physical form, he sure as hell didn't remember.

Was it possible they'd met in the realm of the spirit? Not unless the lawyer had the capability to move between worlds, which seemed highly unlikely.

And then Tyler had gone along to the other man's office, where he'd heard words he'd begun to despair of ever hearing.

"You're the Drakkor," Anabel said, sounding completely unafraid.

The instant Doug confirmed it, Tyler let himself become visible.

Anabel's eyes widened slightly as she saw him, but she made no comment.

The Drakkor looked directly at Tyler and smiled. "A bit late to the party, aren't we?"

Tyler could barely contain himself. He lifted his lip and snarled at the man. "Release my sister," he ordered.

"You know, I just might," Doug said pleasantly. "She turned out to be worthless. She's of no use to me now. Of course, I definitely will want something in return."

"I don't have a lot of money," Anabel put in.

"Oh, I do." Doug continued to smile that shark's smile, his obsidian eyes revealing only a hint of how dangerous he was. "I don't need your money, dear."

"Then what do you want?" Anabel shifted her weight from foot to foot, almost as if she felt the need to assume a fighting stance. Tyler felt that might be a wise instinct on her part.

"Why, I would have thought that was obvious." Doug chuckled, then stood up and stretched, his muscular arms showing his physical prowess. "I want you, Anabel Lee. With your magic and shape-shifting ability, I believe you and I can forge a powerful destiny."

Shocked, Tyler eyed Anabel to see her reaction. Aside from a quickening of her breath, she gave no hint of what surely must be churning around inside her mind.

"Why?" she finally asked. "And you'd better tell me the honest truth."

"A life is at stake," Doug reminded her, appearing amused. "Yet you want to discuss trivialities?"

Anabel remained calm and appeared unimpressed. "I understand a life is at stake. First off, I don't even have proof that Dena is still alive. Second, since you're basically asking me to turn myself over to you, I need to know what you intend to do."

The attorney towered over Anabel, his expression thunderous. For a split second Tyler feared he might strike her. Instead he strode to the door and yanked it open.

"You have forty-eight hours to decide. If I don't hear from you by then, I will kill the girl and be done with it."

Standing straight and tall, Anabel continued to face him down. "I want proof of life. Before I can even begin to consider your proposal, I need to know she is still alive."

"Very well." Ice coating every word, Doug swallowed.

Spinning, he fixed his dark glare on Tyler. "You. Contact your sister tonight. I will not interfere. Then you can tell Anabel that Dena is not dead. Yet."

Tyler nodded, hoping Anabel would see the wisdom of making a quick exit right away. Because maybe, just maybe, if he were permitted to interact with his sister, they could figure out a way to learn where she was being held.

Denise still waited in the lobby, apparently enthralled by a television show in which people rushed to fix up a dilapidated old house. She blinked when Anabel appeared, before going back to staring at the TV. Anabel wondered if the Drakkor had placed her under some kind of a spell.

"Hey." Anabel touched her friend's arm, making Denise jump. "Are you ready to leave?"

"I…uh… Yes." Moving as if she had just woken from a deep sleep, Denise shuffled toward the office door. This time, Anabel thought it might be prudent to take the elevator.

"This way." Taking her friend's arm, Anabel helped her outside and into her car. Tyler had materialized again and sat silently watching from the backseat.

As each minute passed, Denise seemed to come more and more awake. Anabel felt relieved and grateful. She'd worried Doug had done something to her friend that she wouldn't be able to reverse.

After she'd dropped Denise back at the restaurant to retrieve her own car, she glanced at Tyler. "You might as well reappear up here in the front," she said. "We've got a lot to discuss."

Instantly, he was wedged in the front passenger seat, looking both angry and worried. "I'm wondering if we can use this situation to our advantage," he said. "Since he's promised to back out when I contact Dena, I'm thinking maybe we could figure out where she is being held."

Anabel nodded. "I was thinking along those lines myself. If we could free her, then I wouldn't have to even worry about trading myself for her."

"You're not going to think about that, no matter what," Tyler ordered. "I refuse to even consider such a thing."

"You're not in control of me," Anabel pointed out, as gently as possible. "Your sister is young. She has much to live for. Me, I've lost my mate. No one around here likes or respects me. This would be a good trade."

Tyler shook his head. "I thought you were done with feeling sorry for yourself."

Stunned—and a tiny bit hurt—Anabel swallowed. "I'm just being realistic."

"No. You're not. When I came to you for help, you trading your life for hers was never on the table."

"Really? Why not? I already see and hear ghosts. Maybe I'd like to be one." And then she also could find David.

"This is about your husband." As usual, Tyler intuitively understood her thoughts. "I already promised you that I'd find him and bring him to see you."

She bit her lip. "What if that's not enough?" she whispered.

Pain, stark and deep, flashed across his handsome face. "It's not your time."

Wondering at the desperation in his husky voice, she sighed. "Maybe not. Either way, I can't just sit by and let him kill your sister."

"You don't have to." Fierce determination rang in his tone. "We will get her out of there. Before the forty-eight hours are up. But first, I'm going to contact her and make sure she's still alive."

Chapter 13

Once upon a time, Anabel Lee had believed in fairy tales. She'd known love and happiness and had greeted every new day with delight. She'd also known sorrow, lost her confidence and had a mental breakdown. Picking herself back up from the ashes, she'd learned self-reliance. More than that, she knew she could never count on others.

Part of her still believed this. But the few days she'd spent hanging around with a ruggedly handsome ghost had shown her otherwise. Tyler and Juliet had both been essential to her learning her way around her newfound abilities.

But Tyler had taught her something else. How to feel again. He'd plucked her up from the pit of self-pity, depression and despair and forced her to care about someone other than herself. For that, she would be forever grateful.

When the sun set this evening, six days would have passed since Tyler had appeared begging for her help. Six long days while a young woman suffered, hovering at the edge of death.

If she could do one thing right in her life, Anabel knew she had to figure out a way to save her.

Leroy meowed, his standard warning, before leaping in her lap. She caught him easily, taking comfort in the strong vibration of his purr. Holding him, she suddenly remembered the old wives' tales about witches and their familiars. Was that what Leroy was meant to be, her familiar? Was she truly a witch?

Thinking along these lines, she grabbed the phone to call Juliet and fill her in on what she'd learned. Before she could even look up the contact, her phone rang. Caller ID flashed Juliet's name.

"Talk about ESP," Anabel teased. "I was just about to call you. I've learned something about the Drakkor."

"I've learned something about the Drakkor too." Juliet sounded both excited and wary. "I think I know why he's capturing Pack women. As a race, the Drakkors are slowly dying out. It seems their females are being born sterile."

Appalled, Anabel grimaced. "So they're looking for fresh breeding stock."

"Exactly. But from what I've been able to learn, their seed doesn't take root in any other races. The female, whether human or shape-shifter, sickens and eventually dies. I'm afraid that might be what's happening to your ghost's sister."

Anabel glanced around the room, looking for Tyler. For once, he didn't appear to be anywhere in sight. "Now it all makes sense," she said. "I met the Drakkor today. He wants to trade the sister for me."

Juliet gasped. "You met the... Please tell me you aren't even considering this."

"How could I not? There's a young woman slowly dying who needs my help."

"No. Let someone else save her."

Anabel couldn't believe what she was hearing. "How can you even say that?"

"Because you are the last in line of a powerful group of shape-shifter witches. You have within you magic, the kind that can change the world. If you let this Drakkor sink his claws in you, not only will your line die out, but there's a very real chance he will be able to breed with you. If he does, any child born of such a union will be horribly deformed, both physically and mentally. You cannot allow such a thing to happen."

Again, the weight of the world had come to rest on Anabel's slender shoulders. On the one hand, she couldn't let Dena die. On the other, what if Juliet spoke the truth? Would she be doing her own kind a horrible disservice by trying to help Tyler's sister?

"Is there an alternative?" Anabel asked.

"Of course there is." Juliet's voice rang with certainty. "Learn to use your power and vanquish the Drakkor once and for all."

"And I'll help," Tyler said, startling her. "For whatever reason, it seems when I'm with you, your power is stronger."

She had to admit he was right. After relaying this to Juliet, she waited while the other woman considered.

"I'm not so sure about that," Juliet finally said. "But either way, it couldn't hurt. You say you've met the Drakkor. Who is he?"

"Doug Polacek."

Juliet cursed, something she never did, which startled Anabel. "I should have known," Juliet said. "I've only met him twice, but I got a bad feeling both times."

"He's a piece of work."

Juliet laughed. "Yes. Yes, he is. In the meantime, I've located an ancient book I think you should read. There's a lot in it about the Drakkors. I'll run it over to you in a little while."

After hanging up, too restless to sit still, Anabel took a quick shower, feeling the need to cleanse herself after her brief visit with Polacek. She'd just finished drying her hair when the doorbell rang.

Juliet stood on the doorstep, handing over the heavy volume as if it burned her. "Sorry I can't stay and visit," she said, sounding breathless. "But I have errands to run. Please, my intuition is telling me you've got to read this book. Promise me you'll take a look at it as soon as possible."

Mystified, Anabel promised, standing in the doorway and watching as her friend hurried to the car and drove off. Her cell rang, making her jump. Setting the book on the end table, she grabbed her phone and answered.

It was Denise.

"Oh my God," Denise said, first thing after Anabel answered the phone. "I'm guessing your little visit with him made him angry. You are so not going to believe what Doug Polacek is doing now."

Since Denise had no idea who or what the attorney actually was, Anabel sighed. "Probably not. What is it?"

"He's asking for an emergency city-council meeting. Tonight. He's telling everyone who will listen that he feels you need to be run out of town."

Stunned, Anabel didn't know how to respond at first.

If she hadn't known his ulterior motive, this action would have seemed incomprehensible. But now it actually made perfect sense. Doug Polacek was merely tightening the noose. The fewer options she had available, the more likely she'd be to give in to his demands.

"Are you going?" Anabel asked. "To the city-council meeting? Are you planning to go?"

"I can." Denise sounded grimly determined. "You need someone to speak up for you, after all."

"Thank you." Relieved, Anabel took a deep breath. "What time is this meeting? I'm done hiding away while total strangers malign my character. I'm going to put in an appearance myself."

"Good for you." Denise sounded pleased rather than afraid.

Anabel wondered how much of their visit to Doug Polacek's office the other woman actually remembered.

"They're going to try and hold it at seven this evening. I'll see who else I can round up. I want you to have an entire section of supporters."

Wishing her friend luck (and meaning it), Anabel hung up. She'd consider herself lucky if Denise could find two or three others. She turned to find Tyler watching her, arms crossed. "Did you hear that? Doug Polacek is somehow pulling enough strings to make the city council hold an emergency meeting."

"He's turning up the heat." Tyler sounded as furious as she felt. "I wonder what happened to the forty-eight hours he promised you. I haven't even had time to verify she's still alive."

"You do that while I'm at the city-council meeting. As for the time, I'm going to insist I still have it. He was very specific. He didn't say he'd leave me alone for that long, just that I had forty-eight hours to make a decision. Of course, if your sister has passed—and I pray she hasn't—then all of this is moot."

Pain flashed across his features, making her heart ache. Tyler grimaced. "She has to be alive. She has to be. I'll know soon enough." He swallowed, visibly fighting his emotions. Though she knew she should look away, give him privacy, instead she waited silently, wishing she could offer him a hug or something.

Finally, he swallowed again and met her gaze. Determination now shone in his eyes. "What are you planning to do at the meeting?"

"This is the first battle of the entire war," she said, feeling very tall and strong. "It's vitally important that I win."

And then she did something that surprised even herself. She walked over to Tyler, willing him to be solid, and kissed him full on the mouth.

Stunned to the core, Tyler felt dizzy as Anabel broke off the kiss and flashed him a mischievous smile before she strolled away. She closed her bedroom door behind her, a signal telling him to stay out. Which was okay with him because he doubted he could even move at that point.

His existence had changed in so many ways in just six short days. He'd be forever grateful to the higher power who'd given him an opportunity to save his baby sister. What he hadn't imagined would happen would be that he, after having already finished his life, would meet his mate.

Tyler knew Anabel considered her former husband, David, to have been her mate. Whether she knew it or not, she was wrong. Tyler doubted any other man could love Anabel as much as he did. She'd have come to realize this too, if only Tyler hadn't been a ghost.

The bitter irony of this had to be some sort of penance he must pay. That, and the fact that he most likely would succeed in saving his sister, but to do so must sacrifice the woman he'd come to love...

He took a deep breath, trying to focus. First, though, he had to contact Dena.

Once again he reached out, praying to the Creator of all to help him. Energy zinged through him, bolstering his own limited supply. He reached out, through the river of time and place, searching for that one particular spark that belonged to his sibling.

When he finally located her, the dimness of her life force shocked and angered him. Though not much time had passed since he last saw her, the deterioration in her condition made him want to weep.

Polacek might have given Anabel forty-eight hours, but Tyler realized Dena would not make it that long. Something had to be done much more quickly.

Though it killed him, he left his sister lying there, almost a skeleton, curled into a ball on the floor. Nearly a week had passed since he first made himself manifest to Anabel, nearly seven days while Dena got weaker. He couldn't help feeling like a failure.

No longer would he remain a shade of the man he'd once been. He was a soldier, a man of action. Not some wispy, ethereal being who could do nothing but float around and watch. Dena didn't need a ghost. She needed her brother, in the flesh, to fight for her.

Tyler knew what he must do. While Anabel got ready to attend the city-hall meeting, he left the earthly plane and returned home. He planned to make his case to his spirit guide. He prayed he'd be successful, even if he was granted only a few days.

Though Anabel had always loved her flowing dresses and lacy outfits, once again she dressed in tight-fitting jeans, sneakers and a cotton, button-down blouse. She brushed her long, dark hair until it shone and then put it back in a sporty ponytail. A pair of diamond ear studs and a pretty silver watch completed what she hoped was a polished look.

When she arrived at city hall, to her surprise the place was packed. She ended up having to park a good three blocks over. Surely all these cars weren't here because of her? Her heart sank—her life had become more than a spectacle, and now she was about to learn just how greatly her neighbors feared and hated her.

Taking a deep breath, she squared her shoulders and stepped out of her car. As she walked toward city hall, she kept her gaze straight ahead, afraid of what she might see if she allowed herself to look left or right.

There were exactly thirteen stone steps leading up to the entrance of city hall. Anabel knew because she counted each one. Pushing open the double doors, she stepped into a crowded room reminiscent of a mob at a sold-out concert. Not only were there hundreds of people—had everyone in Leaning Tree turned out?—but the noise level was so loud she wondered how anyone could hear themselves speak.

Bracing herself, she murmured apologies and began the considerable task of plowing through the crowd. Somewhere in this melee, she should be able to find Denise and

Juliet, and maybe even some of the members of Juliet's coven if she was lucky, her small group of supporters.

As she maneuvered herself into a clearing, she saw the city council had assembled at a U-shaped desk up on a raised area at the front of the room. Five men and two women, they all stared out at the crowd with identical expressions of amazement.

Someone tapped on a microphone, causing most of the conversations swirling around to stop. "People, please take your seats. The meeting is about to begin."

Even though she looked everywhere, Anabel couldn't locate either of her friends, so she took a seat next to a total stranger. All around her, everyone hurried to find a chair. The room had grown so crowded that many people had to settle for standing against the back wall.

Anabel's stomach twisted. She'd been aware of the dislike and mistrust many of Leaning Tree's residents felt toward her. But to have this many people show up at a city-hall meeting? Despair flooded her, which she resolutely pushed away.

Feeling someone staring at her, she looked up and met Doug Polacek's flat black gaze. One corner of his mouth curled into a mocking smile and she realized the brilliance of his plan. This entire thing had been engineered to demoralize her and make her more prone to agree to his terms.

Not today, Drakkor, she mouthed. *Not today.*

He turned away and took his seat in the front row without responding.

When the room had become relatively silent, the mayor walked over and took the microphone from the other man. "Welcome, everyone. I must say, we usually don't get this big a crowd to a council meeting."

Several people laughed.

"We are here today to discuss many issues," he said and then cleared his throat. "But first and foremost, one of our up-and-coming citizens, attorney Douglas Polacek, has some very serious concerns he wishes to bring to our attention. He has alleged that these concerns affect all of us and can have an adverse effect on our entire town."

The murmurs started up again, growing to a roar. The mayor waited a moment for them to die down and then when they showed no sign of doing so, cleared his throat again. "People, please. We have a lot of discussion to get through."

For the first time, Anabel wondered how many of those in attendance actually knew what these so-called serious concerns were. Surely all of these people didn't really view her as a threat to their way of life, did they?

She guessed she was about to find out.

"We'll open the meeting by asking Mr. Polacek to take the mic and outline these concerns."

Smiling graciously, the Drakkor (Anabel had trouble thinking of him as anything else right now) took the stage. "Most of us here in the beautiful town of Leaning Tree are God-fearing people," he began, sounding as if he were presenting a case to a jury. "And what I've recently discovered has the possibility of shaking our town's very foundations."

Wondering what the heck he might say to follow this broad statement, Anabel caught herself leaning forward in anticipation, exactly like all the others in the audience.

"Witchcraft." The single word hung in the air, taking on a dark life of its own. "I've learned witchcraft is being practiced here within our very own city limits."

Though a few people gasped, most of the faces Anabel saw contained a healthy dose of skepticism, a few outright hostility. For the first time, she had hopes that her enemy's plan would backfire.

She actually had to put her hand over her mouth to keep from laughing out loud.

"Witchcraft?" a woman called out. "Please tell me you aren't referring to our resident Wiccans."

Polacek frowned, as if he hadn't ever heard the term. Anabel guessed maybe he hadn't bothered to bone up on the current atmosphere of tolerance and acceptance.

"I'm speaking about witches," he said, his voice booming like a television preacher. "The kind who cast dark spells."

Someone giggled. Someone else shouted out a "Get real."

"This *is* real," he countered. "Those of you who are regular churchgoers know about Satan's influence on this world."

Several people gasped. The room grew quiet.

"Demons are real," Doug continued. "As are witches. In our small, family-friendly town, there are those who are doing evil's work."

The fact that he himself was one of them made his statements infuriating. Anabel had to battle the urge to stand up and denounce him. Only the certainty that if she did so he'd publicly brand her as one of the evildoers made her remain silent. That, and the painful knowledge that most of the townspeople assembled here would believe him.

As if he'd read her mind, Doug Polacek swiveled around, searching the crowd. The instant his gaze locked on her, her stomach sank. She knew exactly what he intended to do.

"That woman here." His arm came up, finger pointing accusingly at her. Everyone turned to stare. "She is one of the witches, using her dark magic. She has attempted to stalk me and make me do her bidding. I refuse to stand for it. Anabel Lee must be stopped. It'd be better for everyone if she were to move away from our town."

"Our town?" Anabel finally had had enough. "Not only are you talking like a crazy person, but your accusations are outright lies. I've only met you once, and this was long after you were going around inventing stories about me."

Doug laughed, the infuriating sound full of derision. "I think the good people of Leaning Tree know enough about your character to know who's telling the truth."

Anabel looked at all the faces around her and saw that he was right. Her heart sank.

"Anabel is telling the truth." A single voice came from the left side of the room. "This man, for whatever reason, has decided to target her with his hateful lies. Maybe we should think about who's really the evil one here."

Juliet. Standing tall and unafraid. Next to her, another woman stood. Denise.

"I can second this. I went with Anabel to confront Mr. Polacek and find out why he was spreading around so many lies about her. She'd never even seen him before that day."

More people stood. Not only the women from Juliet's coven, but the receptionist from Anabel's doctor's office, the dental hygienist who cleaned her teeth and the woman who worked in the library and indulged Anabel's love of a good British mystery. Each of them, calmly and rationally, offered good character references, refuting what Polacek had said about Anabel.

Tears stinging her eyes, Anabel stood and listened. Her chest and throat felt tight, but she kept her shoulders back and her head high. Today, Doug Polacek wouldn't win. Not this battle. And hopefully not the war either.

The final straw for Doug was when an elderly man stood, adding his voice to the women's. "Young man, I understand you are an attorney."

Warily, Polacek nodded.

"Then I'm sure you know all about lawsuits for slander and libel. I think you'd better ponder this before you say or write anything else about this fine young woman, who also happens to be a native of Leaning Tree."

Several people applauded. Soon, nearly the entire room had begun clapping.

Unable to stop her tears, Anabel wiped uselessly at her streaming eyes. Doug continued to stare her down, his eyes blazing.

Finally, Juliet came and took Anabel's arm, turning her away from the Drakkor's gaze. "Let's get you out of here," she said. Nodding, Anabel sniffled, trying to keep from bawling like a baby. She allowed Juliet to shepherd her outside, down the steps and into the shade of a huge, leafy oak.

"Come here." Juliet hugged her. "You are loved, my friend. More than I think you realized."

All Anabel could do was nod. Juliet handed her a tissue and she took it, using it to blot her eyes before blowing her nose. "Thank you," she said again, her heart full. And then, as she thought about what Doug Polacek had done, she let anger fill her.

"We've got to stop him," she declared. "Not only to free Dena Rogers, but to make sure he never does this again."

"I agree." Watching her carefully, Juliet glanced back toward the building. "Have you been practicing any of the exercises outlined in the books?"

"Yes. And I think I'm getting better." Or at least she

hoped she was. "I need to get home and discuss this with Tyler."

"Oh, he's not here?" Juliet sounded disappointed. "Then by all mean, discuss with him and then give me a call."

"I will. We've got to go on the offensive before Doug Polacek tries something else."

Juliet nodded.

As Anabel headed toward her car, someone called her name. Denise.

"I need to tell you something." Breathless, Denise wouldn't look directly at her.

"Okay." Bracing herself for anything, Anabel waited.

"As I was leaving the meeting, Doug Polacek stopped me," Denise said, sounding worried and bemused.

Heart sinking, Anabel waited.

"The weird thing is, he was very nice. Even though he must know we're friends, he, uh, asked me out." Finally meeting her gaze, Denise blushed.

Staring at her friend, Anabel nearly choked. "Please tell me you said no."

"I can't." Denise gave an embarrassed shrug. "I know you don't like him and vice versa, but he's the first guy I've met in a long while who makes me tingle inside when I look at him."

"Yes, I get that he's good-looking," Anabel argued. "But he's well-known for dating a lot of women. He's supposedly a master at loving them and leaving them."

"That's actually okay with me," Denise said quietly. "I'm not really looking for anything deep or serious. I'm only in town for a few weeks. I just want to have a little fun."

Ah, crud. Anabel contemplated the best way to tell her friend that Doug Polacek was not only bad news, but downright dangerous. She could only imagine why the man had contacted someone close to her. Next thing she knew, he'd be asking Juliet out too.

One difference there. Anabel knew Juliet would definitely have said no.

"Denise, come over and let's talk," she began, about to at least tell her friend that Polacek was a Drakkor.

"No, wait." Denise held up her hand, her expression pleading. "I'm going out with him. It's just a dinner date, not a wedding. Can you please be happy for me?"

Inhaling sharply, Anabel finally nodded. "I'm sorry," she said. "But at least promise me you'll be careful."

Denise only nodded in response and hurried off.

Anabel drove home in record time. Parking in her driveway, she practically ran inside, shouting Tyler's name. She needed to talk to him. Right away. While she refused to let Doug Polacek win any sort of victory, imagining what he might try next would turn her into a nervous wreck if she didn't strike first.

But when she got back inside her house, she couldn't find Tyler anywhere. She even tried summoning him, using that nifty focusing trick that Juliet had taught her, but she only succeeding in making herself dizzy.

Great. Just great. Patience had never been one of her virtues, but it appeared she'd have no choice but to wait for him to put in an appearance.

Spotting the book Juliet had brought over earlier, she figured now might be a good time to look through it. She grabbed it and sat down on the couch, carefully opening the beautiful cover.

Judging from the brittle, discolored pages and the beautiful script, the book was very old and possibly valuable. This made her slightly nervous to handle it, but Juliet had been insistent, so she continued to read. Soon, she found herself lost in the tales. She had to skip several, as they appeared to be in another language, but the ones she did read were veritable history lessons.

Somewhere in here, she knew she would find the answer to her dilemma. She just didn't know where. And there was just so much.

As she read, she kept waiting for that one particular story to jump out at her. When it finally did, she had to read it again, and then a third time, to make sure.

Chapter 14

A knock on her front door made Anabel jump. It came again, before she even had time to head in that direction, a sharp rapping of knuckles indicating the visit might be urgent. She carefully bookmarked her place and put the book back on the coffee table.

Again the hard knocks, in rapid and impatient succession.

Thoroughly out of sorts, she yanked the door open without even using the peephole.

A man stood on her doorstep, his uncertain smile achingly familiar in his handsome rugged face. His hazel eyes blazed with emotion. At first, she could only stare, not entirely sure of what she might actually be seeing.

Was it possible? Could it be? Reaching out, she braced herself. When her hand connected with his muscular arm and warm skin, she actually gasped out loud.

"Tyler?"

"Yes." His smile spread. "It's me."

Even his voice sounded deeper. Richer. More…alive.

Still gripping his arm—his reassuringly solid arm—she tried to tear her gaze away from him. "How is this possible? You're even more real than you were when we—" Breaking off, she felt her face heat.

"I've been granted an indulgence."

Again, she couldn't seem to stop staring. "A what?"

"It's like a favor. I get to be human for as long as it takes to save my sister." His gaze locked on hers. "And to keep you safe."

Normally, she would have bristled, but seeing this, this Tyler, this *nonghostly* Tyler, was the closest to a miracle she'd ever come.

"You're alive," she said, just to make sure she understood correctly.

"Temporarily. And I've been wanting to do this for a long time." He pulled her closer.

Aching, she allowed him to. Truth be told, she helped. As his strong arms wrapped around her, she realized just how much she'd longed to feel him like this. Exactly like this.

He kissed her then. Capturing her mouth with his, demanding a response. A blaze of need roared through her, making her dizzy even as she continued to kiss him back.

Just as quickly as it began, it ended. Breathing as heavily as she, Tyler stepped back. "I swear to you, once, just once before I give up this form, we will make love."

Ducking her head, she didn't protest. Her entire body screamed assent, but she kept her mouth shut.

"Now tell me what happened in town," he said.

Speaking quickly, she told him what had transpired at the city-council meeting. "He's trying to get people afraid of me again." And then she relayed what Denise had said.

"He's going to use her somehow." Tyler frowned. "I

don't know exactly how, but he'll figure out a way to use her to get close to you."

"That's what I'm afraid of." She didn't bother to try and hide the glumness from her tone. "And worse, Denise acts like she thinks I'm jealous. Any words of caution I tried to relay, she brushed away with anger."

"You don't have a choice. Just keep an eye on things, I guess. You can't keep her from going."

He began to pace, his form solid and masculine, making her mouth go dry and her arms ache. "I wouldn't worry too much about the town. From what you've told me, he's only managed to get people thinking he's the one that's crazy."

How had she not noticed how broad his shoulders were or how narrow his waist? Clearly, he'd worked out when he was alive, judging by the toned muscles on his arms and the way his shirt strained over his chest.

She forced away her decidedly sexual thoughts and tried to concentrate on the conversation at hand.

Tyler didn't make thinking any easier. He perched on the edge of her couch and gazed at her, his hazel eyes glowing in the soft light. It took every bit of restraint she possessed not to jump his bones.

Her gaze fell on the book she'd been reading. "I found something out about the Drakkors," she said. "I think I know why Polacek is capturing women. The reason none of us have heard of them is that they're becoming extinct. I'm not sure how many actually remain—for all we know, he might be the last. I think he's trying to find someone he can mate with, someone who is strong enough to carry his child."

Tyler's tanned complexion turned ashen. "You think that's what he did to Dena?"

She didn't answer. How could she? Though she'd given

him what she believed was the truth, doing so felt as if she'd ripped out her own heart.

Instead she went to him and pulled him close. Not speaking, she held him, stroking his hair and hoping her touch could offer some comfort. Amazing how good his being alive felt. She still had trouble believing it. Touching him turned her on. Aware now was the worst possible time, she made herself move away.

Deep breath. "How will this help?" she finally asked, as soon as she could think clearly. "You being human. How will it help us save your sister?"

Strolling over to her couch, he sat on the edge of one arm, looking way too ruggedly sexy for her peace of mind. "It's like this. You were right, apparently. I believe I have magic too. Even as a ghost, I could feel it. Now, in this human form, my magic will be stronger, more of a complement to yours. Together, we can use our magic to fight the warlock, who also happens to be a Drakkor."

Though she hated to ask, she knew she had to know. "And then what? Once Dena is free?"

His smile dimmed slightly, tinged with a hint of sadness.

"Then I go back where I belong. But I won't forget my promise to you. I'll make sure no ghosts ever bother you again. And I'll find Dave and make sure he goes to you."

Though hearing him say this made her want to cry, she kept her expression serene and nodded instead. "Then let's get your sister out. I have a plan."

He shook his head before she could elaborate. "If your plan involves you being some sort of sacrificial offering, then no."

"What?" She stood up straight, pulling her inner strength and that intangible something that made her magic powerful into her core. "You forget what I am. What you are. Together, we can win."

Though he crossed his arms, he nodded. "I'm listening. Tell me what you've got."

One thing Tyler had managed to forget about being human was how much more intensely people *felt* when they were alive. Sensations were everywhere. Emotions too. The instant his gaze locked on Anabel's whiskey-colored eyes, desire slammed into him. If he hadn't been prepared, the force of it would have sent him to his knees.

He managed—somehow—to continue to breathe and act normally, except for his body's violent reaction. This woman, whom he'd known just shy of a week, had rapidly become his everything. Looking at her, he knew he could drown in her gaze.

As he tried to unscramble his brain enough to formulate words, Anabel sniffed and held up her hand.

"What are you cooking?" she asked. "It smells like it's burning."

Puzzled, he frowned. "Cooking? I'm not."

"Sorry." She gave a sheepish smile. "I swear, I smell smoke. I asked out of habit. David used to love to whip up various concoctions whenever the mood struck him. He was terrible at it, and everything always burned."

Her mention of David—her deceased husband and love of her life—helped him get his thoughts back on track. Except she was right. Now he smelled it too. Acrid. "That does smell like smoke. Something is burning." For a split second, he wondered if this was David's way of popping in from the spirit world.

"Look." She pointed. Gray smoke seeped out from under the closed door to her spare bedroom.

His heart stuttered. "Something's on fire."

"Nothing's in there but furniture. Nothing that could possibly catch on fire at least."

He hurried to the door, reached for the knob and then cursed and let go. "It's hot. Call 911, find Leroy and you wait outside."

She'd already hustled over to snatch up her cat, who'd been sleeping on the top of the couch. With her other hand, she grabbed the books Juliet had lent her and stuffed them into her tote bag. Slinging this over her shoulder while struggling with her irate cat, she punched the numbers into her phone, moving toward the front door at the same time.

Confident that she'd be safe, he headed toward the garage.

"Wait," Anabel called after him. "What are you doing?"

"Going to grab your fire extinguisher. I remember seeing one in the garage." As he reached for the knob, he didn't hear whatever she shouted in response.

Already too far into the motion, he registered the knob's heat a second too late. As he yanked the door open, a wall of flame roared at him.

Cursing, he jumped back, trying to shut the door on the orange monster.

But once given entrance, the inferno would not be denied. Flames leaped into the room, a ball of fire. Reaching out and catching hold of her drapes, he knew that soon the entire living room would be ablaze.

"Get out now," he hollered at her, still standing frozen in the hallway. "Go!" He ran toward her, even as she took off for the door.

They both made it outside before the roof caught. As it did, the fire took hold with a loud crackle. Inside, something crashed, sending up an array of sparks into the night sky.

Leroy yowled, squirming in her arms. She held on to him, almost too tightly.

"You have a death grip on that poor cat," Tyler pointed out, putting his arm around her shoulders.

"Sorry. I don't want him to escape. I should have grabbed his carrier. But it was in the garage." Which now was totally engulfed in flames.

In the distance, they could hear the siren wail as the fire engine approached. As the seconds ticked by, Tyler thought everything seemed to be moving in slow motion.

"It's going to be a total loss," Anabel moaned, standing rigid in his arms while clutching her cat. "My house. All I have left of David."

Though the words cut through him like a knife, he made sure that didn't show. Not only did he have no business feeling jealous of a dead man, but poor Anabel really had more than enough on her plate.

"You know who did this, don't you?" she said, twisting out from under his arm to face him, eyes blazing. "Doug Polacek. It's another one of his scare tactics, to force me into a decision."

"You might be right," he allowed. "Though how'd he do this so quickly?"

"He's a dragon. All he had to do was change and then open his mouth and breathe fire."

He shot her a quick look but didn't argue.

Lights flashing, the fire truck pulled up in front of the house. Right behind came an ambulance, followed by two police cars, all with lights on.

The next hour passed in a blur. Firefighters, hoses spraying water, stubborn hot spots refusing to go out. A man came up to Anabel and introduced himself as an arson investigator.

Nodding, she didn't bother to even try to act shocked.

"I'm glad you're here. I happen to think this fire was deliberately set."

The man narrowed his eyes. "Are you insured, Ms. Lee?"

"Of course. What does that have to do with—"

Tyler saw the second she realized what he meant.

"I can assure you that I'm not the one who set this fire. I believe Doug Polacek did."

Stony-faced, the fire investigator stared her down. "Doug Polacek?"

"Yes. He's an attorney in town. Earlier, he accused me of being a witch."

"I see." Clearly, he didn't. Touching a finger to his forehead, he dipped his chin. "If you'll excuse me, I have work to do."

Watching him stride off, Anabel turned to face Tyler. "I didn't think of that," she said, her voice hoarse. "Of course Polacek knew people would think I did it. Almost everyone in town already thinks I'm crazy."

"Not almost everyone," he corrected her. "You said you had quite a few people stand up for you at the city-council meeting."

"True. But there are still plenty of others."

Again he put his arm around her, unable to shake the crazy thrill—even now—at actually being able to do it. "First they have to prove it. And since we both know you didn't set the fire, you don't have anything to worry about."

Leroy let out a yowl, almost as if he were trying to tell them something. "Shhh." Anabel stroked his fur with her free hand. "Don't worry, boy. We'll figure out someplace to live."

"Wolf Hollow Motor Court Resort," he said. "I used to know the McGraws. They're good people."

She winced. And then he remembered.

"I take it they haven't forgiven you."

"I don't know," she replied. "Even if they have, it would be really awkward staying with them." Expression miserable, she turned her gaze back to the smoldering ruins of her house.

He wished he could fix everything for her, make the fire and Polacek and all of her problems disappear. Since he couldn't, all he could do was distract her. "But theirs is one of the only hotels in town."

She turned her gaze back to his. "There's the Value Five Motel, out near the thruway. Muriel Redstone has always been kind to me. And I'm pretty sure she wouldn't have a problem with Leroy staying with me."

Inwardly he winced. Built in the late seventies, the Value Five was one of those cheaply constructed budget motels with no personality to speak of. The last time he'd driven by there was right after high school. He could only imagine how the place had held up over time.

"At least it's not expensive," she said, almost as if she knew his thoughts. "Especially since I've been off work all this time with no income."

Clearly his fault. "I'm sorry." He waved at the ruins of her home. "I had no idea this would take so long. Or be so dangerous."

Now she shot him a look that clearly said she didn't believe him. "Warlocks, magic and ghosts. What could possibly be easy about that?"

She had a point.

A shout from the firefighters drew both their attention. A huge shower of sparks came to life with a roar, sending a fresh round of flames skyward as the roof collapsed.

"That's it," Anabel said. "I can't stand to watch any more. My house is gone, along with everything I own. I'm going to head over to the motel and see if I can book a room. Are you coming?"

He nodded. "Wherever you go, I go too." Though he kept his tone light, he had never been more serious.

On the way to the motel, they stopped at Walmart. She asked him if he'd mind waiting in the car with Leroy while she picked up a few things. Of course he didn't mind.

When she returned, she had a litter box, cat litter and cat food and a few items of clothing for herself. As she slid into the driver's seat, she tossed the bag in the back.

"I got underwear too," she said, then looked stricken. "I'm sorry. I didn't think about asking you if you needed anything. Would you like me to go back in and get you a few things?"

He hadn't thought of that at all. Yet the thought of Anabel selecting his underwear made him feel...weird.

Something in his expression must have clued her in.

"How about I give you some money and you can run in and buy whatever you need?" she offered.

Though he also hated taking money from her, he didn't have any other options. When she tried to hand him fifty dollars, he took only a twenty. "I don't need much," he said.

Her smile looked like a shadow of her normal self. "That's good," she said. "Because twenty bucks won't buy much."

Inside the store, he bought the most inexpensive packet of underwear he could find, a couple of T-shirts that had been marked down to three dollars and a pair of shorts. With tax, he figured the total would come in just under twenty dollars.

As he got back into the car, he tossed his bag next to hers. "Thank you. If I can ever find a way to repay you, I promise I will."

"No worries," she said, starting the engine. "Let's go take a look at my new temporary home."

The Value Five Motel looked better than he remembered it. The place had clearly undergone a renovation. "Wow," he said out loud.

"I know." Her tired smile spoke of her weariness as she parked. "Let's see what I can get. I hope it won't be too expensive. My savings are rapidly dwindling."

According to Muriel Redstone, there were only three other guests staying at the Value Five. She let Anabel have her pick of rooms, her curious gaze locked on Tyler.

He simply gave her a friendly smile back.

Once Anabel had selected a room, paid the discounted long-term monthly rate, he followed her to the one she'd chosen. It was in the back of the motel, out of sight from the road, and the window looked out onto a large field and lushly wooded expanse of forest.

"It feels a little less like a motel this way," she said, catching him gazing out into the woods.

"And an easy route to go if you needed to change."

Her dark look lightened. "That's a great idea. Let me get Leroy settled in and then we will. I think being wolf for a while will really help take my mind off things."

Once inside, he saw that the interior rooms had also been redone. "This isn't bad at all," he said.

Clearly distracted, she set Leroy down. Tail held high, the cat promptly stalked off to explore. They unpacked their meager belongings. All he could think about was running in the woods as wolf with her. The experience had been indescribable when he'd done it before as a ghost. He couldn't wait to hunt with her as a flesh-and-blood wolf.

Mate. The word echoed inside him. Sadly, he knew it was true. He and Anabel were mates, even though such a thing had become an exercise in futility. He didn't know what had happened with Dave or why she'd believed the other man to be her mate. All he knew was the truth of the here and now. By all that was right and holy, Anabel should have been his.

"Okay." Dusting her hands on her jeans, she turned to face him. "Let's get out there and hunt."

As he opened his mouth to respond, her cell phone rang.

She glanced at it, and her composure cracked. "It's Polacek." She sounded miserable.

Mentally cursing the other man, Tyler fought the urge to tell her not to answer. Instead he watched her, waiting for her to make the choice.

"I'm not in the mood to deal with him," she announced, tossing the still-ringing phone on the bed. "Come on. Let's get out in the woods before something else happens. We can start doing some exploring, looking for those landmarks. As wolves, we can cover a lot more ground much faster than as humans."

When she held out her hand, he took it. Together they ran across the field, letting the welcoming shadows of the forest envelop them.

"This time, we'll change together," she said, lifting her chin, her gaze locked with his.

Heat shimmered between them. Mouth dry, he nodded. As she pulled her T-shirt over her head and stepped out of her shorts, he couldn't breathe.

"Hurry," she urged him, a hint of amusement in her voice. Riveted, he could no more move than stop his heart from beating.

The bra came off next and then finally her panties. She stood before him, unabashed, looking like some sensual wood nymph.

He actually took a step toward her.

"I'm going to leave you behind," she warned, dropping to all fours and casting him a reproving look before initiating the change.

Hurriedly, he shed his clothes and did the same, gritting his teeth at the remembered pain.

When he opened his eyes again, he was wolf.

Alive. Narrowing his eyes, he looked for her, not seeing her. Which was okay, because as wolf, his nose told him exactly which way she'd gone.

As he raced after her, his powerful muscles working perfectly, four paws pounding the damp earth, he marveled at the joy of feeling so alive. For just this moment, he'd immerse himself in the experience. For this space in time, he'd simply live.

They ran and played, hunted and shared the rabbit he caught. Though he hesitated a moment at taking a life, since he'd been given one on borrowed time, it wasn't in the nature of wolf to let prey escape. From the laughing look in Anabel's exotic wolf eyes, he suspected she approved.

When they'd had their short recreation, the hunt was on. Even though the light was fading, they could see well enough, guided by their sense of smell.

Ranging far and wide, he felt they'd covered a lot of ground. And saw nothing like the landmarks Anabel had drawn.

He didn't know how much time had passed, but finally they turned around and made their way back to the clearing where they'd left their human clothing.

At the thought of what might happen next, his heart began pounding. All shifters knew the change from wolf back to human made the physical body aroused. Whether or not they chose to act upon it was up to the individual.

He knew what he wanted. But would Anabel want the same?

Chapter 15

Aware that once he became man, desire would overcome his body, Tyler knew watching Anabel become human would prove too much for him, so he turned away. With so much urgency driving him, he used every ounce of self-control he possessed not rushing his own change. Instead he focused on the uncomfortable sensation of wolf turning to human.

This helped, at least during the shape-shifting. But once he'd finished and pushed to his feet, stark naked and more aroused than he'd ever been, and turned to look at her, all his resolutions vanished. The raw longing on her face as she watched him gave him his answer.

She wanted him.

A part of him knew she could just need to blow off steam. That same part realized, in the end, this could only make the pain worse once he left her. But with desire pulsing through every cell in his body, he couldn't walk away.

Elation mingled with raw wanting as he slowly climbed

to his feet, trying to control the dizzying current racing through him. Her gaze soft as a caress, she held out her arms. He went to her, sweeping her into his arms.

His.

He slid his hands up her arms, heart thudding a rapid tattoo. The dizzying feel of her, this woman, made his fingertips tingle as he touched her. The jolt of her hip brushing his thigh, the warmth of her body as she curved herself into him, invited more.

First, he kissed her with his eyes, his featherlight touch. And then, as his mouth covered hers hungrily, he traced the inside of her mouth with his tongue and kissed her there.

Her answering shudder told him what that did to her.

As she moaned and kissed him back, he realized he finally understood what all the books and movies said about love.

He loved this woman. Anabel, his mate. Though he knew he shouldn't, couldn't, he made a vow never to leave her. And then he sealed that vow with another deep, drugging kiss.

Naked, skin to skin, flesh to flesh. His. She belonged to him, as much as he belonged to her.

Gently, he outlined the circle of her nipple, before taking it in his mouth. He slid his hand down the silk of her belly, tangling in her womanly curls, before parting the folds between her legs and stroking the dampness there.

Her gasp was a reward of sorts, but the tremors that shook her and the rush of honey that followed nearly sent him over the edge.

Then he knelt before her and put his mouth in place of his hand, using his tongue to continue the caresses as he drank her in. Head back, body arched, she cried out as pleasure overtook her in waves and she came apart.

Again he barely restrained himself. Only the knowledge that he wanted more kept him sane. Aware he could never have enough of her—however many days he'd be granted alive would never suffice—he knew he had to sink himself deep inside her. At least once.

Finally, she shook her head and pulled him to his feet, her gaze smoldering, the sleek caress of her body a blatant invitation as she tugged him to the ground.

Wrapped around each other, his arousal pressing against her desire-slicked skin, he tried to hold back, tried to maintain some semblance of control before he entered her.

And then she pushed him onto his back and climbed onto him, taking him inside her in one smooth motion. He froze as wave after wave of pleasure engulfed him, desperate to prolong the pleasure.

But she began to move, her body wrapping around him as if she'd been made for him. He cried out, bucking her slow, deliberate motions, driven by the need to move faster, harder.

"Wait," she said, lifting herself just above him, her hands on his wrists, holding him down. "Please. Wait."

Shuddering, he managed to wrest control over his body and managed—just barely, chest heaving, heart pounding— to keep himself still.

With a seductive smile, she leaned close, claiming his mouth in a passionate kiss and writhing just out of his reach. The sleek caress of her body as she deepened the kiss made his senses reel.

"Now," she gasped, still raised up over him. "Now."

As she came down hard on his arousal, her body slick and hot and welcoming, he groaned. And then he took over, rolling so he was on top, plunging himself into her hot, wet depth.

She arched her back, meeting him thrust for thrust.

He cried out in sweet agony, her voice echoing his, and power—magic—spiraled around them, through them, between them, intensifying every touch, every stroke. All at once, he could see images of what she wanted, and the instant the thought occurred to him, he did exactly that.

Pleasing her became more important than breathing, and when her body shuddered and clenched around him as she reached her climax, he used the magic to maintain an iron control on his own body.

This, he thought, was how sex should be. This was how true mates made love. And then as she began to move again under him, he didn't do much thinking at all.

When he finally let himself go, he drove into her, fiery sensations pure and explosive, and shattered into a thousand stars.

After, as he held her in his arms, both too exhausted to move, he understood the true meaning of satisfaction. More than simple bodily pleasure, more even than the give-and-take between two perfectly matched people. This.

No, what he and Anabel had just shared was a kind of vow. A promise of shared sunsets, cuddling next to each other while the snow fell, of laughter and joy, shared tears and hope and dreams. Unfortunately, sorrow filled him as he realized it was a vow he could never keep.

Stirring, Anabel kissed him lightly on the cheek as if she understood. "Come on," she said softly. "Let's go back to the motel and clean up. I don't know about you, but I'm starving."

"I am too," he said, getting to his feet and pulling her up. He spoke the truth, only he didn't say that he was starved for much more than food.

An hour later, they finished the fast food—a burger for him, a salad with fries for her—they'd picked up and brought back to their room. Leroy snoozed on the bottom of one bed and Tyler and Anabel sat together on the edge of the other.

Only then did she glance at the cell phone she'd tossed aside earlier when Polacek called. "He left a message."

"You don't have to play it back," Tyler began. "He's a bully. He gave you forty-eight hours. I don't think your time is up yet."

"It's not." She bit her lip. "What if he has something to say about your sister?"

Considering, he finally held out his hand for the phone. "Let me listen to it."

Without hesitation, she handed her cell over. "I'm going to go take a shower," she said. "I'm sure you'll tell me if he has anything to say that I need to hear."

He waited until he heard the shower start up before pressing the play button on the message.

Instead of calling to gloat, Polacek had left a simple message asking Anabel if she'd made up her mind. On impulse, Tyler pressed the callback button.

Polacek answered immediately. "Ah, so you have reached a decision," he began.

"No, she hasn't," Tyler said, trying to remain calm. "But she would like to know why you set that fire."

"Fire?" The other man sounded genuinely puzzled. "Who are you and what are you talking about?"

"Someone set Anabel's house on fire. And I'm Anabel's friend. Her *close* friend."

Polacek went silent. "I can assure you I did not do that. Now I'd like to speak to Anabel herself if you don't mind."

"I do mind. And Anabel is in the shower."

There was an even longer silence this time. "I wasn't aware she had a boyfriend."

This time, Tyler kept quiet. For effect.

"This might be a problem." Quiet fury rang in Polacek's voice. "Have you and she been intimate recently?"

Instead of answering, Tyler pressed the end-call button.

The shower went off. Getting up, he carried the phone over to the dresser and set it down.

He actually believed Polacek. From what he'd seen, if the Drakkor had set the fire, he'd have been bragging about it.

A few minutes later, Anabel emerged from the bathroom, her long hair damp. She gave him a sleepy smile. "Well, what did he have to say?"

Grimacing, he relayed the gist of the conversation. "I'm not sure what he's up to. But clearly, he's worried I might have impregnated you."

"Wow." She dropped onto the bed next to Leroy, startling the cat awake. "I didn't even think about that."

"Neither did I." Though he couldn't imagine anything more wonderful, if he were really alive, he kept that admission to himself. "We didn't use any protection."

"You're a ghost." Her indignant protest made him wince.

"I *was* a ghost," he corrected her. "Right now I'm a man. And because of this, your getting pregnant is a very real possibility. Unless you're on birth control?"

She shook her head. "I wasn't exactly planning on this happening. However, since it has, it might work to my advantage. He'll want to wait until I have proof I didn't conceive with you. That will buy me some time."

Everything inside him quieted at her words. "What are you planning to do? Surely you're not thinking of going to that monster."

"I know you don't like the idea of me agreeing to exchange myself for Dena," Anabel said, holding up her finger the instant he started to interrupt. "But hear me out. I think if we work together on this, with a little bit of luck, we can make this work."

"I'm not a big fan of luck," he replied, his chest aching. "Still, I'm listening."

She grabbed her tote bag and pulled out one of the books she'd borrowed from Juliet. This particular volume appeared older than the others, with a well-worn, heavily embossed leather cover.

Placing it on the bed, she locked gazes with him. "You're familiar with the mythic story of Persephone? She was one of the few living beings to travel to the underworld."

"She was the daughter of a goddess. Demeter, if I remember right," he said.

"She alternates between living and dying. She dwells in the afterlife part of the year."

"It's *myth*. Not real. There is no underworld."

"Symbolism. Underworld, afterlife, it's all the same. Anyway, the story of Alcestis is what interests me most. When Alcestis traveled to the underworld to offer her own life in place of her dying husband's, Persephone sent her back and spared them both."

"Okay." He kept his tone even. "I still don't see what this has to do with our situation."

Her smile turned mysterious, fascinating him. "Well, according to this book, Alcestis was Pack."

Skeptical but intrigued, he moved closer. "Show me."

Still smiling, she flipped open the heavy book to a place she'd bookmarked. "Here. Read this."

Skimming it, he saw the author—or authors, since the tome appeared to be a compilation of ancient stories and myths from numerous races and species—claimed Alcestis had been a shape-shifter, one of the earliest members of a rudimentary pack.

"That's impressive," he said, looking up from the book.

"And while I usually enjoy learning new bits of our ancestral history, how is this going to help us win against Doug Polacek?"

"When I read this, my plan occurred to me."

Though he still didn't follow, he waited.

"As far as I can tell, we have two choices. The books say dragons have two weak spots—their eyes and their unscaled belly. They can only die one of two ways—by being stabbed there or by poison. So option one is to figure out a way to kill Polacek."

When she didn't continue, he pressed. "Or?"

"Or we've got to make him think I'm dead." Finishing triumphantly, Anabel beamed at him, her copper eyes expectant.

At first, Tyler wasn't sure he'd heard correctly. "Dead? How on earth do you propose to do that?"

"I was hoping you could help."

"Oh no." Just thinking about it, he felt his gut churning. "I have no idea what you have in mind."

"Look at you." Shoulders back, she circled around him, her movements gracefully and no doubt unintentionally sexy. "You were dead and magically became alive."

He stifled a groan. "There was no magic involved in that."

"Really?" Clearly, she didn't believe him. "Then how'd you do it?"

"I asked. I'm limited as to what I can tell you of the afterlife, but there are beings with much more power than you and I."

"Magic." She flashed a triumphant smile. "If they can make you alive, then surely they can briefly make me dead."

This time, he let his frustrated groan escape. "Let's just say, hypothetically of course, that they could do this.

How would you being dead help us with the Drakkor or in freeing my sister?"

"He wants me for breeding. If I'm dead, I'm of no use to him."

He admired her creativity, even if what she wanted was impossible. "And if you're dead, he has no reason to set Dena free."

"Timing," she informed him with an arch look. "Timing is everything. I won't have them make me pretend to die until after the exchange has already been made."

"You have no idea what you're saying."

"Ah, but I do." Eyes glowing with determination, she continued to pace, looking like a caged wolf.

He didn't tell her he'd never heard of such a thing, outside of ancient myths and legends, because if he did, he'd have to admit he'd never heard of a ghost being allowed to briefly return to a living body either. Actually, his very presence was proof that her idea might be possible.

But that didn't make it palatable. He knew if he tried to use emotion to convince her, she wouldn't listen. Her decision appeared to have been made with emotion. Instead he tried to sway her with logic. "What if they agree? Then what? How do you know that such a thing is not irreversible?"

She whirled and hugged him, a quick, brief, impulsive wrapping of her arms around him that made him feel as if he had been set ablaze.

"Because of you," she said. "You being here right now with me, alive and real, is all the proof I need."

It was then that he realized he'd made a horrible, awful mistake.

"I can't risk you," he said, throwing logic to the wind, his voice cracking even though he willed himself to sound steady. "Surely we can figure out another way to save Dena without placing your life at serious risk."

Her beautiful face went serious. "Look, do you want to save your sister or not? Time is running out. Unless you've come up with another plan, we've got to set mine in motion or your sister will die."

She was right—at least about part of it. Though Polacek had given them forty-eight hours, he knew better than anyone that time was running out. They had no guarantee Dena would survive too much longer.

"I want you to live," he said, his voice cracking.

"I want to live too. But I can tell you this. If I do have to trade myself for your sister, I'd rather be dead than suffer what she did at his hands."

"There's got to be an alternative."

Anabel moved closer, wrapping her arms around him and standing chest to chest. Her scent—a musky combination of cinnamon and flowers—made him dizzy. Another part of her appeal that had been hidden to him as a spirit. "If you think of one, let me know."

Pushing away the longing and yearning, he allowed himself to hold her for the space of a heartbeat and a breath, before pulling out of her embrace. "I'll try to contact my spirit guide," he promised. "I'll tell you as soon as I hear if your proposal is even possible."

Eyeing him, she nodded. "Remember, we have a deadline. If my idea doesn't work out, I have no choice but to offer myself in place of your sister. If I don't, her death will be on my conscience. And every instinct I possess, magical or otherwise, is telling me it's not her time to die."

Tyler nodded. "I'm going to go for a walk."

Eyes wide, Anabel slowly nodded. "It's sort of weird that you can't just vanish whenever you want to."

Damned if her comment didn't feel like a knife to his

chest. Apparently, when they weren't making love, she preferred him as a ghost. "One of the things about being alive," he said, keeping all his voice empty of emotion, "is that I'm limited to the earthly plane. I'll be back after a while."

To her credit, she didn't ask him to be more specific. She simply nodded and went back to studying her book. No doubt she needed some time alone with her thoughts. What they were considering was not something that could be done on a whim.

Walking out the front door, Tyler realized he hadn't felt so alone in a long time. As a spirit, he'd been constantly aware of the existence of other spirits and the shimmering chord of energy that bound all life. Human again, he could tell his awareness of this had become blunted. Though he felt his loss sharply, he knew he'd gladly give this up if he were to be permitted to remain with Anabel.

"If magic really exists," he said out loud, to no one in particular, "why can't I use it to free my sister? Why can't things be simple?"

He didn't expect an answer, so when one came, he jumped.

"You know better than that." The familiar rich voice washed over him like warm oil. He turned, eyeing the hooded figure with a mixture of reverent awe and consternation. His spirit guide, appearing as an elderly wise man. Tyler couldn't help noting the rather obvious symbolism, but that was par for Elias's sense of humor.

"I didn't expect so much pain," Tyler began and then stopped. He didn't want to complain. After all, he'd been blessed to even be allowed to return to earth as a spirit. Never mind now, as a live man.

But Elias simply smiled. "You don't have to do this all alone. You know better than that. You're never alone."

As those words sank in, all the worry and trepidation disappeared. "Everything will happen that is supposed to happen," he whispered, not as a question since he already knew the answer.

"Yes, it will. With your help." The guide's eyes sparkled, even though his voice was stern.

Taking a deep breath, Tyler outlined what Anabel wanted to do.

After Tyler left, Anabel immediately closed the book. How could she even concentrate at a time like this? She knew what she had to do, and no amount of discussion or thinking was going to change that. Even if she wasn't permitted to momentarily die, she couldn't let Tyler's sister suffer.

She might as well get this show on the road. Then, before she could chicken out, Anabel picked up the phone and dialed the number Doug Polacek had given her.

He answered on the second ring. "Hello, Anabel Lee." The evil reverberating in his flat voice sent a shudder through her. After taking a deep breath, she didn't bother wasting time on pleasantries. "I've made my decision. I will agree to the trade. But I need proof of life."

"You already have that," he said. "Your ghostly friend was in contact with his sister. I sensed his presence. Go ahead. Ask him."

Stunned, she couldn't keep from glancing over her shoulder, looking for Tyler. Of course, he wasn't there. And she could no longer summon him by simply thinking of him. "He's not around right now," she said—smoothly, she hoped. "But I promise you I will ask him when he gets back."

The silence on the other end of the line fairly crackled with impatience.

"Tell me about your boyfriend," he said, a thread of ruthless anger in his voice.

She took another deep breath, grimly aware of the way her skin crawled even talking to this horrible man on the phone. She couldn't imagine letting him touch her.

"I don't have a boyfriend," she began.

"Don't lie to me." Snarling, he cut her off. "He called me. We talked while you were in the shower. When I asked him if the two of you had been intimate, he hung up."

Stunned, she tried to gather her thoughts. "I had no idea he called you. But that was Tyler, my ghostly friend, as you put it. How can one be intimate with a ghost?"

Polacek went silent while he considered her words. She waited with bated breath. After all, she hadn't lied. At least, not outright.

"So help me," he finally said, "if I find out you're not telling the truth…"

As threats went, it was an empty one. There couldn't be much worse than what he'd already proposed to do to her. She shuddered.

Forcing the thoughts away, she knew she had to focus on the task at hand. If she was going to succeed, she had to be extremely careful. "In the meantime," she said, "let's discuss specifics. I want Dena Rogers out of there so she can get immediate medical help. How do you want to do this?"

"You do understand that I can't personally be involved?" Was that amusement in his detestable voice?

"If I can, then you can," she countered.

"I'm a public figure in this town. An attorney with a successful practice, with hopes of being elected to the city council soon. While you are…" His voice trailed off.

Horrified, she stifled her instinctive reaction. "While I am what?" she asked, pleased her voice sounded level.

"Overwhelmingly despised and regarded with contempt."

Once, she might have felt his words like sharp knives. Even worse, she would have agreed with him. "You can say that after the show of support I received in the city-council meeting?" Her careless laugh came out perfectly timed, which did her heart good. "Anyway, we've already established that we don't like each other. I asked you how you plan to get Dena out. Are you going to answer?"

He went silent for so long she began to think he might have hung up.

When he finally spoke again, his flat, emotionless tone was back. "My assistant, Tammy, is going to help me. I believe you met her when you visited Dena's apartment."

Stunned, she couldn't speak. Although she'd feigned ignorance, Dena's roommate had already known Dena was being held prisoner when Anabel and Tyler had visited. That seriously pissed Anabel off. Still, since she could do nothing, she bit her tongue and stuck to the topic at hand. "How is she going to help?"

"Tammy, as Dena's roommate, is going to claim she found her lying in the field near the apartment parking lot. She will take Dena to the hospital and make sure she gets medical care."

This sounded too simple. "And what do you want me to do?"

Now the faint edge of malice tinged his tone. "You will enter the apartment and remain there while Tammy drives to the hospital."

Way too easy. Which meant it actually wasn't. "And you will be there waiting for me, I'm guessing?"

"Exactly. If you don't show up, Tammy will arrange a little accident for Dena."

A thousand possibilities opened up with his scenario.

"Oh, and don't even think about calling the police," he continued, as if he'd read her mind. "I've carefully set up everything to make it appear that you have been the one who's kept poor, little Dena Rogers prisoner and tortured her. Who do you think the Leaning Tree Police Department will believe?"

She couldn't resist. "Well, after your tirade about witchcraft in town, I'm thinking more will actually lean toward believing me."

"Do I have your word or not?" he said snarkily, clearly not finding any humor or truth in her comment. This time, she didn't bother to hide her own amusement.

"You first. I want your word." Even though she privately considered it meaningless.

"I give you my word."

There. Now it was her turn. "Me too. You free Dena and get her to the hospital, and I'll wait for you in the apartment."

"Bound by oath," he intoned.

"Whatever," she muttered. "Now that we've settled that part of it, I need to know when."

"Tonight. And you'd better believe I will use a cloaking spell. So if you are foolish enough to call the police, Dena will die and Tammy will disappear."

Her move. She glanced at the clock. Short notice, but if Tyler would get back here, she thought, that might be doable. "Nine o'clock," she said. That would give her enough time to talk to both Juliet and Tyler.

"No." Crushing her hopes, Doug Polacek spoke firmly. "Now."

"No," she said back, using the exact same tone. "I need more time."

"For what?" Clearly, he had no intention of waiting for her to answer. "Either you be at the apartment in half an hour or Dena dies."

Even as she began protesting, he ended the call.

Crud. Half an hour. Thirty minutes. And with Tyler nowhere in sight.

Chapter 16

Heart pounding, Anabel scribbled a quick note to Tyler, snatched her purse and car keys and ran for the door. She'd call Juliet along the way. Without Tyler, she had no clue if her admittedly bizarre plan would even work.

Or if she even really wanted it to.

In the car, as soon as she started the engine, she scrolled through the contacts until she located Juliet. Punching Dial, she put the car in Reverse, after scanning one more time to see if she could catch sight of Tyler. Nothing, so she went ahead and backed out of her spot and pulled into the road.

Once Juliet answered, Anabel filled her in, leaving out the part about dying and then returning. What she had to tell her friend was already more than enough.

"No," Juliet immediately protested. "You can't go there alone. You must find Tyler. He has enough magic to help boost yours."

"I'm pretty strong," Anabel said grimly, surprised to realize she spoke the truth. "For whatever reason, I feel like a badass."

"Good for you. But you need to remember what Doug Polacek actually is. A Drakkor will kill a wolf anytime."

Stunned, Anabel considered her friend's words. "Are you saying you think I should change?"

Instead of answering, Juliet posed another question. "In what shape are you stronger? Human or wolf?"

Anabel didn't even have to think. "Physically, wolf. Magically and intellectually, human."

"What you need to figure out is what will best defeat him." Juliet's cryptic words were no help at all. "Tell me how to find this apartment and I'll come help you."

Horrified, Anabel thought fast. "There's not enough time. I've got to go." And she ended the call.

She made it to the apartment building in record time, parked and jumped out of the car. She sprinted up the steps, only stopping to take a breath when she stood outside the unit.

When she'd lifted her fist to knock, the door swung open before her knuckles even connected. She took a deep breath, collecting herself. One last time, she glanced over her shoulder, wishing for Tyler the ghost to appear, though she would have welcomed Tyler the man.

But it seemed for now, she was completely on her own.

Taking a deep breath, she lifted her chin and went inside.

The second she set foot in the apartment, Anabel felt the power coil around her like a hungry python. The stifling air lacked oxygen and light. She barely had time to gather her defenses before realizing she couldn't fight this. The Drakkor was too damn strong. She could only hope he'd kept his word and that Dena had been freed.

Though she knew he wouldn't kill her—at least not yet, not until he'd tried to use her as a breeding machine—evidently he meant to use his power to intimidate and hurt her.

Her last thought before she blacked out was of Tyler, of his chiseled, rugged face, fierce with love for his baby sister. And, if she dared to believe the impossible, also with love for her.

Though Tyler knew Anabel considered her plan a sound one, the powers that be did not agree. His request on her behalf had been denied, no matter how much he'd begged and pleaded. And all he was given by way of explanation was a few words of affirmation.

Trust in yourself.

Just that. *Trust in yourself.*

That was all well and good, but he would have appreciated a bit more assistance than that, maybe even including some detailed instructions on how to proceed.

Standing at the front of the motel, he ran through explanations a few times in his mind. He wasn't sure how she would take knowing her plan had been nixed. One thing for sure, they'd have to come up with something else. Meanwhile, the clock continued ticking. He could only hope and pray his sister continued to fight to live.

Knocking on the door to her room, he waited. After several seconds had passed, he knocked again. Then he tried the knob, which turned easily since it hadn't been locked.

"Anabel?" he called, not wanting to startle her. With the human body came new considerations. "Anabel?"

No answer. So he went ahead and entered, knowing she'd want him to.

The instant he stepped back into the room, he could tell something had happened. The entire atmosphere felt off—

tainted, even. And when he saw Anabel's note propped up against the coffeemaker, he understood why.

She'd gone to meet Polacek. She'd even noted the time. Ten minutes ago. Thankful for small miracles, he bounded outside, eyeing the various cars parked in the motel lot and a few down the street.

There. The 1986 Camaro. Notoriously easy to break into and hot-wire. After he muttered a quick prayer of forgiveness for stealing, it took him thirty seconds to get the door open and another thirty before he had the car running.

And then he took off, heading for Dena's old apartment. Praying he wouldn't arrive too late.

He made it across town in seventeen minutes, glad the owner of the car had left the radar detector inside. Though Anabel had a decent head start on him, he hoped he could catch her before she did anything foolish.

On the way to the staircase, he looked around for Tammy's car, which Anabel had written would be carrying his sister to safety.

He saw nothing and no one.

Furious and frustrated, he took the stairs two at a time. He wasn't sure how late he was, but the churning in his gut made him wonder if Doug Polacek had lied yet again.

Worse, Anabel had to be already inside the apartment. Alone, with a monster.

At the door, he didn't bother knocking. Instead he tried to remember how he'd seen it done on television and attempted to kick it in. It barely budged. Now he definitely questioned the wisdom of him asking to be human. If he'd been his usual ghostly self, he'd already be inside.

He kicked again, cursing. Then he tried ramming it with his shoulder, which hurt like hell and accomplished absolutely nothing.

The door held solid.

Frustrated, he eyed the floor-to-ceiling window. Since he could see no other option, he ran downstairs, back to his stolen car and grabbed the metal toolbox from the backseat floorboard. As he'd suspected, it was heavy.

He lugged it all the way back upstairs, swinging it as he prepared to shatter the window.

Instead the apartment door swung open. Dropping the toolbox with a clatter, he rushed inside.

The apartment was empty. No Anabel, no Polacek, no Dena.

Empty. How in the hell was such a thing even possible?

After searching every single room twice, he stopped, his heart pounding. He'd lost her. The unbearable crushing pain inside him made him raise his face to the ceiling and howl. His body responded instantly, initiating the shift to wolf.

Clothes tearing, he hurriedly pulled them off so he'd have something to wear later. He'd barely shed them in time. The change took over, his bones lengthening so quickly he felt as if he were being pulled in several different directions all at once. At first he was too stunned to react. After an instant's consideration, he went with the flow, aware he could use his beast's heightened senses to try to track where Anabel and Doug might have gone.

As soon as the change was complete, he again made a search of the apartment, this time using his nose. Here. And there. Anabel had recently been inside. Along with Doug Polacek and one more. Another person. Female. Another few seconds, and he realized who it was. Tammy, Dena's roommate.

Of course she'd been. She lived there, after all. But he had no way to answer the million-dollar question—had she been there at the same time as Polacek and Anabel? And what about Dena?

The Drakkor had promised to free his sister. If he'd lied... At the thought, anger filled him. With the fury came something else—power. As a ghost, he'd never felt its physical effects; nonetheless, he recognized them now. The tingling of his skin. The tightness gathering strength behind his eyes. And the roar of it through his blood.

As his lupine physical body vibrated, he wondered fleetingly if he'd turn back into a ghost, a wolf shade. Then he realized it didn't matter. He was here on borrowed time anyway. He needed to focus only on accomplishing what he'd come for. First he must make sure his sister was free and that she got medical attention.

And then he would locate Anabel. No matter what it took, he would find her. And Tyler vowed to make the Drakkor pay for daring to touch what should have belonged only to him.

A cell phone rang. As wolf, he located one lying on the carpet near the sofa. Anabel's.

Quickly he initiated the change back to human. Even though changing back and forth was exhausting, the chance that the call might be important was too great to risk letting it go unanswered.

"Hello?" he answered.

"I need to speak with Anabel Lee, please," a male voice said.

"She's not available," Tyler said cautiously. "May I take a message?"

"I guess so. This is pretty urgent. Please tell Anabel that a young woman matching Dena's description was just brought into the ER," the man replied. It took Tyler a moment to recognize who it was.

"Pastor Jones?" About to ask how the other man had gotten this number, he realized Anabel had exchanged information with him.

"Yes." The pastor's voice changed. "Have we met?"

"No, but Anabel has spoken of you. I'm a friend of hers. And I know Dena Rogers. She's been missing for a while."

"Yes. Yes, she has. And now someone has dumped her off at the hospital. She's very seriously ill."

"But alive, right?" After the other man answered in the affirmative, an awful thought occurred to Tyler. "Why did the hospital call you?"

"She asked them to. Apparently, she said my name and the name of the church before going unconscious."

Alive. Tyler said a prayer of thanks. "How is she?"

"They've moved her to ICU. It's going to be touch and go. Will you please let Anabel know?"

Tyler had to force the words past the lump in his throat. "I will," he promised.

"One more thing. You might head out to the hospital if you actually do know Dena. I imagine she could use as many friendly faces around her as she can get."

Tyler nodded, thanked the other man and ended the call. He wondered how Dena would deal with seeing her dead brother alive again, even though he knew such a thing would be forbidden. Regretfully, he had to stay away.

Plus, he still had to save Anabel. Figuring out where the Drakkor had taken her would be the first step.

Trust in yourself. The voice speaking inside his head was not his own. Yet the words made perfect sense.

He knew what he had to do. As wolf, all of his senses were amplified. He was in prime physical condition and could be a vicious fighting machine if necessary.

Taking a deep breath and praying for strength, he opened the front door and began to shape-shift back to his lupine form. Once again, he rushed the change, making it more painful.

But such pain was easily ignored. Wolf again, he lifted his head and scented the wind. He'd follow his nose and find Anabel.

When Anabel came to and opened her eyes, she was no longer in the apartment. Wherever she'd been taken, the complete and utter darkness felt suffocating. Pushing away the panic, she reached for consciousness, quickly, quietly, trying to regain her bearings without attracting the attention of the powerful Drakkor who'd brought her here.

She wondered about Tyler's sister. Had Doug Polacek kept his promise and set Dena free?

At the thought that he might not have, anger flared up in her, sharp and bright enough to vanquish a small corner of the all-encompassing darkness.

Interesting. Seeing this, she took hope. She'd never been completely powerless. The possibility that Polacek might have underestimated her buoyed her spirits. She was only as weak as she thought herself to be.

Good to know. Now she needed to set her mind to figuring out a way to extinguish pure evil.

"I'm not pure evil." A light clicked on. Apparently reading her mind or her expression, Doug Polacek stood in front of her, looking very ordinary and very human. "I honestly never intended to hurt Dena Rogers. I never intended to hurt any of them."

Of them. She should have been afraid, but instead she clung to her anger. "Yet you did. She's near death, and you still refused to let her go."

"I had no choice. She was my bargaining chip to get to you."

Queasy, she stared, wondering about Denise. Had he stashed her away somewhere too, as a backup plan? "I don't understand," she said, stalling for time.

He circled around her, like a hunter assessing his prey. "Of course you don't. How could you? You didn't even realize your own power until recently."

Though she wanted to lash out, she bit her tongue. Maybe if she learned the reasons for his actions, that knowledge might give her an edge in the battle to come.

"I still don't get it. Even if I am some powerful witch— which right now is highly debatable—what benefit is that to you?"

"Surely you've read up on your history," he chided her. "If so, you must know mine is a dying race. Our females are born sterile. The only way for the Drakkors to have any hope of continuing is to find females of another species who are strong enough to bear our young. A couple of us have been working to impregnate women of various shape-shifter races, in order to accomplish this very important task."

A couple of them? Horror flooded her as she realized what he meant. "You tried to do this to Dena?"

"Of course. Her and the others before her." He shrugged, appearing completely unrepentant. "Both of my colleagues have had the same result. The females always perish, their bodies too weak to contain our seed."

Anabel actually caught herself looking for her cell phone. She needed to call Tyler, Juliet, anyone, and let them know what was wrong with Dena Rogers. That way, whatever hospital they rushed her to would better know how to treat her.

Seeing this, Polacek actually laughed. "I left your phone back in my apartment. You can't call anyone."

"Did you even release Dena?" Anabel demanded, tamping down the rising fury, aware she didn't need to reveal how anger fueled her power.

"Certainly, I did." He seemed affronted that she'd even

asked. "Right about now, Tammy should be dropping her off in front of the Leaning Tree Hospital ER entrance. Of course, she won't be going in with her. She should be back here shortly."

The awful image made her wince. "Surely you don't mean to have Tammy roll her out of the car onto the ground or something, right?"

His answering shrug again filled her with impotent rage. Once more her power simmered, boiling under the surface. Taking note, she tamped it back down.

Clearly not noticing, he moved in closer. "You are very important to me, Anabel Lee," he said earnestly. "With your strength, you might very well turn out to be the savior of the Drakkor race."

"But what about the cost? You are destroying so many women's lives in search of something that might not even be possible."

He froze, rearing his head back as if she'd hauled off and slapped him. When he spoke again, his voice was so quiet she had to strain to hear him. "I do not have a choice."

"We always have a choice."

At her words, he turned away, holding himself so rigidly she figured the control he exerted over his emotions must be very fragile. If so, he could snap at any moment.

He let out a roar, the torment and pain in the guttural cry shaking her to her core. When he spun to face her, she saw his composed mask had slipped. The madness glittering in his eyes had her taking a step back. And then another.

She considered running, aware he wouldn't kill her but would use whatever means at his disposal to stop her, and judging from the condition of poor Dena Rogers, he wouldn't care if he hurt her. In fact, a wounded captive might even be preferable. Less resistance.

Trust in yourself. The voice came out of nowhere, speaking quietly inside her mind. Like balm on an open wound, the words soothed her indecision, enabling her to think clearly once again.

Trust in yourself. More than a mantra, but instruction. She could beat this man at his own game, and maybe if she succeeded, she could prevent other women from falling prey to his kind. Suddenly, she realized her temporary death wouldn't be enough. Even if he let her go, as long as this man—and his buddies—remained free, women would be captured and tortured, raped and killed.

Fighting and arguing wouldn't work. Nor would any sort of intellectual debate. Doug Polacek believed wholeheartedly in his cause and, like all fanatics who'd lived before him, wasn't capable of listening to reason.

He had to be captured, along with the other Drakkor he'd mentioned. As she puzzled out a method, she thought of another way. Convince him she was on his side. Or at least, on the fence, easily swayed in that direction.

"You know," she began, keeping her tone conversational. "I did read up on the Drakkors. I'd never even heard of them. From what I read, they sure were majestic."

"Are," he corrected her proudly. "We *are* majestic. Just because there aren't many of us left doesn't mean we're completely gone."

"How many of you remain?"

Narrowing his eyes suspiciously, he shrugged. "Not very many. Why?"

"Just curious. I mean, those of you that are still around must be very old. The way the books talked, your females went sterile a long time ago. How many years ago was that?"

"Long enough," he said shortly, sounding a bit more reasonable. "And yes, we that are left are aging."

Biting her lip, she decided to trust in her instincts and go for the gusto. "Look, I'm trying to decide if you're right or in the wrong. I still don't have enough information to make a choice whether what you're doing is justified or not."

"It is." He began pacing, muttering to himself. Anabel held very still, trying to remain as unobtrusive as possible, aware his instability continued to make him dangerous.

Finally, he came to a stop in front of her. "There are six of us left. Three males and three females. One female is paired to work with each of us males. Since she is sterile, my female helps procure the women we mate with and attempt to impregnate."

"Tammy?" Anabel guessed, wondering why he spoke of her as if she were chattel.

"Yes."

"She seems young."

He shook his head, his pride apparent in his stance. "Appearances can be deceptive. You of all people should know that. Tammy is over one hundred years old. I myself am approaching two hundred."

She didn't even have to fake her amazement. "All this time, you've been searching for a woman capable of continuing your species?"

His shrug was enough answer. She took that also to mean they'd never succeeded.

Still, there was one more question she had to ask. "How many women?" Voice raw with emotion, she forced herself to unclench her fists, hoping she managed to keep the anger from her voice. "Over the years, how many women have died at your hands?"

"I don't know."

His quiet, unconcerned-sounding answer infuriated her. Until she got a look at his agonized expression and realized despite his actions, some shreds of a conscience remained.

"Then why?" she whispered.

"Don't you see we have no choice? We are the last of our people. We wasted years while the doctors tried to find out what was wrong with our females. Now we do what we must, what we will continue to do until we can no longer function. We cannot let the Drakkor race die. No matter what the cost."

Heart pounding, she pretended to consider. Though his actions were awful, part of her could understand what motivated him. How terrible, to know that you and a couple of others were all that remained of an entire species.

Still, that didn't give him and his two other male Drakkor friends free rein to do whatever they wanted.

"You alone might have the power to change this," Polacek continued earnestly. "Never before have we tried to mate with a woman of magic. All of the others were either human or shape-shifter. None had your power. Our kind are beings of power. We draw strength for it. I believe joining our power with yours might be the key. You alone might have the strength to carry a Drakkor halfling to term."

"Halflings are numerous among shape-shifters," she mused, pretending to be considering the idea while inwardly she shuddered. "Though among all the various combinations of shifter and other, there has never been anything like this."

"Exactly." He couldn't contain his excitement. "Imagine the destiny of greatness a child of ours would be able to achieve. He might even rule the world one day."

He. She wondered what he'd do if they actually were

successful and she birthed a girl child. Smother her at birth?

"True." Managing a smile, she looked down at her hands. "I'll need some time to think about it," she said, as if she truly believed she had options. "Plus, don't you need to wait until my next cycle so you can make sure I'm not already pregnant?"

He laughed, his eyes narrow slits. "I thought you said he was a ghost."

"He was."

"Then how can you possibly be pregnant? Quit stalling. What will happen will happen."

"My forty-eight hours are not yet up. I need at least that much time."

Crossing his arms, he regarded her. "Don't take too long. It's always easier if you participate willingly." The look he gave her made her skin crawl. "Though sometimes it's more fun for me if you don't."

Figures. That was when she knew she'd better start gearing up for a full-on battle. The more time she could postpone it, the stronger she'd be. Hopefully.

Sex. The ultimate sacrifice. Okay, maybe this was a bit melodramatic. Death would actually be the ultimate. But even the thought of letting Doug Polacek put his hands on her made her insides twist into a knot.

The only man she wanted touching her—other than David—would be Tyler. Forever and ever, amen.

As clear as a bell, she heard Tyler's voice, so close he might have been standing right beside her. *"Trust in yourself,"* he said. That same phrase. She tucked those words up, folding them deep inside her to use later, should the need arise. Which she had no doubt it would.

Polacek wouldn't kill her. At least not yet. He couldn't take the chance of ruining his potential baby-making machine. She wondered if he'd even considered what such a child might be. A wolf-dragon? Some sort of hideous combination of the worst of both beings? Or of the best?

No doubt his thoughts ran toward the positive. A child of his would embody all the powerful parts of the wolf and the dragon.

Since halflings—children who were half human, half shifter—were common among the Pack, and she'd even heard of children who were half shifter, half fae, plus a rumored vampire-shifter combination, she didn't really understand why the pairing apparently couldn't happen. It had to mean the Drakkors were on an entirely different level.

Perhaps their line was meant to die out, for whatever reason. What other explanation could there be?

Though she couldn't understand why such a baby could not grow inside any of the poor women's bodies, she knew if they did somehow succeed, any child conceived this way would need both hope and prayers. And love, she thought. She couldn't help wondering if Polacek was even capable of the emotion.

Surely not all Drakkors were like him, were they?

Chapter 17

"What are the others like?" she asked. "The other Drakkors? And how long has it been since any of you have seen a child of your kind?"

One corner of his mouth twisted as his eyes narrowed. "Why do you want to know?"

"Just curious. I mean, if you intend for me to carry your child, I feel like I should know something about them. How will you even know if he or she is part Drakkor?" She held her breath while waiting for him to reply.

"You don't even need to worry about that." The confidence in his voice made her heart sink. "Once you are pregnant, it will be very easy to tell if you carry a Drakkor child or not."

"How so?"

"The same reason why most non-Drakkor cannot survive and carry our child," he continued, his smile full of malice. "Our young grow at a rate twice as fast as other species. And twice as large. Where humans or Pack might have a seven- or eight-pound baby, a Drakkor infant is fifteen pounds when carried to term."

The thought of that made her wince. "I see," she said weakly. "I have to say, that prospect doesn't sound appealing at all."

He shrugged in response. More than ever, she knew she had to figure out a way to beat him at his own game.

"By the way," Doug said, interrupting her thoughts, "I have your friend." He spoke as casually as if he were discussing the weather. "Denise what's-her-name."

Stunned, Anabel reared back. "Why?"

"To make sure I have your full cooperation."

She stared, feeling sick. "Denise is not part of this. Let her go."

"No."

"We had a deal," she began.

"And as you so generously pointed out, Denise had no part in that deal." His smug smile enraged her. "I kept my bargain. Dena is free. Now you keep yours. Or your luckless friend will die."

Hate filled her. "You're a monster," she cried. Under her skin, her wolf began to struggle, trying to break free.

"So I've been told."

"How do I know you don't plan to keep Denise in case I don't work out? How do I know you don't intend to hurt her the same way you hurt Dena?"

His smile spread across his face. "That's just it. You don't. Now take off your clothes."

She froze. Slowly shook her head. "No. I will not. I still haven't made up my mind."

Moving fast, he came at her, using the full weight of his body to knock her onto his bed. He pinned her, with a savage grin on his face. "Time's up. But no worries on the clothes. I'll rip them off myself. Actually, I'll find that more enjoyable anyway."

His heavy body pinning her down made it difficult to breathe. Through a haze of pain and fear, Anabel registered the door opening.

"Stop." Tammy's voice. "Doug, stop. Don't do this."

Numb, Anabel wiped away the stray tears that kept sliding from her eyes. Swiveling her head, she saw the other woman silhouetted in the doorway.

"Not. Now," Polacek snarled, his jaw tight. "Get out."

"No." Tammy stood her ground. Tall and regal, she looked decades older and wiser than the young woman Anabel had met originally. "Get away from her."

"How dare you intrude?" he roared. "You know better. You know this is the only hope we have. Leave. Right now."

"There's no longer any need for you to do this. Our line will go on. I'm pregnant." Though Tammy spoke quietly, the words carried as much impact as if she'd blared them through a megaphone.

For the first time since pinning Anabel to the bed, Polacek faltered. "What?"

"I said, I'm pregnant." Though smiling, Tammy began to cry. "And I've already had this verified, not just through the at-home kit, but at a doctor. I've made it past the first trimester, so it's safe to say I will carry the child to term."

Slowly, Polacek pushed himself up, rolling away from Anabel to climb shakily to his feet. He dragged his hand through his already mussed hair, his expression telling them he still struggled to believe it. "How? When? Who?"

Still weeping as she tried to wipe her eyes with the backs of her hands, Tammy grinned. "The usual way, dummy."

"Is the father a...Drakkor?"

Now Tammy's grin wavered. "No, he's not. Of course not. You males aren't the only ones who've been working at keeping our species in existence. The other two females have been trying, as well."

Afraid to move, Anabel made a sound, low in her throat, enough to draw Tammy's attention.

The other woman moved closer, still wiping at her streaming eyes. "I'm sorry, Anabel. We were trying to save our species any way possible. It's generally been thought the women are sterile. For whatever reason, when we mate with our males, we can't conceive."

Anabel couldn't help wondering if it had ever been even considered that the men were at fault, rather than the women, though she kept this to herself.

When Anabel didn't respond, Tammy turned her attention back to Polacek. "We need to notify the others."

Though he nodded, he didn't appear entirely convinced. Anabel guessed the possibility that he was the one shooting blanks might be a hard pill for him to swallow.

"Who is the father?" he asked, his stony expression matching his flat tone. "You still haven't said."

Cocking her head, Tammy eyed him. "What's wrong with you? This is what we've all been hoping for. The Drakkor line will not die out."

"I want to know what species of being is the father of our next generation. Will the halfling dragon also be wolf or bear? Panther or cougar?"

Tammy laughed. "You'll just have to wait until I tell the others. I can promise you one thing. My child will be very special indeed."

Some dark emotion flared in Polacek's gaze, but he only nodded. "All right," he finally said. "And congratulations. You have the honor of being mother to the savior of the Drakkors."

Dipping her chin, still smiling, Tammy turned to go.

"Wait," Anabel said, struggling to mask her desperation. "Don't leave me here with him."

Tammy's gaze flicked from one to the other. "He has no need for you now," she said.

"Maybe not," Polacek growled. "But I am still entitled to have a little recreation. Leave us."

For half a second, Anabel thought the other woman might refuse, might stand her ground and save her. But Tammy glanced at Polacek and sighed. "Have fun," she said, her voice full of disgust. Leaving the room, she closed the door behind her.

When Polacek turned back to face Anabel, she saw the rage in his expression and shivered. He might say he wanted the Drakkor to go on, might even mean it, but damned if he hadn't wanted it to be because of something he himself had done, not Tammy. Not a woman.

That instant she realized that if she wanted to survive this, she'd have to fight. She needed Tyler, she wanted Tyler, but if she had to, she'd manage to do this alone. She was strong, a powerful if yet untrained witch, and a shape-shifter to boot.

Holding her physical body perfectly still, she dug deep inside herself, reaching out for the spark of creation that resided in everything. This, the source of all, would fuel her magic and give her strength.

Briefly, she closed her eyes, aware he would take that as a sign of surrender.

After counting to five, she opened her eyes and fixed her gaze on him. "I'm ready," she said. "I would also like a chance to have a child who would be revered and considered a savior."

Surprise flashed across his face, making her see he'd been motivated by only his own lust, not of any other potential outcomes. "I like the way you think. Plus, we'll have a lot of fun." His leering smile disgusted her. "I knew you'd come around eventually. Most women can't resist a chance at enjoying my body."

Insane and vain. A dangerous combination. She kept a smile fixed on her face. At least she'd have the element of surprise on her side. Because if he thought she was going to let him lay one hand on her, he had another thought coming.

Since she hadn't been able to get up off the bed, she used her spot to its full advantage. Scooting over closer toward the edge, she pasted what she hoped was a welcoming smile on her face. "Kiss me," she ordered, trying not to gag on the words.

Eagerly, he rushed to comply.

Her fist met his stomach first.

"Oof." He doubled over, the desire in his eyes changing to shock and then rage.

She didn't hesitate, but came at him again, praying the element of surprise would compensate for her lack of strength. Pummeling him with everything she had, she kicked and clawed and punched. She went for his eyes, his man parts, anything she could think of to cause the maximum damage.

At first, he only defended himself, trying to fight her off. When he finally went on the offensive, she knew she was in big trouble. One swipe of his arm as he backhanded her sent her flying into the wall.

Dazed, she didn't move. She tried to figure out an escape route, but first she needed to gather her strength.

Massive legs spread in a warrior stance, he appeared ready to come at her again if she so much as twitched a muscle.

Again her wolf tried to break free. Unsure, not trusting, Anabel barely managed to hold back the beast.

Eyeing the doorway, and noting that he stood between it and her, she wondered nevertheless if she could make a run for it. But even as she began to move to try exactly that, the air around Polacek began to shimmer.

Which meant the man was about to change into the dragon.

She'd had enough difficulty fighting him in his human form. She didn't stand a chance against a Drakkor.

In a few seconds, the flashing light show ended. The Drakkor, now solidified, appeared, his mouth blazing orange and yellow fire, his reptilian eyes glowing red. Despite herself, she noted and marveled at his beauty. He looked like a realistic stained-glass dragon with huge wings spread. Except he was real—and extremely pissed off.

If the intention was to frighten and impress, then he'd succeeded. At least with the *impressed* part. Despite his fury and his evil intent, the dragon was like nothing she'd ever seen. For whatever reason, she was not the least bit frightened. Instead she felt strong. Righteous, even.

Maybe because she'd finally had enough.

As the huge beast circled her, scales gleaming and glittering in an incandescent rainbow, she drew down deep, gathering strength, before beginning her own change into a she-wolf. She had no idea whether or not now was the right time, but since she needed to have faith in herself, she'd decided to trust her instincts. And her instincts told her she needed to let her wolf break free.

The change came too swiftly, just as it always did when she felt threatened. Her bones lengthened, her clothing shredded and she clenched her teeth against the sharp and sudden pain.

Momentarily, the sparkling lights that always accompanied shape-shifting blocked the circling dragon from her sight, a small blessing for which she felt grateful. She'd need every second she could gather to collect her strength and plan her course of attack.

Plan. She drew her lips back and sneered at the thought. As if she could even attempt to formulate a plan against a monster like Polacek. No, this bitch was acting on instinct. Nothing less.

She tipped her head back and howled. Her battle cry, if she ever had one. She was fighting not only for her honor, but for everything else. Everyone else. Especially for the ones the Drakkor had abused and tortured. She had to win to avenge all of the women who'd come before her and any Polacek might be thinking would come after.

He must be stopped. If the Drakkors wanted to try to keep their species from extinction, they'd need to find another way.

She'd fight for her life and her town, for Juliet and the coven, Denise and for Dena, and especially for Tyler. In a nutshell, she'd fight for everything that mattered.

A wolf, she told herself, could trump a reptile anytime.

When her vision cleared, she saw the Drakkor had stopped circling and had reared back, eyeing her the way a hungry predator watched a fatted calf.

Except she wasn't. Nor would she ever be. She'd always been a hunter, never prey.

In her wolf shape, the magic residing inside her had become centralized and more accessible. Teeth bared at her enemy, she probed it carefully, understanding her magic had become a tight core of power, waiting for her to use as she saw fit.

She'd have to use magic if she wanted to stand a chance at winning with the fire-breathing monster.

To her right, something else moved. Registering the blur of motion, she noticed another wolf. Her heart leaped as she recognized Tyler. She didn't have any idea how he'd found her, but she was sure glad he had.

Tracking Anabel's scent, Tyler raced out of the apartment and down the steps to the parking lot. He stopped, sniffing the air, praying Polacek hadn't hustled her into a car.

To his shocked disbelief, the scent continued. Out past the edge of the pavement, through a narrow alleyway behind a convenience store and a fence, and to the open woods.

Something about this forest, this land tickled the edge of his memory. It didn't matter now. Polacek had taken Anabel here. He raced into the trees, following his nose.

A howl echoed in the forest. Not a mournful sound, but more like a battle cry.

He burst into the clearing, stopping short at the metal windmill. One of Anabel's landmarks.

Heart pounding, he spun a circle, scenting the air. Anabel's scent was too faint, though still drifting in the slight breeze.

Trust in yourself.

As he remembered, he went absolutely still, listening. A faint sound came from the west, and he plunged into the undergrowth, heading toward it.

When he came upon the edge of the concrete structure, mostly submerged in the ground, he realized it was much larger than Anabel's drawing had shown. Then he spied the huge metal door, now open, and knew he'd found the Drakkor's lair. Rushing ahead, he ran down the steps into the massive underground room. Just in time to see wolf-Anabel confronted by a massive, fire-breathing dragon.

A quick glance around showed neither Tammy nor Dena anywhere in sight.

Tyler didn't think, didn't hesitate. He just acted. Taking a running leap, he planted himself in between the Drakkor and Anabel.

Trust in yourself.

As he snarled a warning, Anabel moved up beside him, her shoulder bumping his. At the touch, energy flowed, as sharp as electricity, making his entire body tighten. Next to him, Anabel did the same.

They glanced at each other, and then Anabel's mouth curled in a wolfish grin. Just like that, he knew what they had to do.

Side by side, careful that they were still touching, they ran at the Drakkor. The beast only watched them come, a reptilian amusement glimmering in his exotic eyes. Apparently, he believed two wolves were insignificant against his monstrous might.

Normally, he'd be right. But he didn't know they'd read up on him and his kind. They knew his weak spots, where he was most vulnerable.

Polacek sat upright, on his hind legs, leaving his unscaled belly unprotected. From what Anabel had told him, according to the books, the Drakkors could only be killed by being stabbed in the gut or in the eyes, or with poison. Since he and Anabel didn't have any poison, he figured their razor-sharp teeth and claws would have to be enough.

That and their magic.

One more quick glance at Anabel and he knew she understood what they needed to do. Moving as one, they leaped forward and up, avoiding the giant, three-clawed feet, clearly taking Polacek by surprise.

When Tyler connected with the Drakkor's soft underbelly, he slashed and ripped. Next to him, Anabel snarled and growled as she did the same.

Polacek let out a howl of pain, swiping at them with his front talons, knocking them away and sending them flying.

The instant Tyler hit the ground, he rolled and launched himself back up again. From the corner of his vision, he saw Anabel replicate his move.

Great rivers of blood streamed down the dragon's massive body. He shook his monstrous head, swaying as if dizzy. He roared fire at the two wolves, no doubt well aware that only fire or silver could kill them.

Though the flames singed the fur on his back, somehow Tyler miraculously escaped serious harm. Anabel yelped, and he spun to check on her.

Polacek's claw caught Tyler right in the stomach, knocking the breath from him. He felt his insides tear, aware the damage wouldn't kill him, as long as he avoided the dragon's fiery breath. He'd suffer, but he'd heal. What happened to him didn't matter anyway. No matter the cost, he had to protect Anabel and keep her safe.

He landed on top of her as Polacek fell. Pushing her, he rolled her aside just in time to avoid the dragon's last blast of flame.

Tyler tried to push himself off her, to nudge her with his nose and urge her to run, but he'd lost too much blood. As his vision grayed, he prayed the Drakkor would stay down until he healed, at least enough to run. Which, since Tyler was a full-blooded shape-shifter, wouldn't take too long.

That was his last thought before he blacked out.

When he came to, he wasn't sure how much time had passed. Anabel lay in the same spot, clearly still unconscious. The Drakkor also hadn't moved. But the air had filled with smoke, and as he turned his head to discover the source, he saw the forest was on fire.

If he didn't get Anabel out of here, that would mean certain death. He had to save her.

Dragging Anabel by the scruff of the neck, he pulled her as far into the underbrush as he could. Though he hated to leave her, he had no choice. He needed to summon help and he couldn't do that as wolf.

Anabel moaned, drawing his attention. He nudged her with his nose, willing her to wake. As he did, energy surged through him, like a sizzling in his veins, transferring to her. She whined and opened her eyes. The instant she did, she climbed to her feet.

He took a step away, indicating with his paw that she should follow. Once he was certain she could, he took off running with Anabel close behind.

Praying no one saw them, he raced toward the apartment building and up the stairs. He'd left the door open, and the instant they were both inside, he nudged it closed with his shoulder.

And then, side by side, they both began the change back to human.

As soon as he was man, and ignoring his own arousal, Tyler yanked on his clothes and went for the cell phone. He didn't have to look up the number; every shifter had committed the Society of Pack Protectors number to memory.

When the woman answered, he told her everything, including his location. No doubt used to receiving strange phone calls, she didn't even question him. She promised to send Protectors right away.

Relieved and spent, he turned to find Anabel watching him, wearing a too-large T-shirt she must have gotten from the closet, her copper-colored eyes shuttered, exhaustion carving out new hollows on her cheeks.

She looked so fragile he wondered if she'd break if he took her in his arms. Plus, there was his still-obvious arousal, and if there'd ever been a worse time for that, he couldn't think of it.

"Are you all right?" he asked softly.

After a moment's hesitation, she nodded. "I think so. Is that my cell phone?"

"Yep." Tossing it to her, he waited while she eyed the screen, where the last number called was still on display.

"You called *them*?" she asked, not needing to explain since they both knew whom she meant.

"I had to. They need to know about this. They can help us. We can't contact the human police."

Wandering over to the window, she peered out from the dusty drapes as if she expected their enemies to make a sudden appearance. As the thought occurred to him, he went over and locked the front door. Just in case.

When he looked up again, Anabel once again watched him. "What about Polacek? How do you know he didn't escape?"

"I don't. But the Protectors know about him. And the Drakkors need to be held accountable for what they've done."

Wearily, she nodded. "Tammy's pregnant, you know. I'm thinking all along, the problem wasn't with the female Drakkors. I'm not sure what species the father is, but it doesn't matter. The Protectors need to know this so she isn't harmed."

Surprised, he nodded. "Even though their line is now secured, Polacek was still going to…?"

"Yes."

The one word made Tyler blanch. He nearly asked why and then decided he didn't need to. Doug Polacek had revealed his character in so many ways, it shouldn't have surprised Tyler that the man would continue to do such horrible things when the need no longer existed. "We have to make sure the Protectors know."

"I agree." She sighed heavily. "What do we do now?"

He looked around the small apartment, noting the framed photograph of bright flowers in a meadow. Dena had taken that. He noted several other small touches he knew she'd made—the bright yellow pillow on the couch, the book of photographs on the coffee table, the bright pink vase on the bar.

"I want to go see my sister."

She stared at him. "I know she contacted you and everything, but she probably thinks that was in her dreams, if she remembers it at all. Won't she find it weird to see a dead man standing at her bedside?"

Mentally cursing, he realized she was right. Which hurt like hell. But if he had to go back to being dead, he wanted at least a glimpse of his sister before he went.

"Not only that," Anabel continued. "Didn't you say it was some sort of rule that dead people couldn't materialize fully to the one they were closest to?"

He frowned. "I was only guessing." In fact, he'd actually really only said that to make her feel better about David not showing up. As far as he knew, ghosts could frequently visit their loved ones, though most times the person couldn't see or hear them. He wasn't sure why David hadn't bothered to try to visit his wife, especially since she was known in the spirit world as a person of power.

While his sister was captive, he'd made numerous visits to her to try to offer comfort. While she hadn't been able to see him, he'd tried his best.

And now no way would he let this golden opportunity slip by.

"I'd still like to see her," he said. "Even if it's only from a distance. Kind of like a parting present for myself before I have to give all this up."

She nodded, her expression going sad.

All this. Anabel. He got choked up just thinking about it. Which was probably pretty damn stupid. He wondered if Anabel would even miss him once he went back to being dead. Somehow he doubted it, especially if he managed to bring Dave to see her.

Unfortunately, Dave had never appreciated what he had. And now he most likely had only regrets. Maybe the meeting would bring them both closure. For Anabel's sake, Tyler hoped so.

As she watched him, Anabel's expression softened even more. "We can try. Polacek said he had Tammy drop her outside the ER. Let's check there and see if she's been admitted."

Using her phone, she searched for the hospital number and called. After a short conversation, she ended the call. "All the woman would tell me is that she's there. She said privacy laws prevented her from saying anything more."

Suddenly struck by the idea of actually seeing his sister, he took a deep breath. "Why don't you see if you can find something to wear and we'll head over there?"

Chapter 18

A few minutes later, with Anabel wearing an outfit Tyler recognized as one of his sister's flowery T-shirt dresses and strappy sandals, they headed down the steps and out to her car. As human, wedging himself in the front passenger seat felt downright painful.

Neither spoke much on the short drive to the hospital. Preoccupied with worry, Tyler hoped Dena had gotten help early enough to pull through.

Entering the hospital, which smelled, as all hospitals did, of that peculiar combination of antiseptic and sickness, they hurried over to the information desk. There they learned that Dena was in ICU. As for her condition, they'd have to speak to the nurse in that department.

"Are you family?" the head ICU nurse asked, eyeing them both sternly. Her sharp-eyed gaze looked friendly, if stern. "The police have been here and are trying to learn what happened to this young lady. She was left on the pavement outside of our ER, near death."

Tyler almost said he was her brother and caught himself at the last moment. "We're friends," he said instead. "Members of the same church."

The nurse nodded. "Usually, we only allow family in the ICU. But she hasn't had any visitors, so…" She tilted her head and gave a quick glance around the area. All the other nurses appeared to be busy. "I suppose you can take a peek in her room, one at a time. She's in Room 8."

"Is she…?" Tyler almost couldn't finish. His heart thumped so loudly in his chest he thought maybe she could see it. Clearing his throat, he tried again. "Is she conscious?"

"No, sadly, she is not."

"Is she going to be okay?" Anabel asked.

The nurse's face changed, becoming distantly professional once more. "I'm sorry. I can only discuss her condition with family members. Now if you want to have a quick visit, please do so. Otherwise, I'm going to have to ask you to leave."

"Sorry." Anabel gave a placating smile. "We'll just pop in for a quick visit and then we'll get out of your hair."

As they walked away, Anabel took his arm. "You go first," she said. "And be aware that we might be able to help her heal if we use our magic."

He nodded, unable to take his gaze away from Room 8, where the door sat partially open. "I'll do my best, but since I have no idea how to heal anything, I'm hoping you'll have more success than I."

"Just try," she said, propelling him toward the room and the sister he hadn't seen in person for so long.

Just inside the doorway he stopped. Dena looked so tiny in the white hospital bed, hooked up to various machines, every breath accompanied by impersonal beeps. He moved closer, holding his breath, but she didn't stir.

Her eyes were closed and her gaunt face puffy from an array of bruises in varying shades of purple and red.

They'd cleaned her up, he supposed. Her long hair, her pride and joy, still looked lifeless, but at least he could tell it had been washed.

"Dena?" Speaking her name, he couldn't help wondering if she could hear him. He'd read somewhere that people in comas often did, and he took comfort in the idea that on some level, she'd know he'd come to see her.

Remembering what Anabel had said, he moved closer. After glancing around to make sure no disapproving nurse was about to bustle into the room, he touched his sister's arm.

Still soft, her skin felt cold. He wasn't sure exactly what he should do, so he focused on healing. Using the word *heal* as a mantra of sorts, he tried to send her some of the energy his magic provided. But he must have used up whatever supply he'd been given fighting the Drakkor. No sizzle, no spark, no blaze of power. Nothing but the aching worry of his love.

"I love you, sis," he said, over the incessant beeping and drone of the equipment. "You've got to pull through. I'm counting on that."

She didn't stir, but she was free now. She had a chance. He could only pray Anabel had better results, could help her heal fully after what she'd endured.

Turning to go, he took one last look at his sister, hoping he'd be able to visit her as a ghost once she was healthy and whole.

Out in the hall, Anabel took one look at his face. "Don't worry," she said, squeezing him in a quick hug. "She's going to pull through."

He nodded, heart in his throat. Unable to watch anymore, he moved away from the room to wait a short distance down the hall.

A few minutes later Anabel emerged. Her broad smile had his heart skipping a beat. "Come on," she said, taking his hand. His skin tingled at her touch. "I gave her some of my energy. She didn't wake up, but her vitals improved and she will soon."

He chose to believe her and they went to her car. Key in the ignition, she turned to look at him. "We should check and make sure the Protectors got Polacek."

"You mean call?"

Her shrug was artfully careless. "I was thinking more along the lines of we drive out there."

Instantly, he shook his head. "No. No way. If he's regained consciousness, doing that would be putting you right in the line of fire."

As she opened her mouth to argue, her phone rang. "Great timing," she said. "It's the Protectors."

From what he could tell of her side of the conversation, everything was under control. She let them know about Tammy's pregnancy and also about what Doug Polacek had tried to do even though he'd known.

Once she ended the call, Anabel confirmed what he'd guessed. "Polacek is in custody. The society is requesting a meeting of all the remaining Drakkors. From what I could get out of what she was saying, they are going to see if the other Drakkors are as crazy as Polacek. If they aren't, the society might release him to them for punishment."

He thought of Tammy and what Anabel had told him. "Now that one of their females was able to conceive, hopefully the other two will, as well. I do hope Polacek was an aberration rather than the norm."

"Me too. Their beast is beautiful."

"I agree." Oddly enough, he felt at loose ends. Though he didn't want to face up to the knowledge that it might be time for him to go, he knew he'd have to soon. "I think this is out of our hands now."

Anabel smiled sadly. "I guess it is. Now I just need to get my life back on track. I'll start with dealing with getting the insurance to pay so I can rebuild my house."

Without him. Because now that everything had been done, it would be time for him to go.

"I have one question," he said. "Earlier, you had your plan of trying to die and be brought back to life. I was told no, by the way, but I'm curious as to why such a thing would even occur to you."

She bit her lip, finding a sudden fascination with her fingernails. When she raised her head, the emotion blazing from her copper-colored eyes made him catch his breath. "Because I wanted to see if such a thing was possible. Ever. Being without you is unbearable to me."

Humbled, he forced words past the sudden aching in his throat. "You wanted to do this in case there might be a chance I could be brought back to life?"

"Yes."

That single word, so full of hope and yearning, nearly undid him. His heart sank. He knew what he had to do. The longer he stayed with her, the more Anabel would suffer when he left.

He'd been granted all this—from being allowed to contact Anabel as a ghost, to spending time with her as a real, live man. Much more than he'd ever deserved, a gift he appreciated from the bottom of his heart. He couldn't overstay his time and make the powers that be have to be the ones to call him home. He should initiate the process himself and go back where he belonged, leaving with dignity and grace.

Oh, but the thought hurt. Like a fire in his chest, cutting a jagged hole in his heart. The idea of leaving Anabel felt worse than his memories of the actual moment of his physical death. He could barely breathe. Even considering going away from her forever made him feel as if his entire being had been stabbed, shredded, spit out and stomped on.

At least as a ghost, he'd no longer feel physical pain. Though he should have taken comfort knowing that, he didn't care. He'd suffer this a thousand times if he could only stay with her.

No doubt his spirit guide, Elias, would inform him he had some fancy lesson to learn from all of this. Whatever it might be, he felt certain he didn't want to hear it.

He knew the truth. He knew how precious this love was, a love he'd found way too late.

During his time alive, he'd never been a saint, and after he'd died, he learned he'd passed roughly a third of the life lessons he'd needed to learn in this life.

Learning more he could deal with. He'd build on his strengths and overcome his weaknesses, and by the time he was ready to be born again for another try, he'd hopefully do better.

But the one regret he couldn't get past was that he'd never known true love while alive this time. He'd never even realized he wouldn't. Like most men, he'd just assumed that someday he'd meet the woman with whom he was destined to spend the rest of his life. Someday.

He hadn't even dreamed he'd meet her after he was dead. While she was still very much alive.

He'd found love with his eyes and his hands and his skin. With every fiber of his being, an emotion so strong that the sheer power of it had enabled him to briefly become human.

Worse, he'd gotten such a wondrous thing while his sister still suffered. He'd come back to this plane with one purpose—to save Dena. And while he hadn't failed at that, to finally experience the joy of meeting his mate and then being forced to relinquish her, leaving was a mighty bitter pill to swallow.

They pulled up to the motel and parked. As he got out and followed her to the room, he felt a tug inside his core, faint at first. A gentle reminder that he would need to go soon. If he planned to be the one to initiate things, he couldn't put it off. He knew better than to try to fight it.

Back ramrod straight, Anabel unlocked the door and turned on the lights. As she stepped aside to let him past, he took her into his arms. He needed to tell her the truth, say goodbye.

He tried twice to speak, failing each time. Her eyes wide, her mouth fell open. He thought she might have an idea, judging from the frightened expression on her beautiful face. Even her amazing copper eyes looked dull, all the shine gone from them.

"Don't," she pleaded, holding up her hand. "Please don't."

All the color had leached from her face. Worried she might faint, he supported her.

"It's all right," he said, helping her into the fake leather chair. "Take a breath. Let me get you a glass of ice water. You don't look good at all."

"No." As he went to move away, she grabbed his arm. "Come sit. Tell me what's wrong."

He took a deep breath. "We need to talk."

Her worried smile faltered. "Has any good conversation ever begun with those words?"

He only shook his head and went willingly when she

pulled him down onto the chair with her. "Let me hold you," he said.

"For how long?" The sorrow in her voice made tears prick at the backs of his eyes, but he managed to contain them and keep his composure.

They sat that way, neither moving, for the space of several minutes. Breathing in her scent, that particular combination of cinnamon and flowers that would forever make him think of her, he tried to calm his racing mind.

"Whatever it is, we'll work it out together," she said, clearly trying to find a way to help.

The depth of the pain inside made him wonder how he'd bear this. Still... Taking a deep breath, he hoped they'd give him just a little more time. He'd take however long he could with Anabel. Maybe even long enough to give him a few memories to store inside him forever, memories to keep him company when he returned to the cosmos without her. Alone. Completely and utterly alone.

Devastation filled him at the thought. *Chin up,* he told himself. He'd been a soldier, a man's man. He needed to figure out a way to deal.

Except he couldn't. Truth be told, he didn't know how he would survive it. Loneliness wasn't as bad when you didn't know what you were missing. Now he did, which would make being alone unbearable.

Watching the emotions flicker across Tyler's handsome face, Anabel experienced them all at the same time. Soon, Tyler would leave her for good. Intellectually, she knew this. Emotionally, she could hardly face it. Even though they'd known each other only a short time, the deep connection she'd made with him felt like a marriage. Knowing he'd go soon wrenched her insides and made her feel as if she were being widowed a second time.

Since David's death, she'd gradually disengaged from thinking of herself as part of a couple. She'd come to understand there were only two camps—coupledom and singledom.

And when David got killed, she'd unwillingly switched sides. She was now alone—and would be the rest of her life. Now she realized she'd been living life as though she'd given up.

Until Tyler. Now this could end only one way. In pain and fire.

Ah, but the inevitability of it all meant she wanted to figure out a spectacular last day with Tyler. She'd been denied this with David. He'd died and she'd never be able to get back or repair their last conversation.

They'd been bickering. Nothing major. But in the middle of their argument, uncharacteristically, David had grabbed his gear and demanded she take him to the airport for his flight back to Afghanistan. Even though the plane wasn't leaving for another four hours.

Stunned and hurt, she'd snatched up her car keys and done exactly that. When she pulled up to the curb, at least David had leaned over and kissed her goodbye. Except it was more of a peck than a good, toe-tingling kiss between mates.

As she opened her mouth to protest, reaching for him to pull him close, he'd moved away and gotten out of the car. Grabbing his gear from the backseat, he'd dipped his chin in an impersonal nod and disappeared inside the terminal.

This was the last time she'd ever seen him. He hadn't called or anything for two weeks. The next thing she knew, two uniformed officers were at her door, telling her he'd been killed in an explosion. Worse, there hadn't even been enough of his body left to bury. They'd found his dog tags and his wallet and sent them home to her.

Pushing the memory away, she covered her eyes with

her hands. She'd loved David, but he was her past, not her future. Still, that botched goodbye had to be rectified. She needed to see David one last time, even if only as a ghost. She wanted to tell him she was sorry, that she hadn't loved him the way he deserved to be loved.

The way she loved Tyler.

The realization crashed into her, though she'd known this all along. If only her magic, the wonderful gift she'd been given, was strong enough to enable her to keep him with her forever. But she knew it was not. There wasn't a single kind of magic that powerful, even the dark kind. Life was a precious gift from the Creator.

And she would do nothing to dishonor that gift.

Still, she selfishly hoped to keep Tyler with her as long as she could.

Though Anabel seemed lost in her own thoughts, the constant tugging that had begun inside told Tyler he needed to leave this earthly plane.

"Anabel." He touched her arm, unsurprised when she jumped. "It's over." Though he supposed they should have been celebrating his sister's freedom and Polacek's capture, he couldn't keep the sorrow from his voice. "I've got to go back where I belong."

She wouldn't meet his gaze. Upon a closer look, he saw tears streaming silver tracks down her alabaster cheeks.

Pain stabbed him. He refused to go with her like this.

Reaching for her, he pulled her close. Held her, breathed in her scent and smoothed her ebony hair away from her face. Though he ached to tell her how he felt, he knew a declaration of love would only make things worse for her.

So he kissed her instead. When his mouth covered hers, he tried to pour all of his longing and urgency and frustration into the kiss. She returned his kiss with fiery abandon. They both knew what neither dared say. But at least they'd have this, though a single kiss would never be enough.

The celestial tug came again, reminding him he needed to go. Rather than deepen the kiss, he pulled back, though it took every ounce of willpower he possessed.

"It's time," he told her softly, wiping her tears away with his fingers.

She nodded. "Remember your promise," she said, her tone as heavy as his. "No more ghosts."

"No more ghosts." And one other thing, though neither spoke it out loud. He'd promised to find her husband, David, and let her have one last conversation with him.

Though it ripped at his heart, he'd given his word. And since it was what she wanted, he'd move heaven and earth to give it to her.

"No more ghosts," he reminded her. "Except one. I promise I'll find the one you most want to see."

And with that, he stepped out of the motel room and headed toward the trees, wanting to spare her from seeing him leave this second, earthly body forever.

Once there, he breathed the damp, musty scent of forest and gave himself over to what must be.

This time, it didn't feel like dying. Instead, the simple action of stepping out of himself felt more like a caterpillar, shedding dull and tired skin, to finally emerge as another, much more beautiful creature. Being in the spirit contained an almost indescribable joy. Though this time, his transformation was tinged with sorrow.

Briefly, he looked back to see what had happened to his body, but he saw no sign of it. Taking a deep breath, he immediately went in search of his spirit guide, Elias.

When he found the other being, recognizable by his

deep purple hue, Tyler bowed low. "I've completed my task," he said. "My sister is safe."

"And the Drakkors?"

"They have found a way to continue their species."

"Very good." Genuine pleasure rang in the other's melodic voice. "All beings are beloved by their Maker."

Tyler nodded, taking a deep breath. "As I'm sure you already know, I made certain promises to Anabel Lee in order to obtain her assistance."

Elias said nothing, merely continuing to glow his soothing and powerful deep violet hue.

"I've told her no more ghosts will bother her," Tyler began.

Elias laughed. "That is something she herself can take care of. All she has to do is close the door between realms. She herself opened it in her grief."

Though he shouldn't have been surprised, Tyler nodded. "I promised her I would do that for her."

Silence. Finally, Elias agreed.

Tyler wasn't entirely certain how his guide would take his next request, but he'd given his word and would do his best to ensure that he kept it.

"I also promised her she could see her husband's spirit one last time."

Now Elias radiated interest. "That will be easily accomplished," he said, clearly mulling over the right words. "Considering what is happening even as we speak."

Pleased, Tyler waited for instructions.

When Elias said nothing else, Tyler took a deep breath and asked, "Will you find his spirit and bid him to accompany me? I would like to bring him to Anabel Lee tonight, if possible."

At this, to Tyler's absolute astonishment, Elias laughed. "That would be difficult, if not impossible," he finally said. "Especially since David Lee is not here in the realm of spirit."

Tyler's heart sank. "Has he already reincarnated? It hasn't been very long since he died."

"That's the problem, actually. David Lee is not dead."

Stunned, Tyler didn't know how to react. "What exactly do you mean?" he asked cautiously. "Wasn't he killed in Afghanistan?"

"No. He merely made it appear that way. He escaped and is living in the Hindu Kush mountains with his true mate."

True mate? Tyler dragged his hand across his mouth, forgetting for a moment that he was not in his corporeal body. "But he's married to Anabel," he managed, well aware that such a thing clearly no longer mattered to David Lee.

"He is a deserter from his military post. AWOL. Plus, his actions when he set up the explosion to make everyone think he was killed resulted in another's serious injury. Until now, he stayed hiding as he couldn't let anyone know he's alive, or he would have to pay for his crimes. Not at all good for his soul."

Until now?

"I have to tell Anabel," Tyler said, feeling as if a knife had just stabbed him in the heart. "This is going to wound her. She holds her husband in high regard."

"And a traitor like him doesn't deserve that regard." Elias's tone sounded noncommittal, which didn't fool Tyler. He had become intimately familiar with the laws of karma. He knew whatever David had done in his single-minded pursuit of a new life would be something he'd have to face sooner or later. Every single casualty. Including his wife, who'd believed he loved her.

Somehow he had to protect her, if he could.

"I can't let what he's done hurt Anabel," Tyler said. "And yet I can't do her the disservice of giving her a lie."

Instead of reminding him about lessons and karma, Elias nodded. "Sounds like you have quite a dilemma," he mused. "Unfortunately, you will not be allowed to deal with it. This is Anabel's lesson to learn."

Again Tyler felt that tug, even stronger this time. Which made no sense, as he had already left the physical realm for that of the spirit. But it came again, making him stagger. He tried to reach out for Elias, but his guide only smiled benevolently at him from out of reach.

And then blackness.

When Tyler vanished right in front of her eyes, Anabel told herself she wouldn't keep crying. After all, they still had unfinished business. Tyler couldn't go on to his heavenly reward until he kept the promises he'd made to her. She'd see him again, at least once more. She had to.

A few minutes after Tyler left, the phone rang. Not her cell phone, but the hotel landline.

If not for that, she probably wouldn't even have bothered to answer. Knowing what would soon come to pass had made her numb, and Tyler disappearing the way he did made her want to weep.

No one had this number. No one.

The absurd thought crossed her mind that somehow it might be David, calling from heaven. And so she crossed the room to the countertop and picked up the handset.

"Hello?"

The first few words didn't register. She'd been so certain the call would be something from the realm beyond that she had trouble taking in that it wasn't.

Snippets of the conversation finally reached her, spoken in that all-too-familiar, überformal tone used by the military.

The voice spoke a name. David Lee. Her husband. But the rest of what the stranger said seemed incomprehensible.

When the caller asked her if she'd understood, she didn't at first respond. How could she, when she wasn't even entirely sure she wasn't dreaming this entire conversation?

After all, the phone that had rung was a motel phone, not her personal cell. Most likely it was someone making a very bad joke or one of the still-absent remaining Drakkors, trying to extract some sort of bitter revenge at her expense.

Because what the caller said simply could not be true. David wasn't dead after all. David was alive, a deserter, and living in the mountains of Afghanistan with another woman and a child.

When pressed, she finally murmured something in assent. She thought. Yet there wasn't one bit of this making the slightest sense.

She was told David would be court-martialed and tried, most likely there in Afghanistan. She would not be permitted, at least for the time being, to see him.

See him? The only reason Anabel would want to do that would be to ask him for a divorce.

After assuring the caller she'd contact him if she had any questions, she gently replaced the receiver in the cradle and swayed.

Chapter 19

When she turned to make her way back to the living room, she nearly fell. But somehow she reached the couch and allowed herself to drop onto the overstuffed cushions.

Then she tried to think about what she'd just been told.

Allegedly—and as of right now she still couldn't bring herself to believe it was true—her beloved husband, the man she'd considered her soul mate, the soldier she'd held in such high regard, had not only deserted his post, but staged his own death. His doing so had caused others to be seriously hurt. His fellow soldiers, men he'd worked with, men who'd trusted him.

Worse—was there actually anything nearly as bad?— the military had caught up with him. He'd been found living in some remote mountainous village, along with a native girl and their child. Which meant that he'd staged his death knowing he'd gotten the woman pregnant.

The thought that he could do such a thing—not only to her, but to the men in his unit, men who'd relied upon him to have their back as surely as they had his—didn't match up with the man she thought she knew.

Painfully stunned, she wasn't sure how to react. Eighteen months ago, she'd grieved for David. She'd fallen down a well of sorrow so dark that she hadn't known if she'd ever be able to climb back out.

To learn that all that time, while she'd been weeping and trying to figure out how to manage to live without him, he'd been making a new life with some other woman and their child felt like the worst kind of betrayal.

Especially since David hadn't wanted kids. When she brought the subject up not long after they were married, he'd told Anabel he never wanted children. Apparently, he just hadn't wanted them with her.

If the call had even been real. If it hadn't, then the remaining Drakkors really knew how to mess with her head.

Unfortunately, it didn't take long for Anabel to verify that the phone call had indeed been true. Her first hint came from the incessant ringing of the hotel room phone. The second time she answered, it was a reporter from one of the national television shows, wanting to interview her about David.

She didn't know how they'd gotten the number, and after five minutes of nonstop ringing, she no longer cared. Unplugging the phone, she sat down on the edge of the bed and tried to figure out what to do.

Had Tyler known? When he'd promised her that she could speak to her husband again, had he known all along David wasn't dead? She found it hard to believe he would have lied to her, but she also would never in a million years have suspected David of doing what he'd done.

Finally, she began to make a list. Number one on the list was file for divorce. Number two was to find the man her husband had caused to be injured and learn if there was any way she could help. It seemed like the least she could do.

Plus, action might help take her mind off missing Tyler.

A commotion outside the motel had her peeking out from behind the curtains. The parking lot had filled, not only with vehicles bearing the insignia of most of the large news networks, but with people. Reporters carrying cameras and microphones. All camped right outside her room.

She made a quick phone call to the Leaning Tree Police Department, asking Captain Harper for help.

"Unfortunately, you're in a public place," he drawled, sounding not the slightest bit sorry. "If you still had your home, they couldn't come on your property without your permission. But since you're at the Value Five, as long as they don't try to come inside your room, the media are well within their rights."

After vowing not to speak with anyone until she sorted things out, she decided she needed to purchase a laptop computer, even if doing so would tap her already low funds. She put on dark sunglasses and a scarf to cover her head. Then she hurried from her room to her car and did her best to ignore the camera flashes and shouted questions. The way they surrounded her Fiat as she tried to pull away reminded her of what she'd seen on TV with the paparazzi and various movie stars.

Careful not to run over anyone, she finally broke free of the throng of reporters. A few of them tried to follow her, but she knew this town like the back of her hand, and she managed to elude them.

As soon as she'd purchased her laptop and a few other supplies like bottled water and snacks, she headed back. Again her Fiat was instantly surrounded, and she had to battle her way to her room.

Once inside, she locked the door with a sigh of relief

and got set up. Since the Value Five had free Wi-Fi, she got on the internet and read everything she could find about David.

Some sources were reporting that his actions had killed a fellow soldier, while others claimed several other men had been wounded, one of them grievously. The seriously wounded soldier had gone from Kandahar in Afghanistan to the Landstuhl Regional Medical Center at Ramstein Air Base in Germany. Since he'd been badly burned, once stabilized, he'd then been flown to Brooke Army Medical Center at Fort Sam Houston near San Antonio, Texas. As far as Anabel could tell from what she could glean on the internet, he was still alive.

She refused to cry, at least not for David. She'd done all her weeping over him eighteen months ago. But for this man her husband had hurt, she allowed herself to shed a tear or two.

Next, she researched divorce attorneys. As soon as the media storm died down, she planned on filing. Until then, she thought a trip to Texas might be in order. She owed David's victim an apology for what her husband had done and her support and prayers for his continued healing.

The last straw to a very long day was a phone call from a man who identified himself as David's attorney. "I'll be representing him in the court-martial," he said. "Though he has serious criminal violations in the UCMJ—that's the Uniform Code of Military Justice—at least he's not a murderer."

"Yet," she muttered. "I'd like to see the man David caused to get hurt," she said. "The least I can do is apologize for my husband's actions."

"There's no need. Like I said, he's in a coma. He won't even know you're there."

Every instinct, every bit of magic she possessed, urged

her on. "I don't care. I need to see him. Can you arrange this or do I need to start making some phone calls?"

"Doing so might look bad, as if you believe David is guilty."

"Don't you?" she asked, incredulous. "I assume you've talked to him. What does he have to say for himself?"

The silence on the other end of the line told Anabel the attorney clearly just now realized David's wife might not feel too charitable toward his client right now.

Clearing his throat, the lawyer asked if she planned to travel to Texas.

"Yes. I'm driving to the city and to the airport this afternoon." Before she left, she delivered Leroy to Juliet, who'd agreed to watch him.

The uneventful flight, with a layover in Atlanta, gave her time to think. Though she kept her book open in front of her and pretended to read, she couldn't help rehearsing what exactly she'd say. Even though the soldier might be in a coma, she had faith that the magic inside her could help him to heal. After all, she'd been able to assist Dena Rogers.

At the thought of Tyler, her firm, steely grip on her composure slipped. She missed him, more than she would ever have believed possible. She'd have given much to be able to fill him in on this latest development. Assuming he hadn't already known.

Once she arrived in San Antonio, she took a cab to the hospital. Apparently, someone had alerted the media about her arrival. The instant she pulled up to the hospital entrance, she saw they'd assembled in wait for her.

Though the reporters took pictures and shouted questions, she kept her expression remote and stared straight ahead, putting one foot in front of the other and plowing forward. The multiple camera flashes disoriented and disturbed her, but the knowledge that the press—at her request and backed up by the US military—would be denied entrance to the hospital itself gave her a bit of relief.

Once she was inside, the instant the automatic doors closed behind her, the roar of the crowd cut off. That scent particular to hospitals—a combination of cleaning agents and sickness—assaulted her nose.

No matter. She was going to visit the man whom her husband had hurt. Hopefully, the magic inside her would be enough to help him heal.

Somehow she had to make amends. Her magic was all she had.

The two military policemen at her side stopped at a closed door. "He's in there, ma'am," one of them said, inclining his head.

"Please wait outside," she said, keeping her voice gentle yet knowing if they balked, she'd do whatever she had to in order to make sure she entered the room alone.

"Of course," the man replied.

Relieved, she took a deep breath and placed her hand on the knob and turned it.

Entering the room, which was silent except for the thrum and low-level beeping of the machines, she approached the bed. And stared. Hand to her heart, which now had begun beating madly, she looked skyward and muttered a quick prayer of thanks before turning her gaze back to the rugged features of the man lying there.

How could this be? Yet before her eyes, indisputable proof.

Her legs quivered and threatened to give out on her. She sank into the chair next to the bed. Tyler, alive. Not dead after all, even though he'd appeared to her first as a spirit, a shade.

Fleetingly, she wondered how he'd been made human

and then realized maybe with magic and love, anything was possible. In the end, she decided none of that mattered.

He was here, alive, and she might be the only one able to bring him back from his coma with her magic.

Or with her love. Maybe the two were interchangeable.

Trust in yourself. Again the voice in her head, the same one from when she'd had to fight the Drakkor.

So she would, she decided. She'd trust in herself and more. She'd trust in what she and Tyler had made together. She'd trust in them.

Approaching the bed, she took in the various machines keeping him alive. At least he breathed on his own, one blessing. Machines regulated and monitored everything—there were so many she didn't know what each was for.

He didn't move. His wonderful, beloved features looked the same. Puzzled, she eyed the rest of him, swathed in bandages. She'd read that he'd been badly burned in the explosion and she realized the bandages covered his burned skin. Both hands and arms, chest, stomach and legs. Most of his body, as far as she could tell. She wasn't sure how his face had escaped serious injury.

And then she knew. David. David had done this to Tyler. The man from her past and the man she believed with all her heart would be her future, interwoven together like strands of an intricate web. And neither was dead.

Tyler. Her heart sang. The magic racing like a dizzying current inside her veins would help him, save him, bring him back to her, where he belonged.

So she leaned close, inhaling his wonderful scent, fainter now, but somehow still redolent of mint and trees. And then she touched her lips to his and kissed him.

Softly at first, the barest whisper of her mouth. He

didn't respond, of course. Not yet. But she hadn't un-leashed her magic.

Not wanting to overwhelm him at first, she kept the kiss gentle. Slow, and warm and sweet, using her lips to try to coax a response. Still, he didn't stir. The machine continued beeping with his heartbeat, slow and steady. Unmoved.

She broke away, studying his rugged features, so full of love for him her chest hurt, and knew she couldn't fail.

This time when she placed her mouth on his, her kiss became a command. *Come back to me. Come back to me.*

Slanting her mouth over his, she poured everything she had into this kiss, parting his lips and trying to reach his soul. Deliberately drawing his face to hers in another embrace, she stroked a gently growing fire, and when she felt the first answering spark from deep inside him, her pulse fluttered with joy.

Spirit soaring, she continued, stroking his hair, the side of his face, willing him to return. The dreamy intimacy building between them filled her tired soul, and when he finally moved his mouth under hers, tears filled her eyes.

"Tyler." She pulled back, holding his hand as his eye-lids fluttered open. She willed him to feel the almost tan-gible bond between them. "Tyler, it's me."

Finally, he looked at her, his beautiful hazel eyes at first disoriented, gradually becoming sharper when it dawned on him that she was there.

His gaze locked on hers, and a warm glow ran through her. Though she locked her jaw and tried to be strong, she couldn't stop the tears from spilling down her cheeks.

"Anabel?" His voice a rough rasp, nonetheless it was his, sounding the same as he spoke her name. "Is that really you?"

Wiping at her eyes, she nodded, temporarily unable to

speak. He pulled her to him and kissed her again, as if he needed the touch of her lips to convince him she was real.

The machines began wailing, a claxon sound that brought a nurse running. She spoke into a small phone clipped on her belt, and the room filled with people.

"I'm sorry, ma'am," she said to Anabel. "But I'm going to have to ask you to wait outside the room."

Anabel didn't move. How could she leave when they'd just found each other again? Instead she backed up in one corner, making herself as unobtrusive as possible, while a team of people worked on Tyler.

What did this mean? His eyes remained open, and a flicker of annoyance crossed his face as they all poked and prodded at him.

"Stop," he finally ordered. "I just woke up from a coma. I'm starving and I'd really appreciate you getting me something to eat."

Startled, the assembled medical team momentarily fell silent. And then one of the nurses chuckled, shaking her head. "Damned if you don't sound healthy."

"I am healthy," Tyler shot back. "At least as healthy as a man can be who was caught in an explosion and has had numerous skin grafts."

"You remember that?" This time the white-coated man, clearly the doctor, sounded shocked.

"I do. Now if you'll leave me alone with my Anabel—" Tyler cast his gaze toward her, making her smile "—I'd really appreciate it. It's been way too long since we've been together."

The doctor nodded and began inspecting the machines. "Pulse and blood pressure are fine. Oxygen saturation is great. I'd say he's well enough to have something light to eat. And visit with his lady friend."

"Light?" Tyler protested. "I need a steak and baked potato."

The doctor laughed. "All in good time, but not just yet. You've got to give your body time to adjust to regular food." Then, scrawling notes on a clipboard, he motioned to his team and they all left the room.

"Anabel." Tyler beckoned her close. "What the heck is going on? I think I remember, but I can't be sure. I was dead…"

Her heart turned over. When she could find her voice again, it trembled, but she didn't care. "You were never dead. Even when you were a ghost and visited with me to save your sister. Apparently, you've been in a coma all along."

He grimaced. "I wasn't dead," he repeated, confirming her statement. "Does Dena know?"

"I'm sure they must have told her, before all this happened. As soon as either of you is well enough to travel, I'm sure you two can talk about it."

Worry clouding his eyes, he nodded. "How is she doing?"

"Last time I checked, she was being moved out of ICU. Beyond that, I'm not sure."

"And David?"

She tried to speak, failing miserably. But as she gazed at him, she realized she didn't have to. One look at his shuttered expression told her everything. "Did you know all along?" she asked, holding her breath for his answer.

"No. I didn't find out until I left you that last time and asked to bring Dave's spirit to meet with you," Tyler said, his voice gentle. "And that's when I learned that Dave wasn't actually dead."

She nodded. "And his actions nearly caused you to be killed."

Astonishment widened his eyes. "Dave did this?"

Keeping her words as terse and factual as she could, the same way she'd been informed, she told him what she knew. "I mourned a man I didn't truly know. He lied and cheated and almost caused someone else—you—to die."

She took a deep breath. He started to speak, but she waved him away. She hadn't finished yet. "David is not who I thought he was. Everything he did, in the end, was for himself and his Afghan family. He didn't care who else got hurt when he faked his own death. And clearly, he didn't give a second thought to me, the woman he'd left behind, the woman he'd married, who once actually believed him to be her mate."

"Are you all right?" he asked, his voice soft.

"I think I am. I will be." Lifting her chin, she met his gaze. "Even though I realize clearly now that David was never my mate, still I did nothing to deserve to be treated as if I didn't matter. Instead of sadness, all I feel is anger."

"What will happen to him now?" she asked. "Once he's court-martialed? They've assigned him an attorney."

"It will be just like any other trial, only military. If he's found guilty, he'll go to prison."

She nodded. "What of his…girlfriend and their child?"

"They'll remain in Afghanistan." His familiar hazel gaze searched her face.

"I didn't even hear whether it's a boy or a girl."

Watching her carefully, he nodded. "I guess you could ask his attorney."

"Maybe I will." Heart heavy at all the hurt her husband's selfish actions had caused, she walked to the hotel window. Pulling aside a sliver of curtain, she stared out at the parking lot.

"Will I be able to see him again?" she asked, turning

just in time to see a naked look of pain cross Tyler's face before he rearranged his features.

"I'm sure his attorney could arrange that." Tyler shrugged. Then, speaking carefully, he asked, "You still want to see him?"

"Yes, I think I would." Anger still fueled her. "I'd like to demand an explanation. Plus, he'll need to sign the divorce papers once I have them drawn up."

He froze. "You're going to divorce him?"

"Of course I am. Wouldn't you?"

One corner of his mouth lifted. Not quite a smile, so she wasn't sure if he found her question amusing or not.

"You should probably think about this," he said carefully. "Consider whether or not you want to give him a second chance."

"A second chance?" She could hardly believe what she was hearing. "After what he's done? Not only dishonorable, but—"

"You made mistakes too. And I think you've been relieved when people finally forgave you."

What the heck was Tyler doing? Playing devil's advocate? Yet, to her teeth-gritting irritation, he was right. At least about the part where she'd made mistakes. Still, that didn't change how she felt about either man.

She took several deep breaths, trying to see past the righteous and wounded anger. "Forgiveness is one thing," she allowed. "And if I have enough time, I might be able to give him that. But a second chance? I don't think so."

The tense lines on his face relaxed. "As long as you're sure."

"I am." Crossing to him, she gently lowered herself next to him on the edge of the bed, taking his hand. "You're not getting rid of me that easily, my love."

Satisfaction and love blazed from his gaze. "I think

that's my line. I love you, Anabel Lee. Surely you've already realized that."

She couldn't tear her eyes from him. "I love you too. How foolish I was, believing I knew love before you. You're my mate. We were…"

"Meant to be together," he finished for her. "And as soon as you're free, I'd like you to be my wife."

Happiness filled her, wrapping around her like a warm blanket. "As soon as you're well enough too," she teased.

"My strength is returning rapidly," he warned, pulling her down for another kiss. As she opened her mouth for him, thrilling to the familiar shiver of awareness, she dimly registered the sound of someone clearing her throat.

"Excuse me." The first nurse had returned, carrying a tray. "When you said you were hungry, I thought you meant food."

Feeling her face color, Anable scooted back, unable to hide her smile.

Tyler's annoyance vanished, replaced by anticipation. "Great," he said. "We were just talking about me needing to regain my strength."

The nurse placed the tray on his bed table. "Enjoy." Her shoes silent on the floor, she turned and left the room.

Grinning like a kid at Christmas, Tyler lifted the silver cover from his plate. His expression fell as he saw what he'd been given. "Soup?" He sounded incredulous. "And crackers? Oh, look, they gave me lime gelatin for dessert."

Anabel couldn't help it; she laughed. "I'm going to go check into my hotel and give you some time to rest. I'll be back this evening."

He grabbed her hand. "Don't be gone too long," he said. "We've been separated for longer than I ever want to be again."

Heart full, she promised.

In the days that followed, Tyler made a rapid recovery. A miracle, his medical team called it. The skin grafts healed far quicker than they had before Tyler awakened. The hospital physical therapist marveled at his progress— soon he could walk laps around the hospital.

Anabel spent all her time with him, even sleeping in the chair beside his bed most nights. She refused to grant any interviews, giving her standard "No comment" to the reporters when they confronted her.

Finally, Tyler was deemed well enough to leave the hospital. Since the insurance company still had not settled on her house, despite the arson investigator's report that he didn't believe she'd set it, they'd have to return to the Value Five Motel.

"Or—" Tyler's eyes crinkled at the corners as he smiled "—we can see if the McGraws will let us rent one of their cabins at Wolf Hollow. They're so much nicer—and more private—than that motel room."

This time she was willing to consider the idea. To her surprise, the McGraws agreed, stating they had no problem with her staying there. For this, as so many things lately, gratitude overwhelmed attitude. She felt truly blessed.

Tyler purchased a car in San Antonio, using some of the pay that had accumulated during his eighteen-month coma. They drove back to New York together, both still full of wonder at the love they'd found.

David made no attempt to contest the divorce. He signed the papers immediately after receiving them, giving her everything. Which, at the moment, was a whole lot of nothing since she still owed money on the house that was nothing but ashes.

They moved into a lovely and secluded cabin at Wolf Hollow, and the McGraw family made both Anabel and Tyler feel completely welcome.

Once the uncontested divorce became final—rushed through the court system in a miraculous six weeks—Tyler took her shopping for a ring. Despite her protests that she didn't want anything fancy, he purchased her a gorgeous diamond. He said he wanted to find a ring as spectacular as her.

They were married on a brisk fall evening, in a clearing in the woods near their cabin. Though originally Anabel had planned a small wedding, half the town apparently wanted to come, so they made it like a party, with a pot-luck dinner. A local band provided music. There was dancing, and for the first time in years Anabel felt like part of the town, of the local family.

But the best moment of all was hearing the vows Tyler spoke. They'd each written their own, and she'd told him how he completed her and of her great and everlasting love for him. She could have sworn he wiped a tear from his eye when she finished.

"Now my turn," Tyler said, his voice loud and strong and sure. "I love you, Anabel. I vow to protect you and cherish you, for all of our lives until beyond. Because what we have is so amazing and so strong, not even death can tear us apart."

Anabel was sure none of those assembled understood why she laughed. "Not even death," she repeated.

And they sealed their vows with rings and a kiss.

* * * * *

MILLS & BOON®

Need more New Year reading?

We've got just the thing for you!
We're giving you 10% off your next eBook or
paperback book purchase on the Mills & Boon
website. So hurry, visit the website today and type
SAVE10 in at the checkout for your exclusive

10% DISCOUNT

www.millsandboon.co.uk/save10

Ts and Cs: Offer expires 31st March 2015.
This discount cannot be used on bundles or sale items.

MILLS & BOON®

Why shop at millsandboon.co.uk?

Each year, thousands of romance readers find their perfect read at millsandboon.co.uk. That's because we're passionate about bringing you the very best romantic fiction. Here are some of the advantages of shopping at www.millsandboon.co.uk:

* **Get new books first**—you'll be able to buy your favourite books one month before they hit the shops

* **Get exclusive discounts**—you'll also be able to buy our specially created monthly collections, with up to 50% off the RRP

* **Find your favourite authors**—latest news, interviews and new releases for all your favourite authors and series on our website, plus ideas for what to try next

* **Join in**—once you've bought your favourite books, don't forget to register with us to rate, review and join in the discussions

Visit **www.millsandboon.co.uk**
for all this and more today!